"I want you to come to stay with me.

"I've already arranged for a physical therapist to come by and help you. My housekeeper will be there, too. I want to do this, Cathy. The fire really scared me. I was afraid something had happened to you."

Stunned, she replied, "You want me to stay at your house?"

"Unless you have someone else to look after you, you're coming home with me."

Someone else, she thought. As in family or friends. She had neither. "I can't. Look, you don't have to stay," she said. "I mean, I'm sure you have things to do. Important things."

"Right now you're the most important part of my life." Stone took her hand in his. "You never said that you'd come stay at my house," he reminded her. "Say yes."

Cathy wasn't sure if she was dreaming.... Finally she whispered, "Yes."

Dear Reader,

Special Edition welcomes you to a brand-new year of romance! As always, we are committed to providing you with captivating love stories that will take your breath away.

This January, Lisa Jackson wraps up her engrossing FOREVER FAMILY miniseries with *A Family Kind of Wedding*. THAT SPECIAL WOMAN! Katie Kinkaid has her hands full being an ace reporter—and a full-time mom. But when a sexy, mysterious Texas rancher crosses her path, her life changes forever!

In these next three stories, love conquers all. First, a twist of fate brings an adorably insecure heroine face-to-face with the reclusive millionaire of her dreams in bestselling author Susan Mallery's emotional love story, *The Millionaire Bachelor*. Next, Ginna Gray continues her popular series, THE BLAINES AND THE McCALLS OF CROCKETT, TEXAS, with *Meant for Each Other*. In this poignant story, Dr. Mike McCall heroically saves a life and wins the heart of an alluring colleague in the process. And onetime teenage sweethearts march down the wedding aisle in *I Take This Man—Again!* by Carole Halston.

Also this month, acclaimed historical author Leigh Greenwood debuts in Special Edition with *Just What the Doctor Ordered*— a heartwarming tale about a brooding doctor finding his heart in a remote mountain community. Finally, in *Prenuptial Agreement* by Doris Rangel, a rugged rancher marries for his son's sake, but he's about to fall in love for real....

I hope you enjoy January's selections. We wish you all the best for a happy new year!

Sincerely,
Karen Taylor Richman
Senior Editor

Please address questions and book requests to:
Silhouette Reader Service
U.S.: 3010 Walden Ave., P.O. Box 1325, Buffalo, NY 14269
Canadian: P.O. Box 609, Fort Erie, Ont. L2A 5X3

SUSAN MALLERY

THE MILLIONAIRE BACHELOR

Silhouette ®

SPECIAL ▼ EDITION ®

Published by Silhouette Books
America's Publisher of Contemporary Romance

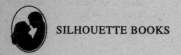 SILHOUETTE BOOKS

ISBN 0-373-24220-4

THE MILLIONAIRE BACHELOR

Printed in U.S.A.

Books by Susan Mallery

*Hometown Heartbreakers
†Triple Trouble
‡Montana Mavericks: Return to Whitehorn

SUSAN MALLERY

lives in sunny Southern California, where the eccentricities of a writer are considered fairly normal. Her books are both reader favorites and bestsellers, with recent titles appearing on the Waldenbooks bestseller list and the *USA Today* bestseller list. Her 1995 Special Edition novel, *Marriage on Demand,* was awarded Best Special Edition by *Romantic Times Magazine*.

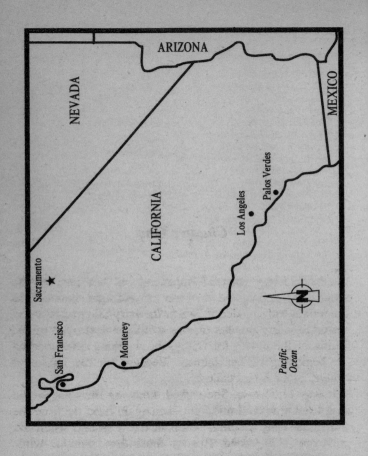

Chapter One

Cathy Eldridge glanced impatiently at her inexpensive watch. She anticipated the hour of midnight as much as Cinderella had dreaded it. While the fairy-tale princess had reason to worry that her dreams would be destroyed by the tolling of the clock, for Cathy, the witching hour marked the beginning of her fantasy. Because on the stroke of twelve, Stone Ward called.

It was 11:23 p.m. She sighed, knowing the time would drag from now until midnight, then again from the time she and Stone hung up until seven in the morning, when her graveyard shift ended. But for those few minutes, while they spoke, time flew. She didn't care that there was nothing between them except what she created in her mind. She didn't care that who he *thought* she was and who she *really* was had nothing in common. It was enough to hear his voice and to know that he enjoyed their conversations as much as she did.

It was a slow night at the answering service. She fielded a call from a worried mother whose toddler had spiked a high fever. After consulting her computer, she contacted the pediatrician on duty, then connected the two. There were two calls from men who had been arrested and wanted to discuss bail. She paged the owner of the bail-bond business and gave him both messages.

The answering service she worked for had an eclectic group of clients. Everything from doctors to a private detective, the bail bondsman, a couple of law offices, even a sizable literary agency that handled screenplays for Hollywood. The service catered to any company that preferred that after-hours callers be answered by a real person rather than voice mail. There were also a few odd clients, like the charming, wealthy but forgetful widow who had the service call her six times a day to remind her to take her medicine, and a traveling salesman who insisted regular messages be left on his answering machine at home so his cat wouldn't feel so alone.

Cathy had been on the job for more years than she wanted to remember and she handled each call quickly and efficiently. She was a favorite with many of the clients. If nothing else, they enjoyed her stories about her exciting life outside of work. Which reminded her...

She opened her large, black nylon carrying case and pulled out her laptop computer. The machine had been expensive and her only indulgence in the past three years, but it had been worth every penny. With a phone line and her laptop, she could go anywhere in the world. No one had to know that she was trapped in a grubby little office, performing a mindless job from which she couldn't seem to escape.

She slipped the plug into a wall socket, then started the computer. When it was ready, she moved the arrow to the correct program and hit the button to connect with her local computer service. From there, she could make her way out into the Internet—a place she didn't understand, but had the power to transform her. She was constantly amazed by the information available. Everything from the latest treatments for a host of diseases to airline schedules to restaurant menus. Tonight, she needed the latter.

She'd spent the weekend researching hotels and clubs in the vacation resort of Cancún, Mexico. All that was left was to find the right kind of restaurant with the right kind of menu.

It took her about ten minutes of searching to locate what she needed. She scribbled a few notes on a pad of paper, took three calls for various clients, relayed messages to an attorney working late, all the while glancing at the clock. Five minutes left, then three, then one, then—

Ring.

Her heart had picked up its pace fifteen minutes before, but now her palms got sweaty and her stomach lurched. The symptoms were familiar—they occurred every time he called. He always made her feel so very alive. She adjusted the mouthpiece on her headset, then pushed the blinking light on the phone console.

"A to Z Answering Service," she said, working hard to keep her tone light and friendly, so he wouldn't guess she was shaking with anticipation. It didn't matter that they'd been talking for months. He still made her nervous.

"Hi, Cathy, how was your weekend?"

She wanted to melt. His voice was low and seductive. It wrapped around her and drifted through her, making it nearly impossible to think or breathe or do anything but sigh out his name.

"Hi, Stone, my weekend was great. What about yours?"

"Nothing very exciting. I worked." She heard faint

sounds over the phone lines, as if he was shifting into a more comfortable position on a sofa or in a chair.

She pictured him in a book-lined study somewhere. The room would be large, paneled in wood with high ceilings and rich leather furniture. She always imagined a fireplace and the scent of burning logs. Which was crazy. This was Los Angeles, and it didn't get very cold, even in the dead of winter. But Stone was her fantasy, and she figured she had the right to conjure up a romantic fire if she wanted one.

"You work too hard," she said. "You need to take some time off. Get away."

"You travel enough for both of us," he told her. "Where was it this weekend? The Bahamas?"

"Mexico. The weather was fabulous." Cathy leaned forward and gathered her notes. According to the Weather Channel, it had been in the eighties all weekend, with clear skies and pleasantly cool nights. She quietly sorted through the information she'd printed out on the various hotels and the sites.

He chuckled. "Not like that week in Paris? No typhoon?"

She joined in his laughter. "It wasn't a typhoon. It was a fall rainstorm."

"If I remember correctly, it was more rain than the city had seen in years. You were practically flooded out of your hotel. You lost power for a day."

Cathy's smile faded as she was again reminded that Stone paid attention. He listened and remembered, as if her life was of interest to him. As if *she* was interesting. She hated that the truth was something different. If only she could be what he wanted her to be—but she wasn't. Not that it mattered. Theirs was a relationship built on fantasy.

At least on her side. She wasn't sure what *he* thought of her.

"This was definitely not Paris," she said.

"So who did you go with?"

"Angie and Brad, Mark, Martin and Melissa."

"Ah, the three *M*s. Was Raoul there?"

Raoul. Her mysterious man of the moment. "He couldn't make it."

"You must have missed him."

"Not as much as you might think," she said wryly, wishing she heard the tiniest hint of jealousy in Stone's voice, but knowing that wasn't going to happen. She had created Raoul—tall, dark, handsome, silent. The perfect man. Actually he was a lot like her image of Stone. Another man she'd never met, but at least Stone existed outside of her imagination. Raoul, Angie, Brad and the three *M*s did not.

"Tell me everything," he said. "Did you wear a bikini?"

"You have to ask?" She'd been playing the game so long, it was easy. The words weren't really lies; they were stories, told to entertain. No one got hurt. She was someone pleasant in Stone's life. A diversion. If he knew the truth about her and her world, he would think her boring. Thin, beautiful Cathy who had fabulous friends and an exciting life was more his style.

"The room was great," she said.

"A suite?"

"Not this time." She consulted one of the sheets she'd printed out about the hotel. "I had a corner room, and it was pretty big. I didn't have anyone staying with me, so that was fine. I could see the pool and beyond it, the ocean. We had a great time. There was a water slide. I practically ripped out the bottoms of my suit on that."

He chuckled. "Wish I'd been there to see that."

"Mr. Ward, I'm quite shocked!"

"Liar." His voice caressed her like a silk glove. "What color is your bikini?"

"Red."

"Low cut?"

The question made her smile. Even though it wasn't real, she enjoyed their flirting. "Are you asking about the top or the bottom?"

He groaned. "You're killing me, Cathy. I can picture it. Never mind, what I'm thinking about is plenty vivid without you providing more of a description. Did you go snorkeling?"

"Yes." She scanned another sheet. "There's a boat at the hotel and it took us out to a wreck. It was great. The wreck is only a few feet below the surface. The water is so warm there, it's easy to swim for hours. There are fish and interesting plants. I could have stayed a lot longer."

"Sounds nice."

It did, she thought. Someday she would actually try to get there. And to Paris and all the other places she'd told Stone she'd visited. In truth, she didn't even have a passport.

"The hotel has a restaurant right on the water," she continued. "Saturday we all went there. It's very formal."

"I'll bet you wore something short and sexy."

"Were you spying me?" she teased.

"I wish. Go on."

"Well, dinner was fabulous. Fresh fish, great wine." She turned to her laptop and double-checked the menu. "They're known for a flaming dessert, and we all decided to try it. Our waiter was obviously new. He wheeled up a cart and began fixing the dessert right there at the table. But there were six of us, and the pan he was using was too small. I guess he didn't want to do it in two batches or ask for help.''

''I sense a disaster.''

''So did we, but we had no idea what was going to happen. So there he is, spooning the brandy over everything so he can light it. But he keeps putting on more and more. Then he lit the match.''

Stone groaned. ''How much of the building went up in smoke?''

She laughed. ''Not as much as you might think, but there was definitely a loud whoosh and a fireball. The entire room took a leap away from the flames. The waiter nearly burst into tears. And the dessert tasted a little burned around the edges.''

''I'll hand it to you, Cathy—your life is very exciting.''

''That's my goal,'' she said lightly, determined he wouldn't ever learn the truth. ''Did you really stay in all weekend?''

''Sure.''

''Stone, there's a whole world waiting for you out there. You should go explore it. You never go out.''

''I like my privacy.''

''It's not healthy.''

''We've been over this before,'' he reminded her. ''You're not going to change my mind.''

''I know, it's just—'' She sighed. ''I worry about you.''

She did, too, which was crazy. The man was an eccentric millionaire. He owned one of the most successful investment firms on the West Coast. He was reclusive to the point of being mysterious. To the best of her knowledge, he rarely left his home, even to go into his corporation's headquarters. All his personal calls came through the answering service. As far as Cathy could tell, no one had his home number, and that included the answering service itself. Its job was to take messages and hold them until he called in for them.

"I appreciate the concern," he told her. "But there's no need."

"If you say so."

"I do. Was Muffin angry when you got home?" he asked in what she figured was an attempt to change the subject.

"She got over it," Cathy said. Muffin was her fictitious dog. A cuddly Lhasa apso who hated to be left alone. "The dog-sitter really takes time with her when I'm gone, and that helps."

"At least you don't have to put her in a kennel."

Cathy cringed as the familiar wave of guilt washed over her. She wasn't devious by nature, and sometimes it was hard to carry on the charade of her charmed life. But she knew she didn't have a choice. Not if she wanted to keep someone like Stone Ward interested in her.

"Did you finish the book?" she asked.

"Last night. You were right—it was great. And I never guessed the identity of the killer."

They took turns recommending books for the other to read. Cathy settled down to discuss the latest plot twists of their favorite mystery writer. She had to put Stone on hold a couple of times while she fielded other calls, but otherwise they talked uninterrupted for nearly an hour.

"It's late," he said finally. "I should let you get back to work."

She nodded without speaking. She didn't want him to go—she never wanted him to go. But she couldn't say that. It was just one more lie of omission.

"You'll be at work tomorrow?" he asked.

"Of course."

"Same time?"

"I'd like that." She had a feeling her voice gave away

too much, but she couldn't help that. His calls were the highlight of her existence.

He exhaled slowly. "You know, Cathy, one of these days I'm going to sneak up to your office and meet you in person."

It was an old threat. The first time he'd made it, she'd panicked, but since then she'd learned he didn't actually mean to do anything; he just liked to tease her.

"I'm on the seventh floor, and security isn't going to let you into the elevator," she replied.

"I have my ways."

She was sure that he did. "Cheap talk," she told him. "Have a good night, Stone."

"Until tomorrow. Good night."

"Bye."

She waited until he hung up the phone, then she disconnected the line. The console light winked out.

Cathy sighed. It was over until tomorrow. Until she watched the clock again and waited to hear from him. She slowly pulled off her headset, rose to her feet and headed for the coffee machine. As she had every night they'd spoken, she would replay this conversation over and over in her mind until she nearly had it memorized. She would analyze his voice, his words, and tell herself that it was okay that he was attracted to a mere figment of both of their imaginations.

She'd brewed the coffee when she'd first come on duty, so it was hot and fresh. She poured herself a cup, then stirred in a package of sweetener. Before she returned to her seat, she raised her gaze up, past the cup and the coffeemaker to the mirror on the wall.

She didn't know what Stone thought of her, but she knew what she'd told him. That she was a five-foot–eight-inch, leggy blonde. He pictured someone who looked good in a bikini. She'd often talked about wearing short dresses or tight jeans. More of the fantasy, she told herself. It didn't actually hurt anyone. She *wanted* to look like that more than anything. She just couldn't seem to make it happen.

She stared at her reflection, at the mousy brown hair that hung halfway down her back. The center part allowed her hair to spill onto her face, concealing her plain features. She wore baggy jeans and a shapeless T-shirt, hoping that the loose clothing would conceal her extra twenty pounds. She'd never worn a bikini in her life.

She lowered her gaze back to her coffee and turned away from her reflection. It didn't matter. Stone wasn't interested in a real person. He liked the pretend Cathy who was only a fun voice on the phone. He had his own world, and she doubted she occupied more than a footnote in the story of his life.

When she settled back in her seat and slid her headset into place, she glanced at the clock. Less than twenty-four hours until she talked to him again.

Stone stared at the printout in front of him, but he didn't actually see the figures there. He, who normally had a nearly supernatural ability to focus on what he was doing, was distracted. It was the time of day. Make that time of night, he amended to himself. Nearly midnight. Nearly time to call Cathy.

Odd how a disembodied voice on the phone had come to be such a large part of his life. For the past two years, she had been his lifeline and his only companion. She often accused him of being a recluse, but she had no idea of the reality of his situation or the fact that he never left his self-made prison. She didn't know that her laughter, the sound of her smoky voice, her impossible tales of a world filled with sunshine and joy were images he clung to. They were the only fantasies he allowed himself.

He wasn't even sure how their relationship had started. He'd always called in late in the evening for messages. One day he'd realized the same young woman answered the phone. He didn't know who had first started talking about something other than business or why. Without him noticing when it had happened, he had begun to anticipate their time together.

He wondered about Cathy. She was obviously bright and funny. She had a great life. So why did she work the graveyard shift at an answering service? Who was she really? Was she hiding out from something or someone? Had she been on the run and settled here? He sensed secrets in her voice. At times he suspected her stories were just that— entertainment. But he didn't mind. He liked listening to her. She made him laugh; she fussed over him. With her, he could be himself and not worry.

Because he didn't want her learning the truth about him, he never pressed her for personal information. It would be easy to have her investigated; after all, he had the staff and the technical resources, but that wouldn't be playing fair. So instead, he took whatever she told him and let it be enough.

He put away the report and glanced at the clock. Only a few more minutes. It had been almost two weeks since her weekend trip to Mexico, and he wondered if she had any other travel planned. Cathy generally went away for the weekend once or twice a month. He dreaded her yearly vacations. Time seemed to drag when she was gone.

He stood up and crossed to the credenza by the window. A carafe of coffee sat on a tray with his untouched dinner. He stared out the glass at the large backyard illuminated by floodlights. Beyond that was empty darkness and in the distance, the lights of the small community of Redondo Beach. During the day, this room had an impressive view of the Pacific Ocean and the beaches just north of the peninsula. At night, water was dark and featureless, although when it was quiet outside, he could hear the pounding of the surf on the cliffs below.

He poured himself a cup of coffee, then returned to his desk. It was time. He dialed the familiar number.

"A to Z Answering Service," she answered.

"Hi, Cathy."

"Stone!" The obvious pleasure in her voice made him smile. "How are you?"

"Great."

"Make a million today?" she asked.

"Just about."

They didn't often talk about his business. She knew that he dealt with investments and real estate, but that was all. He didn't want her having details that might make her too curious about him. It would be far too easy for her to start checking into his past. Once she knew the truth about him, everything would be over.

"How about in your neck of the woods?" he asked.

"The usual. Mrs. Morrison went to the doctor today, so she has a list of new medicines. Do you remember who she is?"

He leaned back in his leather chair. "Yes, the eccentric older lady who likes to be called with a reminder to take her medication."

"Exactly. One of the operators here spent a couple of hours on the phone with her and then her doctor. I'm still not sure we have everything sorted out, but we're trying. Fortunately I only have the late-night call, which I made about a half hour ago."

"Any interesting people calling to get bailed out of prison?"

She laughed. The sound was low and husky and made his gut clench. "Not so far, but that side of the business doesn't usually pick up for a couple of hours."

She talked about her day, about walking her dog, Muffin, in the park, about a movie she'd seen. They argued over the next book they were going to read together. He wanted to choose a spy thriller, while she was interested in a biography about a famous scientist.

"Boring," he insisted.

"How can you know that if you haven't read the book?"

"You think nerds with pocket protectors lead interesting lives?"

"Oh, so we're generalizing, are we? This might be a good time to say something about business tycoons who rape and pillage the economy."

She was so easy, he thought with a grin. Cathy had a temper, and he enjoyed pricking it from time to time. She always responded to the bait.

"I have never raped or pillaged in my life," he said.

"I don't doubt that. I'm just pointing out that generalizations can be limiting."

"Sort of like saying all blondes are bimbos."

"Exactly."

He closed his eyes and wondered what she looked like. "You're a blonde and you're definitely not a bimbo."

"I don't think that's a compliment, so I'm not going to say thank you."

He chuckled. "All right. You win. We'll read the biography. But it had better be interesting."

"You'll love it," she promised. "I'll go to the bookstore—"

A sudden, loud shrieking sound cut through her sentence.

Stone straightened and clutched the receiver. "Cathy? What's that noise?"

"I don't know." He could barely make out her words over the noise. "I think it's the fire alarm. Hold on."

There was a click, followed by silence. Even as tension filled him, he reminded himself that she was on the seventh floor of a locked building. There was a security team on duty. She was perfectly safe. But the tightness in his gut changed from pleasure to uneasiness.

Less than a minute later, she returned to the line. "I'm not sure what it is," she said, obviously worried. He could still hear the alarm in the background, but it wasn't as loud.

"I can't get the security people on the phone," she continued, "But according to the system panel, the smoke detectors have been triggered."

"Did you call 911?"

"No. It's probably nothing."

"Call them right now. Better that they come out on a false alarm than something happens and they're not there. Put me on hold again—I'll wait."

"I don't think—"

"Cathy! Do it."

"All right. Just a sec."

This time she was gone longer. When she returned, her voice was thick with panic. "Stone, there's smoke in the hallway. I went and checked before I called the fire department, and it's creeping up from the elevator shafts. I don't know what to do."

He cursed under his breath. "How far are you from the emergency stairs?"

"They're at the other end of the hall, but they're locked. I don't have a key."

"What? They're supposed to be open at all times, aren't they?"

"Yes. But there were a few break-ins over the past couple of months, so they started locking the stairs at night. Someone from security rides up with me in the elevator when I come on my shift and they check on me several times in the night. When my shift is over, I'm escorted back downstairs. It's never been a problem before."

She'd never been trapped in a burning building before, either.

"It's going to be fine," he told her with a confidence he wasn't sure he believed. "The fire department will be there shortly."

"Stone, I'm scared."

He leaned forward as if he could somehow get physically closer to her. "I know, but I'm right here with you. I won't go away until you're safe."

"Thanks. I know this is silly, but—" She sucked in a breath. "Oh, God, I can smell smoke. It's coming under the door. Something's burning. The odor is funny. I have to get out of here."

Fear tightened his throat. Fear for her and frustration that there was nothing he could do. "Listen to me, Cathy. You told the dispatch person where you were, right?"

"Yes."

"Then they know to come get you."

"Maybe I should go out in the hall. Oh, Stone, there's more smoke. It's filling the room!"

"Stay calm. Put me on hold and call the fire department again. Tell them you're trapped. Put me on hold. I'll wait."

"Okay."

He listened to the silence for what felt like a lifetime. When she returned to the line, she was crying.

"They're nearly here," she said. "But the fire is all over the building. It's going to t-take them a while to get to me. I'm so scared, Stone."

"I know, honey. But I'm still right here."

"They said—" She choked, then recovered. "They said to wet a towel and wrap it around my face."

"You go do that. I'll wait for you."

"All right."

He heard the headset clatter against the desk. He'd never felt so helpless in his life. Stone shook his head. That wasn't true. He'd felt exactly this helpless about three years ago. There'd been nothing he could do then, either, and because of that—and him—Evelyn had died.

He shook off those thoughts and concentrated on Cathy, willing her to be all right. He listened intently and finally heard her rapid footsteps as she returned to pick up the headset.

"There's fire," she screamed. "I can see it. Oh, Stone, what now? I don't—"

A loud explosion cut her off. Involuntarily Stone held the receiver away from his ear. Then he pressed it back in place. "Cathy? Cathy, can you hear me?"

He heard a shriek and a crash, then silence.

"Cathy? Cathy!"

Nothing. There was a click followed by a low, steady dial tone.

Chapter Two

It took Stone several seconds to realize what was going on. He'd been disconnected and had no way of finding out what had happened to Cathy.

The knot in his gut tightened, as did his feeling of panic. Dammit all to hell, he thought grimly as he hit the buttons that would connect him with her office again. Even as he listened to the ringing, he told himself he was wasting time. Something had happened to Cathy. He could feel it as surely as he could feel the rapid pounding of his heart. Even if she was still all right, she wasn't going to waste time or breath answering the phone.

He dropped the receiver into the cradle, then headed out of his office. There was only one thing for him to do, and that was to check on her personally. He would drive to the answering service and make sure that she was all right.

He left his office at the rear of the second story and headed toward the stairs. From there he made his way to the kitchen. Ula, his fifty-something housekeeper, glanced up as he entered. Although it was late, she looked as fresh and relaxed as she had early that morning.

"Mr. Ward, this is a surprise." Her small dark eyes crinkled at the corners, but she didn't smile. "Don't tell me you're actually hungry. It's only been a couple of days since I bullied you into eating something. Usually you make me wait longer before I can force you to look at another meal."

Normally her teasing brightened his spirits, and he would point out that while he didn't eat much food, she rarely slept. But tonight their banter was beyond him.

"I'm going out," he said.

"Now? By yourself?"

He understood her concern. He usually took the limo and used one of the company's drivers. But he didn't have time to wait. "I'll take the BMW," he said. "Don't worry. I'll be fine."

He would be. On more nights than Ula knew about, he took the car and drove until nearly dawn. But he was always careful to be back home before sunrise. It was an odd life. While he didn't have the supernatural powers, he understood the vampire's fear of daylight. The difference was he wouldn't turn to dust. He would merely horrify those who had the misfortune to see him.

"Don't wait up," he said, and grabbed the keys dangling from the hook by the back door. He walked into the garage and moved to the large dark sedan. In a matter of minutes, he was heading east down the winding road. Twenty minutes later, he was on the freeway, driving north toward the valley.

It was well after midnight and there weren't many cars on the road. The BMW ate up miles, the quiet power of the vehicle reassuring him that he would soon be there.

Questions raced through his mind. What had happened? Was Cathy all right?

Even as that worry formed, he pushed it away. She *had* to be okay.

The answering service was on Ventura Boulevard, just east of the 405 freeway. He exited and turned onto the street. Up ahead fire trucks filled the two right lanes. Red lights flashed in the darkness. He saw several emergency vehicles, including police cars and ambulances. Despite the late hour, a crowd had collected. Stone parked as close as he could, then got out and started to walk.

The building stood tall but damaged in the illumination of streetlights. White smoke drifted out of broken windows. Hoses ran across the sidewalk, and water spilled out the front door, then flowed to the gutters. Several police officers held back the spectators.

Stone forced himself to move through the people. He was grateful for the night and for the fact that everyone was staring up at the building. He inhaled the smell of smoke, charred wood, plastic and other materials he couldn't identify. The fear was still there, and with it concern. He had to find out about Cathy.

He made his way to the front of the crowd. A young police officer stood facing the building. Stone tapped him lightly.

"Excuse me," he said. "I'm trying to find out about a friend of mine."

"If you're not a relative, we can't give out any information," the officer said without looking at him.

"I understand. I don't need details, I'm just concerned. I was on the phone with a woman. Cathy Eldridge. She works for an answering service in that building. We were talking when the alarm went off. I stayed on the line with her while she called 911, and then we were cut off. I want to make sure they got her out safely."

The policeman turned toward him. He was young, not yet thirty. His gaze swept over Stone's face, lingering for a moment before moving on. "Two security guards and a woman were taken to a local hospital. That's all I can say."

"No one died?"

"Not that I know of."

Some of Stone's tension eased. She wasn't dead, but she was injured. He considered asking more questions, but didn't think he would get any additional information from the cop. He turned his back on the man. It didn't matter. He could still learn what he needed to know. His hope had been to save time.

He'd nearly made his way out of the crowd when someone touched him on the sleeve. He glanced to his right and saw a young woman staring at him. She was barely out of her teens and judging by her tousled brown hair and mismatched clothing, she'd been awakened by the disturbance.

"I heard you talking to that cop," she said. "They took your friend to the hospital up on Van Nuys Boulevard. The EMT guys were yelling that as they loaded her in the ambulance."

"Thank you," he said, and gave her a quick smile. "You're very kind." He turned toward his car.

"No problem. I hope your friend is—"

When he'd turned, he'd shifted to the left, exposing that side of his face to the streetlight. The young woman gasped and stepped back involuntarily. Stone kept on going as if he hadn't noticed.

It took him less than ten minutes to find the hospital and park in the nearly empty lot. The night staff was slightly more cooperative than the police officer had been and allowed him to wait while Cathy was examined. He settled in a shadowed corner of the emergency-room waiting area. There were plenty of magazines, along with a television. He ignored both and concentrated on Cathy, willing her to be all right. People arrived with friends and relatives as the results of other disasters filtered in. He watched, wondering when her friends would start to arrive. A young couple showed up, and he thought they might know her, but they were there to visit the woman's grandmother.

Time crept along. Stone wanted to pace to ease his restlessness, but he didn't dare. Instead, he sat quietly and wondered about the quirks of fate that had brought him to this place. He hadn't been in a hospital in a couple of years. He didn't like the memories the smell evoked.

Three hours later, a pretty nurse with curly dark hair and eyes the color of chocolate collapsed next to him. "I'm working a double shift," she said, and sighed. "So forgive me if I don't speak in complete sentences."

"You have news for me?"

She nodded and rotated her shoulders. "Cathy Eldridge is one lucky girl. Right now she's being moved up to a room. I have the number." She dug around in the pocket of her blue scrub pants, then handed him a slip of paper. "They're only going to allow family in for a couple of minutes tonight."

He met her steady gaze. "Did I mention we were cousins?"

"I figured it was something like that."

"So she's okay?"

"Like I said, she's lucky. She didn't breathe in too much smoke. She's got a bump on her head that we're hoping is going to turn out to be an inconvenience, but nothing serious. But we're waiting for her to regain consciousness. She wrenched her knee. That's a problem. The ER doctor thinks she's going to have to have surgery and some rehabilitation. However, the prognosis is good.''

He'd been hoping for something better. ''She's unconscious?''

The nurse nodded. ''All the signs are positive. It could have been a whole lot worse. The smoke could have damaged her lungs, or she could have been burned. The firefighters got her out just in time.''

He supposed he should feel grateful, but the news left him stunned. Cathy was injured. He had to get to her.

He clutched the piece of paper in his hand and rose to his feet. ''I'll go up and see her. Thanks for the information.''

''You're welcome.'' She gave him a tired smile.

On the second floor, he found the correct wing, then spoke to a nurse at the main station. ''You know we're not supposed to let anyone in,'' she said matter-of-factly.

''I know, but I need to see her. I was on the phone with her when the fire started. We talked until the line went dead.''

The older woman frowned. ''Five minutes, no more. You wouldn't happen to know about immediate family, would you?'' Before he could answer, her frown deepened. ''Don't even try telling me you're a brother or something.''

So much for pretending to be a cousin. ''Cathy has mentioned several friends to me, but no family.''

''I guess they'll find someone,'' she said.

He took a pen from the counter and wrote on a notepad. ''This is my name and private phone number. If I don't answer, leave a message and I'll get right back to you.''

She stared at the paper. ''What's this for?''

''Until you find family, I'm all that Cathy has. I want to be informed of any changes. Also I'll be responsible for any medical bills not covered by insurance.''

The older woman looked surprised. "You sure you want to do that? It could get expensive."

"I don't care."

He had a lot of concerns in his life, but money wasn't one of them.

"If you say so, Mr.—" she glanced at the paper "—Mr. Ward. Go on in, but you can only stay a couple of minutes."

"Thanks."

Stone walked down the corridor and paused in front of the second-to-last open door on the right. He'd been carrying on a phone relationship with Cathy for over two years, but he didn't know what she looked like. She'd told him she was tall and blond. He'd wanted to picture someone beautiful, like a fashion model, but a voice in his gut had always whispered that wasn't true. So while he'd been able to imagine her body, he'd never had a clear image of her face.

He looked over his shoulder, half expecting to see her group of friends barreling his way. If they showed up, he would step aside. They had the right to be here now. He didn't. If he hadn't been on the phone with her when the alarm had gone off, he wouldn't have known there was a problem. The tension in him increased as he thought of how frantic he would have been if he'd made his call and she hadn't been there. Thank God he'd been with her. Then he sucked in a breath and stepped into the room.

Because of the late hour, the only light came from a dim bulb over the hospital bed. He was careful to stay in the shadows as he moved closer. If she woke up, he didn't want to frighten her.

He took one step, then another until he was within touching distance. After two years of wondering, he finally knew. She was lying down, so he couldn't judge her height.

The first thing he noticed was her face. There were smudges of smoke on her cheeks and forehead, contrasting with pale skin. Her hair wasn't blond at all, but a darker shade. A medium brown. It was long and spilled across the pillow. Her mouth was full, her nose straight. He couldn't tell about her eyes.

She was not the woman he'd pictured, nor was she anything like she'd described herself. Stone stepped a little closer so that he could read the wristband. The name matched. This was Cathy.

Confused by this latest development in a difficult night, he pulled a chair close to her bed and sat next to her. Her arms lay at her sides. He touched the wristband, then stroked the back of her hand. Her skin was soft. He grasped her fingers and squeezed. She returned the pressure.

Stone felt an instant spark, as if electricity had jumped from her body to his. He frowned, not sure what that meant, then he decided it was just a reaction to all he'd been through. He was exhausted, nothing more. Still, he continued to hold her hand in his and he brushed his thumb against her skin. Soft and smooth, he thought, and just as pale as her face. This was not the skin of a woman who had recently spent the weekend in a sunny resort. According to Cathy's stories, she'd spent much of the spring traveling to vacation hot spots. She'd talked about wearing a bikini and getting sun. But there wasn't a hint of a tan.

Stone studied her face again, the nondescript features, the mousy brown hair, then he moved his gaze lower, to her body. The layers of sheet and blanket concealed details, but he had an idea about her general shape. She was rounded. Not unpleasantly so, but he doubted she wore the bikinis and short skirts she talked about.

"Ah, Cathy," he said quietly. "All the times I thought about meeting you, I never thought it would be like this."

He continued to stroke her hand, enjoying the feel of her smooth warmth.

"I'm glad you're doing all right," he went on. "I understand you've been through a shock and that you need to rest, but you're going to have to regain consciousness soon. We need to know that you're fine. I guess *I'm* the one who really wants to know that. So for me, okay?"

For a second it seemed that she was going to stir. Stone froze in his seat, not sure what he would do if she started to wake up. He supposed he would have to duck out of the room before she realized he was there. But she didn't open her eyes and if she seemed more restless than before, it was only noticeable to him because he was watching her so closely.

"Mr. Ward?"

He glanced up and saw the nurse standing in the doorway. "Yes?"

"You've got about two more minutes, then I'm going to have to ask you to leave."

He nodded, then turned his attention back to Cathy. "They want me to go so you can rest. I'll be back tomorrow. It would be great if you were awake for that." Actually he didn't know how he would handle the situation if she was, but he would deal with that problem when it occurred.

He released her hand, then rose to his feet. He moved to the small closet by the door to the bathroom. Inside were a pair of worn jeans and a large, faded T-shirt. A purse rested on a shelf. He pulled it down and stared at the smoky handprints clearly visible on the cheap vinyl. She'd obviously been clutching her purse when they'd rescued her.

After making sure the nurse had returned to her station, he opened the bag and pulled out Cathy's wallet. He made a note of her home address on her driver's license, then checked the remaining contents. She had one credit card and fourteen dollars to her name. He replaced the wallet and returned to the bed.

"I'll see you soon," he promised, then leaned over and kissed her cheek. She didn't stir. On his way out, he stopped and told the nurse he wanted Cathy moved to a private room. He would pay the difference.

Twenty minutes later, he eased the BMW off the freeway and into the silent suburban community of North Hollywood. Despite the name, there was a range of foothills between this city and the tourist and movie mecca of Hollywood proper. Parts of North Hollywood had been renovated in recent years. He checked street names against the map in his car, then, after making a few wrong turns, he found himself on Cathy's street.

He parked in front of the small dark house. It had been built in the fifties, along with most of the other homes on the street. There were mature trees, small lots, older cars. There was nothing wrong with the house—except that she'd told him she lived in a nice condo by the pass.

"Cathy Eldridge, you are a fraud," he murmured in the quiet of the night.

Why had she done it? Why had she lied to him? Even as he asked the questions, he knew the answers could be found in the conversations he had with Cathy. She knew just enough about him to assume he lived an extravagant life-style. His company, Ward International, was well-known. Cathy probably thought she had to create an exciting existence to keep his attention. She probably thought he wouldn't be interested in someone living in ordinary circumstances. Just like Evelyn.

Evelyn. He closed his eyes and willed that memory away. He didn't want to think about her. Not now, not this night.

So Cathy had created a world that existed somewhere between truth and lies. Were the friends real? Any of the travel? Her dog? He stared at the small house and shook his head. If only she'd realized that what drew him to her wasn't where she went or what she did. It was the sound of her voice, her laughter, the sharp wit and obvious intelligence.

He started the car and drove toward the freeway. He supposed he should be angry with her, but he wasn't. Despite the stories, she was still Cathy. He still cared about her, and were she to disappear from his world, he would miss her more than she would ever guess.

Stone watched the first fingers of sunlight creep across the floor of the private hospital room. He stood and stretched, trying to ease the crick in his neck and the dull throbbing in the small of his back. He'd spent most of the previous two nights at Cathy's bedside, holding her hand, talking to her, enjoying her quiet company.

There had been a few times of lucidity, when she'd stirred, opened her eyes and even spoken. He was careful to stay in the shadows then, waiting until she dozed off again before moving close.

He glanced at his watch. Mary, the night nurse, would be by shortly to take vital signs and draw blood. Stone knew that he should be leaving. As it was, he was going to be driving home in daylight. Not to worry, he told himself. Commuters were much too interested in getting to work on time for them to notice him.

He returned to Cathy's side and took her hand. In the past two nights, he'd become intimately familiar with her hand and her fingers. He knew every bump, every curve, every line. He'd traced the shape of her nails, discovered the hollow of her palm. Now his hand curled around hers with a comfortable familiarity.

"Hey, kid, I'm going to have to go soon," he said quietly. "But I'll be back tonight. I know, I know, you're getting sick of my company, but I don't have anything planned so you're stuck with me."

He knew eventually he was going to have to step out of the shadows and let her know he was there. Tonight, he promised himself. When he returned.

He looked at her. Her eyes were closed, her chest barely moving as she drew in each breath. He inhaled deeply, matching his rhythm with hers. As he did, he caught the scent of the flowers that filled every available surface of her room. He'd had them delivered the first day. Not knowing what she liked, he'd had the florist bring some of everything. Sweet smells formed a heady perfume that would always remind him of her.

He'd wondered if any other flowers would join his. Her employer had sent a plant, but no one else seemed to care that Cathy was in the hospital. Stone was no longer surprised.

Curiosity and concern had won over guilt, and he'd asked one of his people to investigate her. Knowing her place of employment, her home address and driver's license number had made the search simple.

Cathy Eldridge, age twenty-eight. An only child. Her father had run off before she started grade school, and her mother had been an alcoholic who had died when Cathy was twenty-one. No siblings, no relatives, no friends. Not even a dog.

At times he thought he should be angry with her for lying to him and for assuming that he would require her to make up an exciting life as a prerequisite for a friendship. At other times the thought of her solitary existence was an all too familiar reflection of his own empty world. She had too little, he had too much and they were both alone. Perhaps that was what had drawn them together.

"Mr. Ward?"

He glanced up and saw Mary hovering in the doorway.

"Ms. Eldridge's doctor is making his rounds. Would you like to speak to him?"

"Yes, thank you." He gave Cathy's hand a quick squeeze. "I'll be back. Don't you go running off without me."

He followed Mary down the hallway to the nurses' station. "This is Dr. Tucker," she said, walking up to a tall, thin man with graying temples. "Dr. Tucker, this is Stone Ward. He's a friend of Cathy's."

Dr. Tucker's pale gray gaze was steady as he offered a hand. "I understand you're about the only friend Cathy has. We've been unable to locate any family."

"She doesn't have any," Stone said. He knew the doctor would assume he was privy to that information because he and Cathy were close, not because he'd had her investigated.

"I see. I've heard that you're taking responsibility for her. Moving her to a private room and arranging for special care when she's ready to leave."

"That's right."

"Fine." Dr. Tucker motioned toward a vinyl-covered sofa in the corner. "Let's have a seat and I'll bring you up-to-date on her condition."

"Thanks."

When they were comfortable, the doctor opened a chart and read a few lines. "Cathy is doing well. She was lucky. There were no burns or damage to the lungs. She wasn't seriously injured in the explosion. I don't anticipate any problems from the head trauma." He read some more. "As far as her leg goes, the knee is going to require arthroscopic surgery, then some physical therapy to get her up and around. I would anticipate a six-week recovery time from that. Maybe two months. She has a lot of bruising, which may slow her down. When we release her, she's going to need someone to look after her for a few days."

"Not a problem," Stone told him. He planned to bring Cathy home with him. Ula would be thrilled to have a houseguest to fuss over.

"Good. We're doing one last CAT scan today and if the results are what we expect, she'll have the surgery tomorrow. That would mean releasing her in three days."

"That's fine. My house is already prepared."

They finalized a few more details, then shook hands. "Very nice to meet you," Dr. Tucker said. "I'm glad Cathy isn't alone."

"Me, too."

The doctor hesitated. "It's really none of my business, but I couldn't help noticing the scarring. Car accident?"

Even as he told himself not to, Stone involuntarily touched the left side of his face. "Yes. About three years ago."

"I thought so." Dr. Tucker leaned close and studied the marks. "There's a very gifted plastic surgeon in my medical building. Her offices are next to mine. If you're considering surgery, I would highly recommend her."

Stone shook his head. "No, thanks."

Dr. Tucker persisted. "There are some wonderful new techniques. She could even out your skin completely and get rid of the thick scars. You'd probably be left with thin, pale lines, but they're nothing compared with what you have now."

Stone rose to his feet. "I appreciate the information.

About this—'' he pointed to his face ''—and Cathy. Thank you, Doctor.''

He headed toward the elevator. He knew Dr. Tucker wouldn't understand his refusal to have plastic surgery. His first doctor hadn't understood, either. He was healthy, and he had the money to pay for the operation. So what was the problem?

What they couldn't know and what he wouldn't explain was that the scars were part of his penance. He carried the scars as a tangible reminder of that night…and Evelyn's death. Just in case he ever tried to forget.

Chapter Three

Cathy stirred. She was pleasantly drowsy in the dimly lit hospital room, yet the urge to open her eyes was strong. She'd been awake on and off most of the day. She supposed she should try to stay up a little longer, but the thought of sleep tempted her.

She shifted, trying to get comfortable. Except for a few aches scattered throughout her body, most of the pain radiated from the bump on her head and her injured right knee. She'd been awake when Dr. Tucker had made his rounds late this afternoon, and he'd explained her condition. She'd been lucky, he'd told her. She could have died.

Cathy knew that was true. She tried not to think about those horrible minutes while she'd waited for the fire department to come rescue her. If Stone hadn't stayed on the line with her, she would have lost it for sure.

Stone. She relaxed and smiled faintly. He'd been so good to her, keeping her calm, telling her that she was going to be safe. He'd sent her enough flowers to fill a greenhouse. That was so kind of him.

She missed him and hoped that he missed her, too. It would be a while before she would be able to work. The thought of them not being able to talk upset her, so she decided not to deal with that right now. There were other pressing worries—her job, for one. Was the company still in business? Plus there was the issue of her medical bills. She doubted all of them would be covered by insurance. Her smile faded and with it, her good humor. She didn't want to think about any of this. It would be better to sleep.

She drew in a deep breath and forced herself to relax. The pain throbbed in time with her heartbeat, but she was due for a shot soon and that would help. In the meantime, she would close her eyes and allow herself to drift away. Her problems would still be waiting when she was stronger.

"They told me you were awake, but I guess they were wrong."

The statement hung in the air. Cathy tensed instantly, not sure if she'd imagined the words or if they'd really been spoken. That voice! It couldn't be. Stone? Here?

Excitement ripped through her, only to crash headlong into the wall of reality. If Stone was really here, then he could see her. Horror flooded her. He might already know the truth, or if he didn't, he would soon figure it out.

No. This couldn't be happening. She'd imagined the voice. After all, she'd hit her head pretty hard and she'd been out of it for a couple of days. That was it. She wasn't in her right mind.

Someone moved into the room. She didn't dare open her eyes, but she felt a presence—*his* presence. A chair scraped against the floor, then he took her hand in his.

The contact was warm, gentle and oddly familiar. Perhaps because she'd imagined it a thousand times, she told herself. Over the past two years, as she relived their phone calls, she'd fantasized about him coming to meet her, about him taking her in his arms and telling her that he felt things for her he'd never felt for another woman. Foolish dreams, she thought, not quite able to believe this was really happening. Stone was here?

"Cathy?" he murmured. "Can you hear me? Mary, the night nurse, said you were awake. How are you feeling?"

She didn't want to open her eyes. If she kept them closed, then he wasn't real.

But he was. Shame filled her. For the deception and the lies, and for the truth he must now know about her. She wasn't sure which would be worse. His contempt or his pity.

"Please go away," she whispered.

"Not exactly the greeting I was hoping for. You could at least put a 'hi' in front of it. As in, 'Hi, Stone. Nice to meet you. Now please go away.'"

Her eyes burned with unshed tears. "You're laughing at me."

"No, I'm trying to make us both feel a little better. Come on, try it. 'Hi, Stone.' How hard could it be?"

He had no idea, she thought, turning away from him. A single tear trickled down her temple and got lost in her hair. She moaned softly. Her hair. It wasn't enough that she didn't have the friends she'd told him, but she didn't look like he thought, either. He was expecting a leggy blonde with a beauty-pageant figure. Instead, she was a dumpy, overweight pale woman with plain features and mousy brown hair.

"I thought you might like some company," he said. "Am I wrong?"

"Not you," she managed to answer as tears thickened her throat.

"I see."

He released his hold on her hand. She was suddenly cold. Silence filled the room. Finally he cleared his throat. "I thought we were friends."

That got her attention. Involuntarily her head swung toward him, and she opened her eyes.

Stone Ward was really in her hospital room. She saw the outline of him in the shadows. She couldn't make out individual features, but she saw he was a powerful man, tall with broad shoulders. His hair looked dark.

"How can you say that?" she asked. "You have to know the truth about me. About what I told you." She sucked in a breath and caught at the hem of her sheets. "About the lies." The last three words came out as a whisper.

He moved toward her, captured her hand and laced his fingers with hers. She felt warm again. Warm and comforted, not to mention confused. She squinted, wishing the room weren't so dark so she could see him.

"None of that matters," he told her.

"But—"

He cut her off with a quick shake of his head. "I mean it, Cathy. No distressing subjects for conversation. What matters is that you're getting better. The rest of it can wait. How do you feel?"

She wasn't sure how to answer the question. She felt lost and uncertain. Her entire world had shifted, and she couldn't find her balance. Stone Ward was here, talking to her, holding her hand, acting as if she was important to him. He didn't seem to care that she'd lied about who and what she was. But he *had* to care. She'd misled him and—

"I don't understand," she said softly. "Why are you being so nice to me? You should hate me or at least despise me." She blinked, trying to see him more clearly. "Or did you always know it wasn't true? Were you laughing at me?''

The grip on her hand tightened. "Cathy, no. Don't think like that. I didn't know anything. But that's all right. Don't you see? It was never the places you went or what you looked like that made me want to talk to you on the phone. It was how we always had a good time together."

She wanted to believe him. The edges of her brain felt fuzzy and she supposed it was the painkillers they'd given her. Suddenly she was too tired and out of it to argue. Later, when she could really think, she would find a way to make sense of all this. For now it was enough that he was here and she wasn't alone. "All right. Thank you for understanding."

"My pleasure. Now, how are you feeling?"

"Sore."

"Your knee?"

"And my head."

"According to your doctor, you're going to need surgery on your knee."

She rubbed her temple. "He said something about that when he was here earlier. He said it won't be any big deal, but I'll be on crutches for a while afterward."

Crutches. She didn't want to deal with that, or the physical therapy he'd talked about. She had insurance through her work, but she wasn't sure how good it was. Maybe the building owners would cover some of the expense, or their insurance would, because of the fire. Or maybe—

She bit her lower lip. She didn't want to think about any of this now. Everything hurt too much, and she was too confused.

"Cathy?"

That voice. She still couldn't believe that Stone was actually here, that he'd seen her and didn't seem angry about her deception.

"Yes, sorry. I'm kind of out of it."

"I understand." He leaned close, but not close enough that he moved out of the shadows. "I don't want you worrying about anything," he said. "Everything is taken care of. The doctor, the surgeon, the physical therapy."

"But it can't be."

"It is. I'm taking care of all the details. All you have to worry about is getting better."

She looked at him, at the shape of him, and tried to figure out why he was being so nice to her. "I don't understand." Any of it, including him.

"It's very simple. When they release you in a couple of days, I want you to come stay with me. My house is large, and you'll have plenty of room. I've already arranged for a physical therapist to come by and help you. My housekeeper will be there, too, and she'll make sure you're completely taken care of. I want to do this, Cathy. The fire really scared me. I was afraid something had happened to you."

She couldn't have been more stunned if he'd suddenly started speaking a foreign language while performing a folk dance. "You want me to stay at your house?" Her voice was a squeak.

"Yes. The doctor said you shouldn't be alone for a few days. Unless you have someone else who can look after you, you're coming home with me."

Someone else, she thought dully. As in family or friends. She had neither. "I can't," she told him.

"Of course you can. We're friends. Friends look out for each other. You'd do the same for me if you could."

He sounded confident, but she wasn't so sure. She couldn't imagine having anything that someone like him wanted or needed. She was just boring Cathy Eldridge. Nothing about her life was exciting or even the way it was supposed to be.

"My housekeeper will be there all the time," he said. "So you don't have to worry about being alone with me."

Oh, yeah, that was her big concern. That Stone would suddenly lose control and want to attack her in the night. If she hadn't felt so weak and tired, she might have smiled.

"It's not that," she managed to say.

"Then what is it? You'll like the house. It has a nice view of the ocean. Think of it as a vacation."

Something she'd never been on in her life. A vacation. Just like those lies she'd told him. She averted her gaze and turned her head away. "I didn't really go to Mexico a couple of weeks ago."

"I know."

"Or Paris."

"I figured that out, too."

"I just thought—"

"I understand," he said. "Please believe me. I don't want to talk about this now. It's not important."

Not important? How could he say that? She felt as if every layer of her being had been stripped away, leaving her flaws bare to inspection. He would study her and find her very wanting.

"Cathy, please. Just trust me. We've known each other two years. Surely I deserve a chance."

She turned toward him and raised the bed so that she was more sitting up than lying down. Then she pulled her hand free of his touch and reached for the light switch.

Instantly he took hold of her wrist. "Don't," he said.

"I just want to turn on the light."

"I know. You can't."

"Why?"

"I'm—" He shook his head. "I was in a bad car accident about three years ago. My face is scarred, and I would rather you didn't see me just yet."

Her mouth opened, but she couldn't speak. Nothing was what she'd thought. Was this the reason he hid away in his house? Did he think she would find him hideous?

"I don't want to scare you," he said, confirming her thoughts.

"You couldn't."

"You don't know that. It's pretty bad. You're going to have to trust me on this."

How bad could it be? she wondered. But she didn't have the energy to pursue the subject. For now she would trust him. And there was a bright spot in the situation. Stone couldn't see her, either. He wouldn't know how plain she was. Not ugly, just not pretty at all. If only she were the leggy blonde she'd told him about. If only she had been to all those places.

"Cathy, don't," he said. "Don't worry about it. I understand why you said those things to me. It doesn't matter."

How could he read her mind? Before she could ask, a nurse came in to give her a shot. They briefly discussed the morning schedule. She would be having her surgery first thing. When the woman was gone, Cathy turned to look at Stone.

"You don't have to stay," she said. "I mean, I'm sure you have things to do. Important things."

"Right now you're the most important part of my life."

He took her hand again and laced his fingers with hers. The touch comforted her and made her want to move closer to him.

"You never said that you'd come stay at my house," he reminded her. "Say yes."

The shot had been powerful. Cathy could feel herself fading. It was an effort to talk, but even as the edges of her mind began to fold over on themselves, she managed a whispered "Yes."

Two days later, Cathy found herself half sitting, half lying down in the back of an ambulance.

"The ride's going to be about forty minutes," the driver told her as his assistant checked the straps on her gurney.

"I'll be fine." She gave the men a reassuring smile.

"Mr. Ward said we were to bring a nurse along if you thought there might be a problem."

"That's not necessary." Over the past day or so, her headache had faded. The only pain came from her knee, but as she'd had surgery on it yesterday, that was to be expected. In the small bag that contained the few items of clothing she'd been wearing the night of the fire was a prescription for painkiller. According to her doctor, physical therapy would start in a few days. Everything was going according to plan.

The driver slammed the rear door of the ambulance, then the men walked around to the front and slid into the cab. Cathy clutched the metal rails on either side of her gurney, not because she was afraid of falling out, but to touch something real and reassure herself that this was really happening. She was actually leaving the hospital to go stay with Stone.

Even as she smiled, she knew tears weren't far behind. She wasn't sure if she was living a dream or a nightmare. Last night after the surgery, Stone had stopped by. She remembered going to sleep wondering if he would visit her again, then she'd awakened some time after midnight and he'd been sitting at the side of her bed.

They'd talked in the darkness, and for a few minutes

she'd allowed herself to pretend it was just like it had been when they'd talked on the phone. But it wasn't the same. For one thing, he'd asked her for the key to her house. The request made sense. After all, someone had to go collect her things, pick up the mail and arrange for the new mail to be held. But she hated the thought of him finding out where she lived or what her house looked like even as she told herself the fact that it was small and old didn't matter. She kept the place clean. The garden was tidy, the hedges neat.

But it wasn't about cleanliness or tidiness, she thought as the ambulance pulled onto the freeway and headed west. It was about being poor. She'd told Stone she lived in a modern condo. Very trendy, well decorated. It had been another part of the fantasy.

"'Oh, what a tangled web we weave...'" she said softly, knowing that the old quote was still applicable today. At least in *her* life. She'd tried to deceive Stone and now she was facing the consequences of her behavior. What she didn't understand was why he wouldn't talk about it.

She'd tried to bring up the subject several times, but he always dismissed it, saying it didn't matter. She frowned. It had to matter. He had to loathe her. Except he didn't act as if he did, so nothing made sense. It was starting to hurt to think this hard.

So instead, she concentrated on the view out the window. They took the 405 freeway south, over the pass and into West Los Angeles. From there, they continued south. She saw large passenger planes fly low over the freeway as they landed at the airport. A few miles past that, the ambulance exited and headed west again.

Her heartbeat increased slightly. They must be getting close. Stone had said his house had a view of the ocean. She'd never lived close to the water before. That would be a nice change. Maybe he was right. Maybe she should think of this as a vacation—a brief chance to visit a world very different from her own.

They drove for several miles, then the road narrowed and they started to climb. Cathy caught glimpses of houses, trees and beyond them, flashes of the blue ocean.

The ambulance pulled into a long driveway. She turned so she could see over her shoulder. Two wide gates kept out the curious. The driver spoke into a small box. A couple of seconds later, the gates slowly opened and they drove onto the property.

Cathy ducked low enough to be able to see out the side window. The house was huge. At least three stories and designed more like a castle than an actual house. The facade was stone, the windows different shapes. Many were beveled. The grounds seemed to stretch on forever. Stone had to have a couple of acres up here, and at the price of real estate in this neighborhood, he'd obviously sunk millions into his home.

She'd always known they were different, but it was intimidating to see those differences played out in such a clear way. No doubt there was a staff in residence. She swallowed. Maybe this had been a bad idea, she thought. Was it too late to change her mind and have the driver take her home to her tiny house in the valley?

Before she could decide, they came to a stop. The driver opened the rear of the ambulance. He glanced from her to the house.

"There are stairs up to the front door, and I'm gonna guess there's a bunch more inside."

"I can use crutches," Cathy said. She'd practiced on them that morning. She wasn't good, but she had managed.

"Naw. That's why I brought help."

His assistant climbed out of the passenger's side of the

vehicle. Both men were strong and obviously used to carrying around patients. Together they slid the gurney out of the back of the ambulance and wheeled her toward the front of the house. As they approached, one side of the double front door opened and a small woman stepped out.

She looked to be in her mid-to-late fifties, with graying hair and coal black eyes. She wore a pale gray dress that looked like a cross between a nurse's uniform and a dress for a maid, and sensible white shoes.

"Miss Eldridge," she said, and smiled. "I'm Ula, the housekeeper. Stone said you'd be arriving this morning. Welcome." Her smile faded as her gaze focused on the two men. "You two be careful with her. She's had quite a shock, and we don't need her dropped on top of everything else."

The two men exchanged an exasperated glance. This was not the first time they'd heard this particular admonition. "Yes, ma'am. We'll make sure the young lady arrives safe and sound."

"Through here, please."

She led them into the house. Cathy had a brief impression of a foyer large enough for a hotel, marble floors and doors and hallways leading to other parts of the house. Before she could absorb anything, they were moving up the stairs, then down a corridor. Ula open a door and stepped aside. The men followed.

Cathy was placed next to a four-poster queen-size bed. She'd barely caught her breath when the men physically lifted her onto the mattress.

"We'll be right back with her things," one of them said as they left.

Ula crossed to the windows and pulled back the thick drapes. Instantly bright sunlight filled the huge room. From her place on the bed, Cathy could see well-kept grounds, the corner of what looked like a swimming pool and an incredible view of the ocean. The water stretched out to the horizon, all glinting and vast. To the right was distant land, probably Malibu, she thought.

"It is pretty, isn't it?" Ula said, drawing her attention back into the room.

Cathy nodded, not sure what else to say.

"Stone told me about the accident," Ula went on. "You were very lucky. He said it could have been a lot worse."

"That's what I heard."

Ula started moving around the room. "Here's the television and video player," the housekeeper said, opening an armoire against the far wall. "We have a satellite dish, so you can get any channel you want." She stepped to her left. "The closet. Your things were brought over and unpacked."

"Thank you," Cathy said, grateful Ula didn't open the door. She didn't want to see her meager, worn possessions hanging in the huge open space. She felt out of place as it was.

"This is the bathroom." Ula did open that door. Cathy caught a glimpse of gleaming tile and a shower big enough to house a football squad. "Let me get rid of those men and I'll be right back." She left the room.

Cathy took a minute to catch her breath. Everything was happening so quickly. From the moment the fire alarm had gone off in her office building until now, she felt as if she'd been spinning out of control.

She sucked in a deep breath and tried to relax. The room didn't make it easy. She'd never been in anything this nice before. The guest suite was about the same size as her entire house. She had her own television and VCR. Amazing. There was a small desk tucked in the corner, a sofa with a nice lamp. That would be a great place to read. Whoever had set up this room had thought of everything.

She heard footsteps in the hallway. Her heart rate increased and for a second, she thought it might be Stone coming to welcome her. She hadn't seen him since late last night. But instead, Ula entered the room.

"They're gone," she said, and smiled. But the smile didn't reach her dark eyes. Cathy had the sense that while the housekeeper might not mind having her here, part of her was holding back.

"Thank you for all of this," Cathy said, motioning to the room. "It's very impressive."

"It is nice, isn't it? Stone hired a brilliant decorator to help him with the house. I always tell him it's a shame that these beautiful rooms stand empty so much. We never have company. You must promise to let me spoil you."

"Thank you. I don't want to be too much trouble."

"No trouble," Ula told her. "Stone doesn't eat enough to keep body and soul together. Three women come in every week to do the cleaning. I get tired of sitting around doing nothing. It's been three years since there was any life in this house. I don't think Stone has had anyone to stay since Miss Evelyn dled."

"Miss Evelyn?" she asked. Who was she? Stone's mother?

"Yes. She died in a car accident nearly three years ago. She was Stone's wife."

Chapter Four

Cathy set her fork down and stared at the plate in front of her. Ula had brought her a huge amount of food, and to her embarrassment, she'd eaten it all. She hadn't thought she was hungry until the housekeeper had shown up with the tray, but then her stomach had growled and she'd taken that first bite. As the savory roast beef had practically melted on her tongue, she'd been lost. Maybe she could explain her appetite. After all, she hadn't eaten much at the hospital, what with being unconscious and having surgery. Before that, well, it had been the end of the month and her money had been tight...as usual. She'd been living on packages of pasta and canned soup.

She pushed the tray aside. The tall table on wheels moved easily. She wondered at the piece of hospital equipment in an otherwise well-decorated house. She hoped Stone hadn't bought it for her brief stay and rehabilitation.

She supposed she could ask him, if and when she saw

him. She'd been in the house since early afternoon and hadn't seen him. Of course, she'd been confined to bed and hadn't been able to go exploring. Not that she would. While the house was lovely and she was sure she would find treasures in every room, she wasn't comfortable here. She wasn't even sure why he'd brought her here.

Cathy shrugged, trying to shake off the feeling of restlessness. She told herself the sensation came from the ache in her knee and too much time in her own company. At least at work, she'd had Stone's phone calls to look forward to. It was ridiculous to think he would call while they were in the same house. Surely he would visit her, wouldn't he? At least to be polite.

Unless he didn't want to see her. That was always a possibility. After all she'd done, she couldn't blame him for that.

Her mind careened in that direction, and she had to pull it up short. She'd spent most of her waking hours beating herself up about the lies she'd told Stone. While she was sure she was going to keep doing that for a while, she wasn't up to it tonight.

She reached for the television remote control, then let it fall back onto the plush covers. She wasn't in the mood for that kind of entertainment. She was restless, but unable to move. Although her crutches were within easy reach, getting out of bed was a slow and painful process. She wasn't going to do it just so she could limp back and forth across the beautiful carpet.

Which meant she had too much time to think. About being here. About Stone. And about Evelyn.

The name still caused a start of painful surprise in her chest. His wife, Ula had said. Somehow Cathy had never thought that Stone might have been married. Which was ridiculous. The man didn't live in a vacuum. But a wife.

She shook her head. She supposed some of her surprise came from the fact that he was a widower rather than divorced. She wasn't sure why, but she knew the latter would have been easier to accept. Maybe because it would have meant he was over her. But to have lost his wife in a car accident—probably the same one that had left him scarred—she couldn't even imagine. Cathy drew in a slow breath. It was no wonder he locked himself away like he did.

Everything was still very confusing to her. Too much had happened in a short period of time. She was here in Stone's house and for all she knew she was never going to see him again. The place was certainly big enough. He hated her and if he didn't, he would soon. She wasn't sure if she still had a job. If nothing else, the answering service was going to have to relocate. What would that mean to her? What had happened to her car, tucked behind the building in the parking lot? What about—?

A knock on her half-open door broke through her long stream of self-torment. She turned toward the sound.

"Yes," she called, wondering if Ula had come to collect the tray.

"It's Stone," the familiar voice said. "Are you up to a little company?"

She wanted it not to matter. She wanted to be able to answer calmly, without her heart pounding and her already spinning thoughts whirling faster and faster. But she couldn't manage any of that. Instead of sounding cool and casual, her voice came out completely breathless.

"Oh, please, yes," she told him, and hated how eager she sounded.

"I need you to turn out the light," he said.

Cathy hesitated. She'd wanted to ask Ula about Stone's scars, but she hadn't had the courage. She'd wondered about them, wondered how bad they must be. She didn't have a whole lot of experience with disfigurement and could only picture things she'd seen in the movies. How bad was his face?

But instead of asking, she did as he requested. With an audible click, the glow from the lamp on her nightstand blinked out and the room plunged into the thick blackness of the night. The only light spilled in from the hallway, and that was muted at best. Cathy strained to see, but Stone was little more than a moving shadow as he pushed open the door and stepped into the room.

"How are you feeling?" he asked.

She watched his shape as he walked over to the sofa by the window. He moved with the certainty of one familiar with the night.

"Better," she said. "A little disoriented. Everything happened so fast."

"How's your head and your knee?"

She leaned back into the pillow. If she closed her eyes, she might be able to pretend they were talking on the phone as they'd done a hundred times before. She might be able to forget he was in the room with her. Stone was actually here. She nearly smiled. The correct statement wasn't that Stone was here, but that *she* was with *him*. She still couldn't believe that.

At least he'd only asked about her head and her leg. He hadn't asked about her heart or her tummy. Both fluttered uncomfortably.

"I still have a bump on my head," she said, gingerly pressing her fingertips against the raised ridge by her temple. "My knee is a little sore and very stiff."

"Physical therapy will help that. You start tomorrow. Aside from that, I want you to take it easy. That's what the doctor ordered. Plenty of rest and time to recover. Ula is excited to have someone to fuss over.''

Cathy thought about Ula's quiet appraising stare and didn't think *excited* quite described her attitude. "I don't want to be a bother," she began, not sure what else she could say. "This is all so…" Her voice trailed off.

Stone raised his hand in what she guessed was a gesture of dismissal. "Don't even mention that," he said. "I want to help you. When the alarm went off while we were on the phone…" Now his voice was the one to trail off. He cleared his throat. "I didn't know what had happened to you. All I could think about was driving to the office to make sure you were all right."

Cathy frowned. "I don't remember much about that night," she admitted. "Everything is a blur. I do know we were on the phone and the fire alarm started. At first I thought it was a test or something. Then I smelled the smoke."

Thinking about it made her head ache. She could almost inhale the scent of fire again and she shuddered. "I remember that you talked to me. I was so scared."

"We don't have to discuss this if it bothers you," he said.

"No, it's all right. I don't remember much after calling 911. They said there was an explosion." Again she rubbed the tender spot by her temple. "I was tossed through the air and landed on my knee and my head."

"I'm glad you're all right."

His voice was low and familiar. Cathy strained to see him, but the darkness was too thick. Was this really happening to her? Was she really in Stone's house, talking with him? Had he really brought her here and arranged for physical therapy, and Lord knows what else?

"Why are you doing this?" she asked him.

"Because I want to. We're friends. If the situations were reversed, wouldn't you help me?"

"Of course, but that's not the point."

"Then what is?"

He moved on the sofa. She watched the shape of him shift, then settle in one place. He was a tall man, with broad shoulders, but he wasn't bulky. His features remained indistinct. He seemed to be in slacks and a long-sleeved shirt, but that was all she could tell. She supposed the good news about their situation was that if she couldn't see him, he also couldn't see her. Although he had been able to see her while she was in the hospital.

She thought about him staring down at her while she was sleeping. Of him seeing the truth and realizing that everything she'd told him was a lie.

"The point is," she whispered, "I'm a fraud. I'm not a pretty blonde with an exciting life. I'm—" Her voice cracked as the tears formed. Even as her throat tightened, she fought against them. "I don't have those people as my friends. I don't really have any friends. Even Muffin was a lie." The last word was barely audible, despite the quiet in the room.

She remembered how Stone had held her hand in the hospital. She wished he would do that now, that he would approach and offer her comfort. She needed that. Otherwise, she would be left feeling a fool and a complete failure.

"None of that matters," he told her.

"I don't believe you." Irritation gave her strength. "You can't mean that. I've deceived you."

"You made up some stories about your life. There's a difference. No one got hurt, Cathy. We all pretend in different ways. I understand how it happens. In business deals, I often bluff."

"This was a lot more than that." She swallowed. The threat of tears had faded. "But you're right about one thing. I didn't mean to hurt anyone." A grim smile twisted her lips. "You, I guess I mean. There wasn't anyone else involved."

"Then if I'm willing to forget it ever happened, why aren't you?"

Because her life had never been that simple or easy. Situations were always complicated for her. But maybe this time it was different, she thought and wished it could be true.

"I suppose I think I should be punished or something," she said.

"You're stuck in bed after knee surgery and you nearly died in a fire. How's that for punishment?"

"I hadn't thought of it that way."

"Consider the idea and then let it all go. We'll start fresh. Hi, Cathy, my name is Stone Ward. Tell me about yourself."

She plucked at the comforter cover. "There's nothing to tell. That's why I made up the stories. The real Cathy Eldridge is pretty boring."

"I think she's bright and funny. Tell me about your family. The hospital said they couldn't get in touch with anyone."

He was trying to make her feel better. Cathy believed that with all her heart. But he was heading in the wrong direction. This line of conversation was even more distressing than the memories of her lies. Then she reminded herself it had been a long time. The past was behind her and had therefore lost its power to hurt her.

"I don't have any family," she said. "My father is gone. I don't know if he's dead or alive. He took off when I was a baby. My mother never said anything about him. I don't even know where he's from. Mom was an orphan. There was always just the two of us. She—''

Cathy paused. How was she supposed to sum up her life in a couple of witty sentences?

''We don't have to talk about this if you don't want to,'' Stone told her.

''No, it's fine. She drank a lot. I took care of her. When she was sober, she was great and that's how I try to remember her. But I never knew what she was going to be like, so when I was growing up, I didn't get close to a lot of people. Kids would want to come visit me at home, and I couldn't take the chance.''

''That sounds lonely.''

''It was.'' She shrugged. ''I adjusted. I guess I've always been a loner.''

''Then we have that in common.''

Cathy stared at him, at the shape of him, and wondered why Stone chose to live like this—so cut off from the rest of the world. He could fit in anywhere. Even if the scars were bad, people would understand. Friends would.

''I used to have a lot of dreams,'' she confessed. ''About what would happen when I was finally on my own. I had this vision of a wonderful life. Sort of like the one I made up for you.''

''You could still make that happen.''

Cathy thought about her job at the answering service. It didn't pay very much, and she didn't have any skills to get another job. She'd once thought about college, but instead of heading off to higher education with the rest of her high-school graduating class, she'd stayed home to take care of her mother. The alcohol had taken its time to ravage the older woman's body—she'd spent nearly two years trying to die.

''In theory those dreams could come true,'' Cathy said.

"But it's been so long now. I've forgotten most of them, and it doesn't really matter anymore."

"I disagree."

She knew from past experience there was no point in arguing with him. "What about your dreams?" she asked. "What do you want?"

"I have everything I need," he told her.

She wanted to point out that want and need were not the same thing at all, but she didn't think that was her place.

Silence stretched out between them, but it was comfortable. She liked hearing his voice like this. He sounded a little different than he did over the phone. Plus she could see him—sort of. At least the outline of him, the way his body moved when he talked. With him in the room, she didn't feel so alone.

"Why did you bring me here?" she asked. "Tell me the truth this time."

"I told you the truth before. I brought you here because I care about you. Over the past couple of years, we've become friends. I don't have many of those in my life and I treasure the ones I've made. I want you to get better and selfishly I brought you here to make sure that happened. Does that answer your question?"

It did, but it also raised a hundred more. Stone said he thought of her as a friend. Cathy didn't know what other explanation there was. She'd tried to think of another motive. He could have easily hung up during the fire and not given her another thought. Or he could have visited in the hospital, done his duty as a client of the service, then let her be. But he hadn't. Maybe she should just stop asking and believe him.

"Thank you," she said quietly.

"You're welcome. Now close your eyes."

"What?"

"You heard me." He chuckled. "Come on. You can trust me."

"I—" Cathy stared at him, but it was a futile effort. She couldn't see much of anything. "All right."

Was he going to turn on the light? Did he want to look at her without her being able to see him?

She sensed movement in the room, then his presence by the bed.

"Keep them closed," he instructed.

His hand gently squeezed hers, then something soft and warm brushed against her cheek. "Sleep well, Cathy. I'll come see you again tomorrow."

And then he was gone. Cathy slowly opened her eyes. Without meaning to, she pressed her fingertips to the place he'd kissed her. She told herself it had been a brief peck, a meaningless gesture between friends. It couldn't be anything more.

Even so, she was smiling as she sank down into the pillows and as she closed her eyes again, she relived the moment over and over until she dropped off to sleep.

Stone walked over to the window in his office and stared at the darkness. The house felt more welcoming tonight, and he knew the reason slept up one floor, at the end of the opposite wing.

Cathy. Her presence here was nearly enough to banish the ghosts, even as she, in some ways, echoed them.

She was nothing like Evelyn. Not in appearance or temperament or even circumstances, save the fact that they'd both grown up in families that barely made ends meet. And yet they were so alike.

He drew in a deep breath and promised himself that this time would be different. This time he wouldn't make the same mistakes. This time he would be aware of what was going on. He could help Cathy in ways he'd never been able to help Evelyn. He could fix her life. In some small way, that might atone for the sins of the past. Maybe if he got it right this time, some of the pain would fade away.

Without wanting to, barely aware of the action, he rubbed his fingertips against the scars on the left side of his face.

This time he wouldn't get involved, he told himself. This time he wouldn't care too much. He liked Cathy. Friendship was safe—nothing else was permissible. He would ensure that they maintained the relationship they'd already established and nothing more.

When she was healed, on the inside, as well as from her injuries, he would let her go. She would walk away stronger because of him, and maybe then he would be left in peace.

Cathy was awake early the next morning. She managed to get to the bathroom and back, although the short trip took about twenty minutes.

"I wish I'd studied dance or something," she muttered as she sat down on the bed and tried to catch her breath. "Or even a beginning class in 101 ways to use crutches."

She was many things, but she'd never been graceful or even athletic. The crutches hurt her arms and shoulders, and she still didn't have the hang of them. If she tried anything complex, like stairs or even a long hallway, she was afraid she was going to fall flat on her face.

She managed to lean them against the wall between the nightstand and the headboard, then she pushed herself back onto the bed so she could swing her legs up onto the mattress. Her nightgown hitched up, exposing pale thighs. Cathy stared at the slightly lumpy skin. All her life she'd been wrestling with the same twenty pounds. Unfortunately she had a feeling that in the past couple of months those pounds had been breeding and now it was more like twenty-five. With all this forced inactivity, the situation was only going to get worse.

Her stomach growled. Great. Now she was hungry.

She wished she were the swearing kind, although she'd never understood how saying certain words was supposed to relieve emotional tension. There was nothing to be done but for her to get through the situation. When she was back home, she was going on a diet for sure. She would even start exercising. Nothing complicated—just walking.

The promise was as old as it was familiar. Cathy pulled up the covers and fought against the accompanying sense of failure. So many lost opportunities, she thought grimly. How many times had she vowed she wasn't going to eat another bite of chocolate until she'd lost a few pounds? How many times had she sworn to herself that she was going to get into shape, only to spend her days reading?

A knock at the door interrupted her pity party, and she was grateful. For a split second, her heart jumped at the thought it might be Stone. Then she remembered that he didn't want her seeing him, so it was unlikely he would show up in the morning, when light spilled into her room.

"Come in," she called.

Ula, the housekeeper, opened the door and stepped inside her room. "Good morning," the older woman said. She was petite, with graying hair pulled back into a sensible bun, and dark eyes.

"How did you sleep?" Ula asked.

"Great. My leg didn't bother me much at all."

The older woman nodded. Her pale gray dress wasn't exactly a uniform, but it didn't look like a fashion statement, either. Cathy shifted uncomfortably on the bed. She wasn't sure if the housekeeper was simply restrained in her manner, or if she resented Cathy's presence. Maybe she thought Cathy was a leech or a charity case. Cathy grimaced. While she didn't consider herself the former, she might definitely be thought of as the latter.

"I wasn't sure what you liked to eat," Ula said. Her stern expression softened. "If you would tell me your preferences, I would be happy to prepare them. Mr. Ward isn't one who pays attention to his food. I don't think he notices anything I feed him."

Cathy thought about the outline of Stone's body. He'd looked lean in the darkness. Ula was slight, too. Great. Here she was waddling through the land of gazelles.

What did she want? Chocolate. About three pounds. That should see her through.

Stop it! she ordered herself. It was time to let go of the excuses and actually do something. This was a perfect opportunity. For the next few days, she wouldn't be able to prepare her own food, let alone shop. Why not get a jump start on the program she wanted to begin when she got home?

She cleared her throat and felt a flush stain her cheeks. "Would it be too much trouble to have you make some low-fat foods?" Cathy asked in a rush. "Nothing complicated. Maybe some grilled chicken or fish. If it's too much work, I'll understand."

"Not at all," Ula said smoothly. "I have several interesting recipes." Her gaze swept over Cathy. "You want to lose some weight?"

It was the obvious question. Cathy nodded.

"I can do that." The older woman hesitated. "It's not my business, but you might want to ask the physical therapist about an exercise program. Perhaps there's something aerobic you can do while your leg is healing."

Cathy hadn't thought of that. "What a great idea. I'll do that. Thank you."

Ula offered her a slight smile.

Cathy gathered her courage. "I don't know what Stone told you about me," she began, then paused, hoping Ula would fill in the blank. The housekeeper didn't, so Cathy plunged on. "Well, we're just friends. I've known him for about two years. Not in person, of course. I know he doesn't go out much. But over the phone. He used the answering service I worked for, and we talked most evenings." She cleared her throat. She wasn't sure why she was explaining herself to the housekeeper; she just didn't think she could bear to live here if Ula didn't approve. Silly, but true.

"Anyway, I was on the phone with Stone when the fire broke out in the building where I work. He was concerned enough to come to the hospital and check on me. Then he brought me here. I don't want you to think that I'm going to make trouble or anything. I'm not. We're just…that is, I'm not very important to him. I understand that."

Ula's expression didn't change. "Thank you for explaining," she said. "It was unnecessary, but very kind of you. Mr. Ward had said you were a friend of his, and as such, you are welcome in his home. Let me know if there's anything else I can do."

She turned to leave, then paused in the doorway. "Perhaps later I'll bring by a list of recipes I can try and we can discuss which ones interest you the most."

As overtures went, it wasn't a huge one, but Cathy didn't think she was much in a position to complain. She smiled. "I would like that," she said. "Thanks."

This time the housekeeper did leave, but when she was gone, Cathy didn't feel quite so alone.

Chapter Five

"You must be Cathy," the young woman said as she bounded up the stairs.

Cathy sat on the patio because Ula had insisted. After breakfast the housekeeper had informed her it was a beautiful day and that the physical-therapy session could as easily happen outside as in. Over Cathy's protests, Ula had hustled her down the hall to the stairs, where she'd slowly made her way to the first floor. Now Cathy sat in the wrought-iron chair, her back to the sun and generally hating life.

Her arms and shoulders ached from the crutches, and her knee throbbed. While she'd enjoyed her low-fat breakfast, she was still hungry and all she could think about was chocolate. To make matters worse, the young woman beaming in front of her looked to be about five feet tall, and maybe all of eighty pounds. Ula was tiny—this woman was tiny.

Had Cathy somehow entered a world of perfect little people, where she was the only troll?

"Hi," Cathy managed to say, hoping her bitterness didn't show.

The young woman grinned. She had short blond hair and the kind of body featured in fitness magazines. A T-shirt and bicycle shorts showed off the sleek muscles to perfection. "I'm Pepper, your physical therapist." Pepper held up her hand. "It's a nickname, and I prefer the soft-drink jokes be kept to a minimum. My mother named me after her favorite aunt, Esmeralda, so Pepper is an improvement. How are you feeling?"

Pepper's voice was as perky as her smile. Cathy fought nausea. "Just great."

Pepper plopped down on the steps by Cathy's feet. "You don't sound great. If anything, you sound tired. Did you sleep well last night?"

Cathy shrugged. "Not great," she admitted. The pain pills had helped, but she'd been restless. There were so many things on her mind. Her job—or the possible lack thereof—her surgery and recovery, Stone. Everything was still too confusing.

"The first few days are the worst," Pepper said. "Your body has to recover from the shock of the injury and from the surgery, as well. On the surface, you'll heal pretty quickly, but remember it takes the body a year to completely recover from any operation. So be kind to yourself. If you get tired, take a nap. Try not to get too stressed."

That Cathy could handle. She looked at Pepper. "What exactly are you here to do?"

"A couple of things. We're going to work on your leg to make sure you don't lose too much muscle tone. I'm going to show you some exercises to strengthen the muscles around your knee. Stronger muscles will stabilize the area while it heals. Second we're going to work on your technique with crutches. Most people are pretty hopeless on them. It takes a lot of balance and upper-body strength, not to mention practice. I'll be making sure you don't injure yourself while you use them. We'll do a little massage, too, to help the muscles." She touched the spot above her left breast. "It hurts right here, doesn't it? And across your shoulders?"

Cathy nodded. "Yes. I try shifting positions when I use the crutches, but it doesn't seem to help."

"While they keep the weight off the leg so it can heal, using crutches is physically unnatural. I want to minimize your pain and suffering in an already uncomfortable situation." She stood up and looked around. "The housekeeper suggested we work out here. It's pretty private. What do you think?"

Cathy followed her gaze. In front of her was a wide view of the ocean. On either side, tall hedges protected this part of the garden from prying neighbors. Behind them was the house, and as far as she knew, only Ula and Stone were inside. She doubted either would find her physical-therapy session interesting. But the real reason she agreed was that the alternative was going up to her room, and she just couldn't face the stairs right now.

"I'm sure we'll be fine out here," she said, wishing she felt more enthusiastic about the whole thing.

"Great. I'll get my stuff."

Pepper's "stuff" consisted of a portable table big enough for Cathy to stretch out on, along with some workout-size rubber bands and a small suitcase. In a matter of minutes, she had the table opened and a clean sheet spread over the plastic-covered padding.

"Hop on," she said, patting the sheet.

Cathy struggled to her feet, took her crutches and lurched

awkwardly toward the young woman. Pepper stepped forward to assist. "They've got the height adjusted wrong," she said. "You'd think they'd check something like that. Don't worry, I'll fix it. But first let's work on your leg."

She gave Cathy a hand up onto the table. Cathy was shocked to feel the other woman's strength. At her look of surprise, Pepper chuckled.

"I know, my size is deceiving. I'm strong. I grew up with five brothers, so it was get strong or get pinned every time we wrestled." She smiled. "I decided to learn how to kick butt. They're all huge, but I've got 'em running for cover."

She had Cathy lie down on the table. They went through a series of stretches. Pepper made several notations on a chart.

"Do you exercise?" the physical therapist asked.

"Not really." The loose sweatpants she wore weren't very flattering, and Cathy figured that Pepper had probably already noticed the fact that she wasn't in very good shape. "I've tried to start an exercise program a few times, but I've never been able to stick with it. Now I don't know what to do."

"We're going to have you up and around in no time," Pepper promised. "In a few months, you won't even know you've had surgery."

"Is there something I can do in the meantime?" she asked, reminding herself again that this was the perfect opportunity to make some changes in her life. "Ula suggested I ask you about that."

"Sure. There are different aerobic exercises for people in wheelchairs. You could do some of those." Pepper wrinkled her pixie nose. "I'll work something up to bring in next time."

"That sounds great. Thank you."

"That's what I'm here for. Now let's work on this leg."

Pepper took her through several exercises and more stretches. When her leg was too sore for them to continue, they shifted to her upper body. Cathy learned how to stretch out the muscles stressed by the crutches, as well as a few ways to build her upper-body strength. She could barely lift a five-pound dumbbell, but she refused to get discouraged. At least she was finally doing something. She eyed Pepper's well-defined arm and wondered if that was possible for her.

When they finished, Pepper applied heat to her neck and upper back. "Just relax for a few minutes. Then we'll start the walking lesson. By the time I'm finished with you, you'll be barreling around on those crutches like a pro."

"I can't imagine barreling, but I would like to move a little more easily."

Pepper glanced at the house. "I would guess so. There must be a ton of stairs inside."

"I wouldn't know."

The therapist looked at her in surprise. "But you live here."

Cathy lay on her stomach, the heavy heat-pack around her neck. She rested her head on her folded arms and grimaced. "No. I'm—" Words failed her. What was she, exactly? A friend of the family? Hardly? A what, then?

"Mr. Ward and I have a business association," she said at last. "I don't have any family, and when he heard what had happened in the fire, he wanted me to stay here while I recovered."

"Nice work if you can get it," Pepper said enviously. "Imagine actually knowing Stone Ward. Wow. I've read about him, of course. This house is amazing. What's he like?"

Cathy hesitated, not only because she didn't know what

to say, but also because she respected Stone's privacy. While she wasn't completely sure about the parameters of their relationship, she *did* consider him a friend and she didn't want to be responsible for gossiping about him.

"He's reclusive," she said. "A very private man, but kind. We're not that close."

That was true, she thought sadly. They weren't close, and everything that had happened between them had only confused her. She wanted their relationship to be different, but she couldn't say how. She just knew that she missed the regularity of their lives before...when she'd known she could count on hearing from him every evening at midnight. Although he'd come by last night, she didn't know when she was going to see him again, and that troubled her.

She missed him. They were in the same house, and she missed him. It was crazy.

Pepper touched the heat pack. "We'll give this another five minutes, then on with your lesson."

Cathy smiled. "Thanks."

Stone stood at the window, watching. Even as he told himself he had no right to spy on Cathy, he found himself unable to turn away. The physical therapist seemed capable, but he barely spared her a glance. Instead, all of his attention focused on his guest.

She moved across the patio, her stride slow and halting. The therapist stopped her and made an adjustment to the crutches. Cathy was able to straighten a little, and that seemed to help her balance.

Her straight hair hung down, concealing her face from him. Shapeless sweats hid her body. She wasn't all she'd claimed to be, but none of that mattered to him. Their relationship had never been about what she looked like. What he'd cared about was who she was inside.

She continued to pace across the patio. With each pass, her mobility improved. It wouldn't be all that long before she would be an expert on the crutches. By then, she would be able to put them aside and walk on her own.

Even though the darkened glass prevented anyone from seeing into the room, after a few minutes he stepped back. He'd wanted to check on Cathy's progress, nothing else. The physical therapist had been as competent as he'd been promised. So now he could forget about his houseguest and go about his business. Everything was on schedule. He was helping Cathy get better. He would fix her—both physically and in any other way she required. That was his goal. To improve her lot in life, to atone.

Yet as he focused on the computer screen in front of him, he found himself thinking about Cathy instead of balance sheets. He found himself eager for the darkness so that he could again spend time with her. As he had a thousand times since the car accident three years before, he cursed the day and the light it brought.

Cathy stared longingly at the tray next to her bed. She'd demolished her dinner in less than ten minutes. The fish had been perfectly cooked in a delectable sauce. Sautéed mushrooms had been added to the rice; even the vegetables had been delicious. The small plate of cut-up fruit with a single scoop of frozen yogurt had been a very nice surprise for dessert. The only problem was, she was starving. She would have sold her soul for fast food, or even real, fat-filled chocolate. If there had been a way to hobble to a local store for a quick fix, she would have done it. However, she was well and truly trapped. She might as well have been at a spa in the middle of the desert. Maybe that's how they were so successful. It wasn't anything more than physically keeping clients away from the food they loved.

Cathy sighed softly and leaned back against the pillows. She wasn't *really* hungry, she told herself. She'd just had dinner. Maybe she should have eaten more slowly so that her brain would have had time to register the food sitting in her stomach. At least that's what all the magazine articles said. Or if that wasn't it, then it was just psychological. While she was physically full, she wanted the rich, fattening foods to provide emotional comfort. She needed something with which to distract herself. In time she would get used to eating less. The results would be worth it.

Cathy stared down at herself, wondering if she'd lost any weight yet. It had been a whole day, and she hadn't cheated once. In her mind, weight loss should be a function of sincerity rather than calories. In this case, she was very, very sincere. Surely that would count for at least a five-pound weight loss.

The phone on her nightstand rang. She jumped slightly and stared at the instrument. She hadn't heard it ring before. Yet Stone must get calls. No doubt he had several lines for business. Maybe this was the house line.

The phone rang four more times. She ignored it and picked up the television guide Ula had brought her. Maybe there was a good movie on tonight. Or something scary. If she was worried about being attacked by aliens or vampires, maybe she wouldn't think about food.

She flipped through the pages but didn't see anything that looked interesting. She'd just tossed the magazine aside when someone knocked at her door. She glanced up as the housekeeper entered the room.

"How was dinner?" the older woman asked.

"Great. I didn't think I liked fish, but whatever you made was terrific."

Ula took the empty tray and smiled. "I'm glad you enjoyed your food. I had a good time finding the recipes. We'll try something with chicken tomorrow."

It was nearly seven in the evening, yet the housekeeper looked as fresh and alert as she had first thing in the morning. Every hair was in place, and there wasn't a wrinkle in her pale gray dress. Who was this woman? Did she live here? Cathy opened her mouth to ask, then closed it. Ula's living arrangements weren't her business. The older woman was just starting to warm up to her. Cathy didn't want to risk shutting her down by asking personal questions.

"Your phone rang a few minutes ago," Ula said. "Were you in the rest room?"

Cathy blinked. "This extension rang, but I didn't think it was for me."

"It was. Mr. Ward wanted to check on you. I told him you probably didn't realize the guest room had a dedicated line. If this phone rings, feel free to answer it."

"Stone called?" she repeated. "Did he leave the house?"

Ula headed for the door. "Not at all. He rarely leaves. He's in his office. I'll let him know that it's all right for him to call back."

"Please," Cathy told her, then took a breath. "Ula, is Stone all right?"

The housekeeper paused and looked at her. "What do you mean?" The smile had faded, no doubt because in her opinion, Cathy had overstepped her bounds.

"He told me about the scars on his face. I mean, they're why he doesn't go out much and..." Her voice trailed off. What was the old saying? In for a penny? She might as well finish. "Is there anything else? Any other lasting effects? Physical ones, I mean, from the accident."

"Oh." Ula shook her head. "He's fine. There are just the scars."

Cathy wanted to ask how bad they were, but she couldn't think of a way to politely phrase it and she wasn't comfortable enough to just blurt out the question.

"He was injured in the same car accident that killed his wife, wasn't he?" she asked.

"Yes."

Okay, so Ula wasn't going to offer information. At least she was answering questions.

Cathy cleared her throat. She didn't want to ask, but she had to know. "He's kept to himself all this time. He must have loved her very much."

"Miss Evelyn meant the world to him," Ula confirmed. Her expression softened, as if she were lost in pleasant memories. "They'd known each other since they were children. She was his best friend. I don't think he'll ever recover from losing her." She paused. "Will you be needing anything else?"

Cathy's throat had closed, and she could barely speak. "Thank you, no," she managed to answer through the pain and disappointment.

Ula gave her another smile. This one nearly reached her dark eyes. Obviously they'd bonded over the sharing of Stone's tragic past. "Then good night."

"Night, Ula."

The door closed, and Cathy was alone with her whirling thoughts. It was her own fault for asking, she told herself. If she hadn't wanted to know about Stone's relationship with his late wife, then she should have kept quiet. What had she hoped to hear? That Stone had hated his wife? That it had been a marriage of convenience and he was glad she was dead? Not likely. And if that were true, he wouldn't be someone she would want to know. Stone was more honorable than that. But still, to learn that he'd loved Evelyn so much he hadn't recovered from her death was not how she wanted to start her evening.

Cathy stared at the ceiling. She wondered what it would be like to care about someone that much. To love and be loved in return. She had no frame of reference, no experience with that. She'd wanted to love someone, but men were not a part of her world. She didn't know where one went to meet them. Even if she did, she wouldn't go there. Aside from the fact that she couldn't start a conversation with a strange man even if her life depended on it, she wasn't the kind of woman who attracted men. She wasn't pretty or especially fun. She didn't have a sparkling personality. She was just average. Her meager life wouldn't impress anyone.

She forced her mind away from that train of thought. Why had she asked? She'd known better, but she'd done it anyway. Just to round off the evening, she'd missed Stone's call. She hated that she hadn't known to pick up, although it was a little strange to think that he'd phoned when he'd only been at the other end of the house.

She flopped back against her pillows and shifted her gaze to the blank television screen. Now what? The evening stretched out in front of her. She refused to spend it thinking about what Ula had told her. She wanted to laugh. She wanted to be happy and feel good about herself. While there hadn't been anything that looked interesting on TV, maybe she could flip channels until something caught her eye. A sitcom or a funny movie. Or she could—

The phone rang again. Cathy snatched at the receiver. "Hello?"

"Hi. How are you feeling?"

The familiar voice sent a ribbon of pleasure all the way to her toes. She forgot about being hungry, or how much her knee hurt, or even the stiffness in her body from the armchair exercises she'd done that afternoon. She forgot about the things Ula had told her and how much she wondered about Stone's late wife. She even forgot she was alone.

"Better," she breathed, knowing he would think she was talking about her injuries, while what she meant was how she felt now that she'd heard his voice.

"I'm glad. Your physical therapy went well?"

"Uh-huh. Pepper is nice and she knows what she's doing. She told me my crutches weren't adjusted correctly and she fixed them. It's made a big difference in my being able to move around the house."

"She came highly recommended. I'm glad she helped. How was the rest of your day?"

Cathy glanced around the room. She'd spent most of her time in here. What could have happened? "I heard from my boss," she said. "Ula took a message while I was with Pepper. They're relocating, and it's going to be a couple of weeks until everything is up and running. He says for me to take as long as I want before I come back."

Eddie had been concerned when she'd called him back. He'd wanted to know if she was having any trouble with the insurance company and if she did, to talk to him. He was a nice man, although she didn't want to have to think about returning to her old, boring job.

"That's one less thing you have to worry about," Stone said. "I know it's a relief."

Cathy tucked the phone under her chin. "This is very strange," she said.

"That we're talking on the phone? We do it all the time."

"I know, but we're in the same house."

"Is that an invitation?"

His voice was low and enticing. Cathy shivered. She wanted to curl up in a little ball and shriek with excitement. Okay, so it wasn't exactly flirting, but it was close enough for her. Stone was just being a friend and a very nice man. She would be a fool to read anything else into his actions. And yet...oh, but she wanted them to mean more. Was it so very wrong to dream?

"Would you like it to be?" she managed to ask, wondering if he could hear her shaking.

"Yes," he said. "I missed our conversations while you were in the hospital. But now that you're in my house, I don't want you to feel obligated."

"I never talked with you out of obligation." How could he even think that? His calls were the highlight of her day! Of her life!

"Then I'll be right there. Turn out the lights."

For a split second, his words created an image of intimacy that made her face flush while at the same time more shivers of anticipation rushed through her. Then she reminded herself about the scars and that he didn't want her to see him. It wasn't anything more.

"I will," she said, and hung up the phone.

For a second she wished she could run to the bathroom and brush her hair or apply a little makeup. But even with her improved balance on the crutches, she would never make it there and back in time. Besides, she didn't have any makeup and it was going to be dark, so what did her appearance matter? But a girl could wish, she thought. So along with makeup and freshly brushed hair, she would wish herself thin and pretty.

She laughed, then clicked off the light. The room was silent enough that she could hear, as well as feel, the pounding of her heart.

There was a single knock, then Stone entered. "Hi," he

said. "Do you always let strange men just walk into your bedroom?"

"You're the first."

"I'll try not to abuse the privilege."

She fought against the urge to tell him to abuse away.

"I come bearing gifts," he said, and she saw him move toward the bed. Something settled next to her.

"What?" she asked as he walked toward the sofa across the room. Her fingers brushed against a smooth, flat surface. "Books. Which ones?"

"The two we couldn't agree on."

She grinned. "We *did* agree. You said you would read the biography."

"Nerds on parade," he said. "I remember. I bought it and the spy thriller I wanted. I thought we could read them both."

"I'll quiz you on the biography," she told him. "Don't think you're going to get away with just looking at the dust jacket."

He sighed heavily. "I figured as much. I'll read it." His long-suffering tone made her smile.

They continued talking about the two new books, then conversation turned to previous books they'd read together. Cathy found herself watching the way he used his hands to occasionally make a point. She couldn't see much of him, but she caught the broad gestures in the shadowy darkness.

Theirs was an unusual intimacy, she thought, liking how they were in the same room. Even though she couldn't see him, she was still close. He'd called *her*. He'd acted as if he *wanted* to come to see her. She hugged the knowledge close, and it comforted her.

"What are you thinking?" he asked when they'd both been silent for a time.

"That talking in the dark is very strange, but I like it."

"I do, too. I don't have many friends, so having you in my house is a real treat."

"You are so incredibly gracious," she said.

"I'm being honest."

"Maybe."

"No *maybe*s. I am. I want you here, Cathy. I want to make sure you get better, and the best way for me to do that is to be in charge."

"So you really want to be the ruler of the Western world?" she teased.

"Something like that."

She laughed. She didn't know why she'd gotten so lucky with him, why he liked her or was so concerned. All she knew was that he was. She wasn't going to question her good fortune anymore—she was just going to enjoy it.

"Tell me about your physical-therapy session," he said. "What did you do?"

As she explained about the exercises and what Pepper had told her about the surgery needing time to heal, she found herself wishing that he were sitting closer. At first the sofa hadn't seemed that far away, but now she felt as if there were an ocean between them. She wanted him to touch her, to kiss her as he had the previous night.

More foolish dreams, she thought, but she wasn't going to let these go. Not yet, anyway. As long as she was here, she could dream.

He mentioned a couple of businesses he was thinking of investing in. They discussed his work, then the weather. Finally Stone rose to his feet.

"It's getting late, and you need your rest. I'll see you tomorrow evening, if that's all right."

"It's perfect," she said, and held her breath.

But unlike last night, this time he merely crossed to the

door and let himself out into the hall. Cathy watched him go, then fell back onto the pillows. She clutched the books to her chest, but they were a poor substitute for the fantasy that was Stone Ward.

Chapter Six

Stone stood at the window of his office, watching as he had every day for the past two weeks. Cathy's improvement was remarkable. She was now able to get around without using her crutches, although she needed a cane going up and down the stairs.

The physical therapist—Stone could never remember her name—led Cathy through several exercises. Cathy bent and turned as instructed. She still wore her shapeless gray sweats and an oversize T-shirt when she worked out. Stone wasn't sure, but he thought the garments might be a little more baggy than they'd been when she'd first started. For the past couple of nights, he'd thought her face might be a little thinner, but in the twilight that was their world when he visited her, it was hard to tell.

Ula had mentioned that his houseguest preferred her to prepare low-fat meals. Was Cathy trying to lose weight? He thought about the vague outline of her shape he'd seen when he'd visited her in the hospital. She'd been a little heavier than she'd described herself, but he hadn't really noticed anything specific. He knew that women tended to worry about their weight more than men did. He leaned against the window frame. If being in his house gave Cathy an opportunity to achieve a personal goal, then he was pleased. He wanted to help in any way he could.

Cathy climbed down from the table. Her therapist said something, and Cathy leaned back her head and laughed. The sound drifted up to him, and he found his mouth curving up in response. He liked her laughter. The expression of happiness added a little life to his otherwise dead world. She reminded him that he was still alive.

There was danger in that, he acknowledged. Danger in wanting too much. The pleasures of ordinary mortals had no appeal for him. He had yet to pay for his sins, and until he did, he would not be spending any time in the light— literally or figuratively. He deserved the darkness. Not only did it allow him to hide, but it also forced him to remember what he'd done.

Evelyn. Everything came back to Evelyn. At first he'd thought he would be able to let it all go and move on. Now he knew better. This was his world—the solitary darkness. For a brief period of time, Cathy would be here to show him what it was like in the light. When she was healed, she would leave him and he would return to the gray silence where he belonged. He didn't have to wait until after death for his punishment. He had his own private hell on earth.

"Cathy is doing much better."

Stone turned and found his housekeeper standing in his office. She was one of the few people who had ever seen his scars. At first he'd been self-conscious about her being around him, but Ula was nothing if not unflappable. As usual, she was dressed in a perfectly pressed gray dress with a white apron. He'd told her many times he didn't care if she wore a uniform or not. She always thanked him, then continued to wear the same thing. After nearly ten years, he knew better than to try to change her mind.

He glanced back out the window, watching Cathy as she sat on the bench and raised and lowered her foot while keeping her thighs still. "Yes, she has really improved. In another couple of months, she'll be back to normal." And then she would probably want to leave, but he didn't want to think about that right now.

Ula walked over to his desk and set down several flat envelopes. "The overnight packages are here."

"Thanks."

Usually she gave him the mail, then left, but this morning she lingered. He stepped away from the window and moved to his desk. "Is there a problem?"

"Not at all." Her dark eyes were unreadable, as was her expression. "I wondered if you would like to go over next month's menus."

He grimaced. "Only if the alternative is a root canal. You know I don't care about that. Fix what you like."

He prepared himself for the familiar battle. Ula didn't think he ate enough. Sometimes she was right. He'd lost weight recently, the result of his absent appetite. But food held no interest. His world had been reduced to his work and his calls to Cathy.

Still Ula didn't leave. He settled into his chair and gave her his full attention. "What's on your mind?" he asked, and motioned for her to take a seat. She ignored the invitation.

"Your guest," she said. She was tiny, not even five feet, yet she didn't look the least bit intimidated by him. She never had. That's probably why he'd kept her around. "Cathy has been here for two weeks. She's well on the road to mending, and I thought she might be getting a little tired of being locked in the house all the time. Perhaps she would like to get out and go shopping, or check on her house.''

Stone had picked up one of the packages, intent on checking his mail. Now he let it drop to his desk as he grimaced. ''You're right,'' he said flatly. ''I should have thought of that. She probably thinks she's a prisoner here.''

''You don't leave very often yourself,'' she said as she settled onto the edge of the chair opposite the desk. ''Why would you think others would be any different?''

''That's not even subtle, Ula.''

''I wasn't trying to be.'' She smiled faintly.

''Okay, I'll talk to Cathy tonight when I go see her. She can have the car and go anywhere she likes.''

''I suspect what she would like is some company.''

''You mean friends?'' He thought about that. To the best of his knowledge, she didn't have any. From what he'd learned, her life was very solitary. ''She's welcome to invite over anyone she likes.''

A brief flicker of something hot burned low in his belly at the thought of a young man visiting her, but he pushed that aside. He didn't care if Cathy had fifty admirers. That wasn't what their relationship was about.

''That, too,'' Ula said. ''But I was thinking of something else. She always eats alone. Perhaps you could join her some evening.''

Without wanting to, Stone touched his left cheek. The ridges were old friends by now. He'd grown accustomed to his disfigurement, but that didn't mean Cathy would be comfortable in his presence.

Dinner. With another person. He hadn't experienced that particular pleasure even once in three years. The longing was as intense as it was unexpected. He forced it away, using the iron control that had yet to let him down.

He snatched up the envelope and ripped it open. "I don't think that would be a good idea."

Ula dismissed him with a wave. "You're making more of your scars than you should. She won't care."

"But I will," he said coldly, letting the housekeeper know she'd crossed over the line with him.

She sighed heavily, then rose to her feet. "Very good, sir."

The *sir* was emphasized, as she let *him* know she wasn't impressed by his attempts to intimidate her. Stone knew she meant well. Ula had been good to him over the years.

He deliberately softened his expression. "I don't think it would be wise," he said by way of a peace offering.

"Why not? You're making all of this—" she motioned to his face "—more tragic than it has to be."

That drove Stone to his feet. He dropped the papers onto his desk and barely noticed when one of them drifted silently to the floor. "It *is* tragic," he said, his voice laced with anger. "Have you forgotten Evelyn died that night? Have you forgotten that it was my fault?"

"I haven't forgotten you want to make it your fault. There's a difference. It's been three years, Mr. Ward. It's time to let it go. Evelyn, too."

"I'll thank you to remember you are simply an employee here. As such, I would appreciate it if you would keep your opinions to yourself."

Ula's temper flared to match his. But the housekeeper didn't respond. Instead, her spine stiffened and she turned on her heel, then left. Stone remained standing for several more minutes, listening to the silence and the pounding of his rapid heartbeat. He felt the threat of the memories, as if the release of his temper had also released the box where he kept them locked up.

As they swirled through his mind, jabbing him, blinding him to anything but the past and his guilt in it all, he sank slowly into his chair and prepared for the onslaught.

"You're quiet tonight," Stone said.

As always, the sound of his voice made her want to dance with delight. Instead, Cathy shifted slightly on the sofa and looked at him. "Sorry. I was thinking."

"About what?"

He was really here. Sometimes she had trouble remembering that, or believing it. Despite the fact that he'd come to her room every night for the past two weeks, she kept expecting to wake up and find that this was all a dream. But here they sat, a scant foot apart.

Ever since she'd given up the crutches and started moving around more easily, she'd taken to sitting on the sofa while he visited. Although she couldn't see him any better, because even though she was closer, it was still dark in her room, she liked to pretend that they were a normal couple on a date. That he had come to see her for romantic reasons rather than because he felt sorry for her, or responsible, or whatever real reasons drew him to her side.

She liked feeling his presence. They were physically close enough that sometimes she caught the scent of his body, the combination of faint cologne and some male essence that left her thighs trembling. She liked that when he talked he used his hands, and occasionally he would reach out and briefly touch her shoulder when he was making a point. She liked that when they argued about books or politics, he would lean forward as he tried to convince her to see it his way. Sometimes she disagreed just to be contrary and to tease. She liked everything about him.

She wished that she could see him. Several times she'd almost asked, but something had kept her silent. Respect for him and his wishes, she supposed. Obviously his need for privacy was great. She had no right to violate that.

So she made up fantasies about him, about what he looked like and how it would be if she could see him. It was like having a crush back in high school.

"Cathy?"

"Huh? Oh, sorry. I was lost in thought." She felt herself flushing. Thank goodness he couldn't see that. "What was the question?"

"What were you thinking about?"

She tried to figure which of her wayward thoughts would be the safest to share. "Um, high school."

"What was that like for you?" he asked.

She thought about all the lies she told on that particular subject and suddenly she was very tired. Did it matter if Stone knew the truth?

"Not fun," she admitted. "I didn't have many friends, mostly because I couldn't do anything with them after school, and that was expected. I didn't mind going to their house, but I couldn't invite them to mine and I always had to be home early."

She paused, waiting for the inevitable questions. Instead, Stone was silent. After a couple of minutes, she continued. "My mother drank a lot. I never knew what to expect." She closed her eyes against the memories, but that didn't help much. They were always there, just below the surface. "Sometimes she would be fine, just like everyone else's mom, but most of the time she was either drunk or passed out. I spent a lot of time taking care of her. I didn't want to have to explain why she was acting strange or asleep on the sofa, so I avoided situations where I would have to. In the end, it was easier to just be alone."

"I'm sorry," he said.

"It's not anyone's fault. It just happened."

"Your father wasn't there at all?"

"No. He ran off when I was little. I never knew if it was because my mom got pregnant or her drinking or what. She never volunteered the information, and I was too scared of the answer to ask." The last sentence came out in a whisper.

Cathy clamped her lips together. She'd said too much. Stone would be shocked or disgusted. She drew her good knee to her chest and wrapped her arms around her leg.

"My growing up was different," Stone said, his voice conversational. "I grew up in a beautiful home. There was quite a bit of money, but very little attention. It's not that they were neglectful of me. I think it was more that I didn't cross their minds very often. As long as I obeyed the rules, and the housekeeper, they pretty much left me alone."

He stretched out his arm along the back of the sofa. His fingers were only inches from her shoulder. He didn't seem to be doing more than sharing about his life—as if that's what they were doing—exchanging stories. Was it really that simple? Had he just listened and accepted what she'd told him?

"I was popular in high school," he said, then shrugged. A low laugh filled the room. "Fortunately I didn't peak then. At least I hope I didn't. I've always felt sorry for people who had their best year when they were seventeen."

"I'll bet you had tons of girlfriends," she teased.

"Not tons, but enough."

They couldn't have been more different. She'd never had a boyfriend in her life. Her entire romantic experience consisted of getting drunk at a party in her senior year and playing a kissing game. Apparently the experience had been forgettable because all she remembered was spending the next day throwing up and wishing she could die.

"Do you have any brothers or sisters?" she asked.

"No, there was just Evelyn. She was my best friend from grade school. Eventually we married."

Cathy's stomach tightened at the sound of the other woman's name. She told herself he trusted her enough to share the details of his life with her. That was a good thing, right? But it didn't feel very good. If only she could see Stone's face and know what he was thinking. "That must have been nice," she said.

"It was. She died three years ago. I still miss her." His tone gave nothing away. Before Cathy could think of how to ask for more information, he changed the subject.

"But enough about that," he said. "The past is over. Let's talk about the future. Specifically, tomorrow."

"What do you mean?"

"You've been cooped up in this house for two weeks now. You must want to get out, at least for a few hours."

Cathy blinked. "I hadn't really thought about it." That much was true. The house was so huge, it was impossible to feel trapped, much less cooped up. Then something unpleasant occurred to her. "Do you want me to go?" She cleared her throat. "After all, it *has* been two weeks. I'm sorry. I should have thought of that. You've been more than kind and I—"

He leaned forward and pressed his index finger to her mouth. The action silenced her as effectively as a gag.

"Enough," he told her. "I'm not trying to get rid of you. I've told you before. I like having you around. But as Ula pointed out to me this morning, you've been in the house for two weeks. If there's somewhere you'd like to go, or some people you'd like to visit with, I'll be happy to put the car and a driver at your disposal."

The pressure of his finger was soft and warm. She could practically taste his skin. Her heart rate increased, as did her breathing. He'd meant the touch as a simple way to get her attention, but to her it was intimate and very special. When he finally dropped his hand to his lap, she had to bite back a whimper of protest. At least it was dark, she told herself as she licked her lips, hoping for some lingering proof he'd really touched her like that.

"You're not putting me out," he said. "I want to do this."

"I appreciate that," she told him, forcing her mind away from the pleasure of what had just happened and focusing on what he was talking about. The truth was she didn't have anywhere she wanted to go. "I don't think—"

He raised his hand. "I insist," he said, cutting her off again.

He insisted. Great. Now what? "I'm sure I could drive myself," she started, only to be silenced by a tilt of his head. She knew what he was going to say. She wasn't up to driving. When she'd seen her doctor last week, he'd told her it would be at least ten more days. Maybe she could go home and check on the house and then out to a movie.

"Thank you," she said, injecting her voice with an enthusiasm she didn't feel. "I'd like that."

"Anything for you."

She stared into the darkness and wished that were actually true.

"So what are your plans for today?" Ula asked as she poured more coffee.

"I'm not sure. Stone said I can have the car for the whole day. I thought I might check on my house." Which would take all of two hours, including driving time both directions. The day stretched out endlessly. She didn't want to get back too early and have him think her life was so incredibly pitiful that she couldn't fill a few hours away from the house.

Ula took the seat opposite. Cathy had been joining the housekeeper for breakfast every morning for nearly a week. The older woman wasn't overly friendly, but she was loosening up a little. If nothing else, Cathy was fascinated by her always perfect grooming.

"I have a suggestion," Ula said. "If you wouldn't think I was butting in."

"Butt away," Cathy told her. "The only thing I've come up with is a movie, but I'm not too excited about going alone."

"Well, I know a salon on the west side. They do great work with hair. I thought you might like to get a cut and style. It would be fun."

Cathy knew the housekeeper meant well. In her gruff way, Ula had befriended her. Still, the implied criticism hurt. Cathy knew she wasn't much to look at. Her mousy brown hair hung down to the middle of her back. The best thing she could say about it was the center part was straight and her hair was clean.

She pushed the small serving of fruit around on her plate and tried to figure out how to respond to the housekeeper's suggestion.

"I'm sorry," Ula said. "I didn't mean—" She pressed her lips together. "It's just that you've done so well on your diet and with your exercises. You're a lovely girl but you don't do anything to accentuate the positive. I can't figure out if you don't think you're worth it, or you just don't know what to do."

Cathy raised her head and stared at her. "I'm not lovely."

Ula snorted. "Oh, please. You have perfect skin and big green eyes."

"They're not green." Cathy wished they were. "They're sort of a muddy moss color."

"With the right hair and clothes, the green would stand out," Ula told her. "Your smile lights up the room, you're smart and funny. Why don't you give yourself more credit? Sit up straight. Enter the room as if you have the right to be there. Don't be afraid."

Her comments made Cathy straighten in her chair, but she wasn't so sure about the rest of it. Ula's assessment of her was startling. Did the older woman really think she had potential?

She fingered a strand of hair. "What kind of cut?"

Ula poured them each another cup of coffee. "Something layered. Your hair is fine, and layering will give it more volume. I can call the owner of the salon right now and see if he can squeeze you in."

Two hours later, Cathy found herself covered by a purple vinyl cape and staring at herself in a wide mirror. Ernest, the well-dressed middle-aged man who owned the salon, tsked as he stood behind her.

"The seventies were over years ago," he said. "Long straight hair disappeared with the decade. A cut." His tone was sure. "Some color, maybe a little red with a touch of honey to warm up your features."

His own hair was receding, but what was left had been grown out and pulled back into a ponytail. Earrings glittered from both ears.

He pressed his hands to her shoulders and leaned forward. "Ula told me about the fire and your surgery. You poor dear. We're going to fix you right up. Would you like a latte while you're waiting?"

"Um, sure."

"I'll take care of everything." He smiled at her in the mirror. "Just trust me, honey." He turned away. "Selena, a latte for Cathy, please, then we're going to work some magic."

Four hours later, Cathy found herself back in the same chair, staring at herself in the same mirror. While calling it magic was a stretch, Ernest had definitely made a difference.

"You like?" he asked with a wink.

Her hair hung in soft layers to her shoulders. The cut had freed up a wave she hadn't known had been there. Honey red highlights brought out the green in her eyes and made her skin glow. Selena or Marta or one of the women—they were all dressed in black, incredibly beautiful and impossible to tell apart—had applied makeup. Not a lot, just enough to emphasize her cheekbones and her mouth. She was a vastly improved image of her former self.

Cathy smiled back at him. "I like it very much."

"Good. Then you'll need to make an appointment for six weeks from now. Trim every six weeks, color every twelve. It takes time to be beautiful, but it's worth it."

Cathy followed him to the front of the salon. Once there, she made an appointment for the trim and didn't even wince when they announced the total for her credit card. She'd never done anything like this before in her life. She'd never thought she was worth it.

As she turned to leave, she caught her reflection in the mirror by the entrance and had to smile. She was standing straighter. Not so much because Ula had suggested it, but because she felt better about herself. She knew she'd lost a few pounds, too. Not much, but enough that her clothes were loose. She'd always worn them baggy, hoping the excess fabric would disguise her bulges. Now her old jeans were practically falling off. A new pair would be another nice treat. Nothing expensive. Maybe they could stop at her favorite discount store on their way back to Stone's house.

As Cathy approached the gleaming BMW waiting for her on the curb, she had to laugh. Here she was being driven around the city in an expensive car, and on her way back to the fabulous mansion where she was staying, she wanted to stop at a bargain store. What on earth was wrong with this picture?

Cathy hurried up the front stairs as quickly as her healing knee and her cane would allow her. She was beaming with excitement and happiness. The shopping trip had been so successful, she'd worn her new jeans out of the store. She kept glancing down in disbelief. They were a whole size smaller.

Granted, she wore baggy clothes and for the first time in years, she'd bought something that actually fit, but it was still a size smaller! She'd splurged on a couple of new T-shirts, too, wanting to celebrate. When she'd studied herself in the full-length mirror in the dressing room, she would have sworn she saw the first hint of muscle definition in her arms. Her stomach wasn't as round, and her thighs looked a tiny bit more trim. Maybe it was the lighting or her imagination. She didn't care. All she knew was that she'd actually been eating right and exercising for two whole weeks, which was about thirteen and a half days longer than she'd ever managed before. She loved her new haircut, her makeup and most especially her new attitude. For the first time in a long time, things were looking up.

She headed toward the kitchen to share her new look with Ula, then, on a whim, headed up the stairs. She wanted Stone to see her. After all, the last time he'd seen her in the light had been when she'd been in the hospital. Not exactly a flattering image.

As usual, the door to his office was closed. Cathy hesitated, fighting back sudden shyness. What would he think about her new haircut? Would he hate it? Would he think it was silly that she wanted to share her news with him? Maybe she should wait for tonight, or—

"Stop it!" she whispered fiercely. "Do it or don't do it, but for once quit dithering."

That decided, she knocked firmly, then pushed the door open.

"Stone, I'm sorry to bother you, but Ula suggested I get a haircut and I did and—"

Her gaze settled on him at the exact moment she realized what she'd done. In all the excitement of the day, she'd simply forgotten about the fact that she'd never seen him before. At least not in the light. And there was a very good reason for that.

He stood by the window. The drapes were pulled open, and harsh afternoon sunlight spilled into the room. He looked up, and his dark eyes bore into her. She told herself to apologize or run or something, but all she could do was stand there and stare at him.

Chapter Seven

The scars were on the left side of his face. She had a brief impression of thick, harsh red lines scoring his skin from his cheekbone to his chin. His hand came up and covered them, while at the same time, he turned away.

Cathy's breath caught in her throat. Not because his disfigurement had been worse than she'd imagined, but because his profile from the right side was incredibly handsome.

If men were allowed to be called beautiful, the description would fit him perfectly. His hair was dark and a little too long—at least down to the middle of his collar. His nose was straight, his mouth well formed, his eyes an unusual shade of blue gray. He could have been a male model, or a heartthrob in the movies, she thought with some dismay.

He was tall and lean. Ula had hinted that Stone didn't eat much, so his shape didn't surprise her too much. However, she hadn't expected the layer of muscle that was obvious even though he wore a long-sleeved shirt and jeans. He must work out, but not too much. He looked strong but not overly developed.

She knew she should say something. After all, she'd barged in on him. The realization made her flush. She'd wanted to show him her new hairstyle and makeup, but what was the point? Even with the scars, he was an incredibly handsome man. She hadn't thought much about what he might look like, and when she had tried to picture him, she'd foolishly assumed he would be fairly average. Someone in her league. She'd been wrong.

Stone Ward was many things, but mostly he was out of reach. Rich and now good-looking. What on earth would he see in someone like her?

The crash of her dreams was as audible as the echo of the tide on the shore below. She felt defeated and more than a little foolish. All this time, she'd thought she meant something to him. Instead, he was only being kind. He must despise her.

"So it's that bad," he said lightly. "I've left you speechless." He gave her a mocking smile. "I don't suppose I should be surprised."

At first she thought he was angry, but then she realized he was as embarrassed as she was—but for different reasons. He thought she was horrified.

Compassion filled her. She was still feeling off guard and more than a little foolish, but his pain mattered more than hers. She would worry about herself later.

So instead of running, which was what she wanted to do, she squared her shoulders and walked toward him. "They're just scars, Stone. To be perfectly honest, I'd imagined something a lot worse."

He half turned toward her, then stopped himself, as if

wanting to keep that side of his face away from her. She sighed as her heart went out to him. So much for self-preservation where this man was concerned. Maybe it was her lack of experience with the opposite sex. Or maybe it was Stone himself.

"Shades of the Elephant Man?" he asked.

"That would have been an improvement over my imagination." She paused in front of his desk. "I didn't mean to barge in and disturb you. I just wasn't thinking. I'll leave if you want me to."

Stone gave her a quick glance. He didn't know what he wanted. Now that Cathy was here, he didn't want her to go. But he also didn't want her to see him. Unfortunately it was too late for that. She *had* seen him. And while she'd seemed surprised, she hadn't run screaming from the room.

"Why did you come to see me?" he asked, as if the reason would be significant.

She bit her lower lip. He thought she might be blushing, but it was hard to tell. "This is going to sound really stupid, but I got my hair cut and I wanted to show you."

Her chin dipped toward her chest and she stiffened, as if expecting punishment for her confession. They were, he realized, a sorry pair. If nothing else, maybe they could work on healing each other's wounds.

"Please stay," he said.

She raised her head. "Only if you'll look at me."

He knew what she meant. Sometimes looking at someone was the hardest thing he'd ever done. The bright afternoon light didn't offer any shadows in which to hide. There was no point, anyway. Her intent was clear. She wanted to stare at him until he wasn't unfamiliar anymore.

He moved toward his desk, then settled into his chair. At the same time, he motioned for her to take the seat opposite his.

She did as he requested, and they stared at each other. Cathy smiled first. "I'm really nervous. What if you don't like my haircut?"

Her comment, so unexpected, broke the tension between them. He relaxed back in his chair and grinned. "Guess you'll be in trouble."

Then he actually looked at her hair. It was different than it had been in the hospital. He recalled medium brown strands that were straight. When he'd observed her during her physical-therapy sessions, he'd noticed that she wore her hair parted in the center. The simple style allowed her hair to fall forward and shield her face.

The new cut left her face exposed. Fringed bangs hung down her forehead, but the sides curled away. Her layered hair was a rich brown with lots of red highlights.

He'd only ever seen her eyes in the shadows, but he never would have guessed they were green, or so large and pretty. Her skin glowed. There was something else different, too. Something…

He frowned. "Your face is thinner. In fact, all of you is thinner. Have you been losing weight?"

Her mouth stretched into a smile, and she looked as if he'd just handed her a salary's worth of stock options. "Yes," she said, and grinned some more.

He recalled Evelyn's complaints about wanting to lose ten pounds. She'd looked fine to him. From what he'd heard, Evelyn hadn't been alone in her quest. "Are you eating enough? Women obsess about their weight. I've never understood it."

Cathy made an *X* over her heart. "I swear, I'm eating plenty."

"Hmm." He didn't know what to say. Cathy had been more rounded than some women but less rounded than others. He'd thought she was fine. But he knew better than to say that. Instead, he focused on her new haircut.

"I like it," he told her. "The color is nice. It brings out your eyes. You look very pretty."

This time he didn't have to guess at her blush. She ducked her head again, but it wasn't from fear. His compliment brought her pleasure.

Something unfamiliar flickered through Stone. A need he couldn't define. He wanted...what? To say the right thing? To offer her a—

To touch her.

The thought came from nowhere, and once he'd acknowledged it, he couldn't let it go. He wanted to touch her hair and see if it felt as soft as it looked. He wanted to touch her smooth cheeks, her neck. He wanted to pull her close and taste her mouth while his hands stroked the generous curve of her hips. She was so incredibly female and alive and whole and he wanted her.

The fire stunned him with its intensity. One minute he'd been admiring a new hairstyle; the next every part of him was alive. He was hard and ready to take her. He cursed silently. It had been so long since he'd had that kind of a reaction that he'd begun to assume that part of him had ceased to function. But everything was working now. The ache was nearly unbearable.

He forced himself to remain calm. He didn't want to give away his thoughts or his condition. Cathy would be appalled. In her mind, he must be a brute. A flawed shell of a man. His desire would horrify her.

She raised her head and looked at him. "I want to ask about the accident but I don't want to pry," she said.

He'd nearly forgotten. About the scars, about the fact that she was seeing them for the first time. "What has Ula told you?" he asked.

He didn't think his housekeeper would betray anything personal, but Cathy and Ula seemed to get along. It was natural that they would have talked.

"Not much," she admitted. "I know you were in a car accident." She hesitated, as if not sure how much to mention. "I know that your wife died when you were injured."

His wife. He still had trouble thinking of Evelyn that way. As his wife. To him, she would always be his best friend, the shining part of him that was his conscience and his sounding board. When he'd listened to her, he'd done well. When he'd ignored her advice, he'd often paid the price through failure. Right up until the end, he thought.

The pain was an old, familiar companion. He knew it would always be there. The regrets he could never forget. The sins for which he could never atone. Not that the latter kept him from trying. If only, he thought sadly. If only he had it to do all over again.

"We'd been at a party," he said flatly. "I'd had too much to drink, so she was driving us home. There was a crash."

He remembered all of it. The harsh words and accusations, the way she'd kept asking him "Why?"

"She ran off the road," he continued, but the story had no meaning to him. He was simply repeating what the police had told him. "They were never sure if there was another car involved and the driver left the scene, or if Evelyn just lost control."

"Was it raining?"

He shook his head. "The night was clear, but it was late." Although she couldn't have fallen asleep. They'd been in the middle of their argument when they'd crashed. He knew that for certain. Nothing had been resolved. Evelyn, perhaps the only person he'd ever loved, had died thinking him a complete bastard. The hell of it was, she was right.

"I'm sorry," Cathy said. "I shouldn't have asked."

He dismissed her comment with a wave. "It's fine. The accident was a long time ago. I don't mind talking about it." Another lie. Another familiar companion. At least their conversation had one desired effect—the need he'd felt had faded, along with the physical manifestation. Perhaps it had never happened at all.

The phone on his desk rang. Cathy stood up. "I'll let you take that," she said, and walked out of the room.

He picked up the receiver and dealt with the call. Then he sat alone in the office and thought about what he should do next. Cathy had seen his face and she hadn't been disgusted. Perhaps now they could spend some time together.

The spark of pleasure he felt at the thought was different from desire, he told himself. Safer. He was only interested in being her friend…in helping her get her life back together. Nothing more. Friendship was allowed. That was how he'd set the rules.

He rose to his feet and crossed to the window. The grounds were beautiful in the spring afternoon. Flowers bloomed, the bright colors contrasting with the green leaves and lawn. The house was a showplace. He hadn't much cared when they bought it, but Evelyn had been excited about the purchase. The huge mansion had been a far cry from the double-wide trailer where she'd grown up.

He would have given her the moon, if he could have. Because he couldn't give her the one thing she'd wanted from him. He'd tried to be a good husband. Spending time with her had been easy. After all, she'd been his best friend. But that wasn't enough. Affection, even love. They couldn't make up for the simple truth—he'd never wanted her the way a husband was supposed to want his wife.

He closed his eyes, but it was too late to stop the memories. They flowed into his mind, as inescapable as the tide. Flashes of them growing up together. The way they'd always studied for tests together, first in high school, then in college. He smiled faintly, remembering his outrage when she'd done a little better. Not enough to make a difference, but a couple of questions here, a couple there. She'd been smart, and he'd respected that.

His smile faded. Maybe his mistake had been in trying to get around his family's wishes. A couple of years after he'd graduated from college and joined the family firm, his parents had picked out a young woman for him to marry. Someone suitable. At least in their minds. He'd rebelled. His lone rebellion in an otherwise agreeable existence. He'd wanted to marry for love. Barring that, he'd wanted to marry someone he could respect. On a whim, he'd proposed to Evelyn.

The second she'd accepted, he'd known. The truth, carefully concealed until that moment, had brightened her eyes until the light had nearly blinded him. He didn't know when she'd first fallen in love with him, when the bonds of friendship had become something else for her. Something more romantic. He'd known instantly that marrying her was going to be a mistake, but it was too late. He wouldn't have hurt Evelyn for the world.

Instead, he'd killed her.

The pain began behind his eyes and moved through his head. There was no physical cause, he knew. It was guilt. Oh, he hadn't been driving the car, nor had he actually caused the accident. He'd done worse. He'd betrayed her.

"Don't go there," he said aloud, but it was far too late.

He saw them on their wedding day; Evelyn's happiness had surrounded her with a nearly visible glow. He felt her body under his later that night. She'd been sweet and pretty and had all the right curves, but he'd never wanted her. The first time had been difficult for him, and it had never gotten better. He'd made love—enough, he'd thought, but he'd been wrong about that, too. She'd sensed his disinterest and over the years it had destroyed her self-confidence. While she'd talked of children, he'd tried to think of ways to tell her it wasn't going to last. It couldn't. He couldn't give her what she deserved. But to let her go meant losing his best friend. He didn't know what life would be like without her.

Everything had been destroyed anyway that last night. That damn night. His hands curled into fists as the self-loathing filled him. He'd had too much to drink. It wasn't an excuse—he knew that. But it was all he had.

He remembered standing alone in a corner of the party. One of his client's wives had come over to him. The woman—he couldn't even remember her name—had been attractive and obviously interested. Stone had felt a spark of response.

He'd known it was wrong and stupid and beneath him. Yet he'd let her lead him into the back room, and when she'd kissed him, he'd kissed her back.

He remembered thinking all he wanted was to feel a flash of passion. He had no intention of bedding the woman. No matter how bad things were with Evelyn, he wouldn't have done that to her. The kiss had been mildly pleasant, not memorable, except it had shown him it was time to come clean with his feelings. He was playing his best friend for a fool. She deserved better than that, and better than him.

He'd put his hands on the other woman's shoulders. His intent had been to push her away. Then he'd heard it. The gasp of surprise. He'd looked up and seen Evelyn standing in the doorway, staring at him.

She'd been so pretty that night. Her silky blond hair pulled back into a chignon. The sleeveless black dress had shown off her curves perfectly. Curves he couldn't make himself want. She'd stared at him as if she'd never seen him before. Perhaps she never had. He'd never betrayed her before except perhaps when he'd proposed on a whim.

He'd destroyed her. He knew that now. If they hadn't been arguing on the drive back, they probably wouldn't have gotten into the accident. If only... He had a thousand of them. All useless after the fact.

"Evelyn," he said aloud. "I'm sorry."

But the apology merely faded into the silence of the room. It was too late for that. Evelyn was gone, and all the apologies in the world weren't going to bring her back.

"Mr. Ward wondered if you would care to join him for dinner tonight," Ula said.

Cathy looked up from the book she'd been reading. She was in the library on the first floor of the house. For a second, she just stared at the housekeeper as her mind absorbed the words. "Stone wants to have dinner with me?" The last word came out as a squeak.

The older woman smiled. "That's what he said. About seven, if that's convenient."

Convenient? As if she had a social calendar that was close to full? "Sure, no problem."

"I'll let him know. Seven o'clock. In the dining room."

Ula left as quietly as she'd come. Cathy stared after her. She'd been nervous about what had happened when she'd barged in on him. She hadn't been thinking, and he would have had every right to be annoyed with her. But if the invitation was anything to go by, he'd forgiven her.

"Dinner. With Stone!"

She put her book on the table by the leather wing chair, then stood up. They were going to eat dinner together. Just like a real date!

"Don't start that," she murmured to herself. "He's being kind. This isn't a date."

She knew it wasn't, but as her entire dating experience had come from living vicariously through the experiences of other people, either on television or in books, she figured it wouldn't be such an awful thing if she pretended. As long as he never knew.

She glanced at her wristwatch. It was nearly six. She wanted to take a shower and get dressed. Now, what was she going to wear? One of Stone's staff members had gone to her house and brought back most of her clothes. She didn't have much that classified as appropriate attire for dining with a millionaire. There was that green dress, she thought as she slowly climbed the stairs. Her knee was better, but at the end of the day it often ached.

When she got to her room, she moved to the closet and looked at her meager selection. Unfortunately the shopping fairies hadn't brought her anything wonderful. The green dress was still her best bet, she thought. However, it was tight and it pulled at the waist and around her behind.

"We'll be sitting down," she mumbled. "Maybe he won't notice."

She stared at the dress, knowing it was that or a frumpy skirt and blouse, both of which had been old and out of style three years ago.

She sighed, then stripped off her shirt and new jeans. She unzipped the dress and dropped it over her head.

As she went to the mirror, she tugged at the waist. To her astonishment, it was loose. She could actually pull a little fabric away from her skin.

She drew in a deep breath. Her rib cage expanded, but didn't press against the bodice. Cautiously, barely daring to hope, she turned and stared at her profile. The dress hung smoothly off her hips and the small of her back. There was no bunching, no snugness.

"It fits!"

She grinned at her reflection. All the low-fat food and exercise had been worth it! She crossed her arms over her chest and hugged herself as she spun in a circle.

"Mr. Stone Ward, here I come."

An hour later, Cathy entered the dining room. Ula had set the large table with two place settings, next to each other at the far end. Fine crystal and glass glowed. There were candles but little other lighting.

For a single heartbeat, Cathy allowed herself to believe this *was* the romantic dinner she'd fantasized about in her shower. Maybe Stone had been swept away by her transformation and he'd—

Get over it, she thought, and firmly squashed the thought. The light was dim because Stone was nervous about his scars. For no other reason. She reminded herself that her imagination was allowed free rein only when she was alone, but when she was with Stone—especially now that they were going to be in the light instead of in the protective cover of shadow—she had better keep her mind on reality. She wouldn't want to embarrass him, or herself.

"Good evening."

She spun toward the sound and found him standing in the entrance to the dining room. He'd replaced his more casual shirt and jeans with a dress shirt and slacks. She was grateful that she'd thought to change into a dress, and even more grateful that it fit her well.

"Hi." Butterflies took up residence in her tummy. It was the new circumstances, she told herself, hoping the soft-shoe show they were performing against her rib cage would be a short one.

He walked toward the table and held out one of the chairs. It took her a second to realize he meant for her to sit in it. She swallowed hard. She'd seen men do that in the movies, but she hadn't known anyone did that in real life.

By the time he poured her a glass of wine, she didn't know if she was going to shriek with delight or just quietly swoon. Neither sounded appealing, so she followed his lead and when he raised his glass to her, she did the same.

''To friends,'' he said.

''Friends,'' she echoed, and took a sip. The white wine was tart but smooth, and she liked the way it made her tongue tingle. She'd had wine before. It had always been served at the answering service's holiday party. But she knew that whatever Stone had in his home was very different from the boxed liquid she'd had in the past.

Ula brought the first course—a salad with cut-up fresh vegetables. By now Cathy was used to the flavor of the fat-free dressing the housekeeper served. She gave the woman a smile, then picked up her fork.

As she chewed, she looked around the oversize room. There were two chandeliers, a buffet against the opposite wall and a built-in china cabinet at the far end of the room. Beneath her feet was an Oriental carpet that probably cost more than she'd made in the past three years combined.

''You're looking serious about something,'' Stone said. ''Want to share your thoughts?''

She finished chewing, then spoke. ''I'm a little out of my element here,'' she confessed. ''Sometimes I feel as if I've gotten caught up in one of those glitzy made-for-television movies or something. I'm just plain Cathy Eldridge, from North Hollywood, What on earth am I doing in your world?''

''You're recovering from your accident.''

She looked at him. He'd seated her so she faced his right side. She couldn't see his scars. Knowing they were there wasn't enough of a distraction. He was still too good-looking by far.

"I don't belong here."

"Of course you do. You're my guest." His voice had a note of finality, as if the issue had been resolved.

"It's not that simple," she told him. "I still don't understand why you're doing this. Why aren't you furious with me?" She took a sip of wine, hoping the alcohol would give her courage. "I lied to you."

"We've been over this, and I told you it doesn't matter. I understand." He leaned toward her. "I mean that, Cathy. I do understand. More than anyone. You think I haven't wished I could hide behind a mask? In a way, I do that every day. This house is my refuge, but it's also my prison."

"It doesn't have to be. Yes, you have scars, but they're not so terrible. I'm not kidding. I expected them to be much worse. A few people would stare, but they'd get over it. I wish you wouldn't lock yourself up here. It's not healthy."

"No, but this salad is." He speared a mushroom.

"You're trying to change the subject."

"I'm doing more than trying. Don't worry about it," he told her. "Just accept that you're here. I'm glad I could help."

"You have. You've been wonderful."

He must have heard something in her voice because his gaze sharpened. He stared at her.

"Don't," he said. "Don't make me more than I am. The reason I hide away is that I'm little more than a beast."

"Don't say that. You're not. You're gentle and kind and—"

He placed his hand on hers, but the gesture wasn't romantic or even friendly. He meant it as a warning.

"I'm many things, but I'm neither gentle nor kind." He motioned to his face. "These aren't the only scars. You would do well to remember that. I can be dangerous. If you forget that, you do so at your own risk."

Chapter Eight

Cathy squinted at the readout on the calculator, but it didn't help. No matter how she looked at the numbers, there wasn't very much in her checking account. Living with Stone kept her expenses minimal, but she still had to pay the mortgage and basic utilities on her house. While her salary had never been very high at her job, the temporary disability payment she received during her recovery was even less. There was always her savings account, she thought, then wondered if the meager amount would cover the bills still left to pay.

She dropped the calculator onto the glass tabletop and resolved not to think about that any more today. The bills would still be waiting for her in the morning. It was a beautiful afternoon, and she wanted to enjoy the sunshine.

She stretched her arms over her head, then turned to look out at the ocean. Blue water sparkled in the warm sunlight. Pepper had worked her hard that morning during their physical-therapy session, and her muscles ached pleasantly. Cathy no longer minded sweating or pushing herself during their workouts. She was seeing the results more quickly now. Not only was her knee healing, but the rest of her muscles were also toning up. She was able to do some aerobic exercise, and that had helped speed up her weight loss. Thankfully her stomach had gotten used to Ula's sensible portion sizes while her brain had ceased screaming for chocolate every five minutes. She knew she still had a long way to go before she would be at the weight she wanted, but she was definitely getting healthy and feeling good about herself.

"You look like a cat preening in the sun."

She turned toward the voice and saw Stone walking toward her. He moved with an easy grace she envied. Not only because her knee still gave her a little trouble, but also because he was so physically amazing. She barely noticed the scars on his face, and when his right profile was to her, he was incredibly handsome. Despite the time they'd spent together, or maybe because she was getting to know him and liking him more, she found that he still took her breath away.

There was something inherently masculine about his easy stride, his tall, lean body. Worn jeans hugged his hips and thighs. His white shirt was rolled up to the elbows, exposing muscular forearms. He was the kind of man women dreamed about, and she was no exception.

He pulled sunglasses out of his shirt pocket and slipped them on, then took the wicker chair opposite hers.

"I saw you sitting out here," he said as he smiled at her. "You looked so comfortable and content, I thought I'd join you."

"I didn't know you ever went outside during the day,"

she said without thinking, then could have cheerfully bitten off her tongue. Talk about an insensitive remark!

"Sorry, Stone," she said quickly. "I didn't mean it like that."

"I know what you meant," he told her. "I don't usually go out much at all and when I do, I prefer the shadows of night. But my scars don't seem to bother you, so I didn't think you'd mind."

"I don't. I like spending time with you." She nearly groaned out loud. Talk about having a case of foot-in-mouth disease this morning. "What I mean is we have fun together. And I don't notice the scars. They're not that bad anyway."

Ula appeared on the steps and called out an offer for something to drink. Stone accepted for both of them. Cathy took the moment to try to compose herself. Being around him always made her feel fluttery. Sometimes when they were talking about politics or books they'd read, she could go toe-to-toe with him and hold her ground in the discussion. But when she remembered their differences in position, or that he'd been to college and ran a multimillion-dollar business, she became tongue-tied.

Stone relaxed back in his chair. She was pleased that he was so comfortable with her. It had been little more than a week since she'd first walked in on him and seen his scars. Since then, they'd been spending more time together. They'd shared all their dinners and most lunches.

Cathy was willing to believe that Stone liked her—at least as a friend. He'd been good to her. He'd even warned her away from him.

She remembered that conversation, which they'd had the first night they'd eaten dinner together. He'd told her he was little more than a beast. She'd thought about it a lot, and she'd finally figured out what he really meant. He'd been gently telling her that he wasn't for her. No doubt he'd realized she had a huge crush on him and he didn't want to embarrass either of them by encouraging her to act on her inappropriate feelings. While she was a little chagrined he'd read her so easily, she was grateful he'd found a gentle way to let her down. The crush was still alive and well, but she was working hard to keep him from knowing.

Ula returned with their drinks. Cathy took a sip of her low-cal soda on ice. Every time she wanted a sugary drink or felt a hunger pang, she reminded herself that her body was burning calories and if she could hang on just for the rest of the day, she would have accomplished something. That's what she was trying to do—go it one day at a time. As her mother had often said, on those rare occasions when she'd been sober, clichés were clichés for a reason: they were usually accurate assessments of life.

Stone downed half of his iced tea, then pointed at the papers in front of her. "What are you doing?"

She wrinkled her nose. "Paying bills. Or trying to. I'm getting disability until I go back to work in a couple of weeks. At least the house payment is tiny. The place is old, and my mom never took out a second mortgage. That helps." She spoke lightly, not wanting Stone to think she was trying to beg or borrow money. "I'll be fine."

He set down his glass and leaned forward. "The doctor cleared you to go back to work in two weeks?"

She'd had an appointment earlier in the week. Cathy nodded. "Actually he said I could return whenever I wanted. My boss gave me the extra time. He wants me a hundred percent when I return." She smiled. "Eddie's kind of gruff on the outside, but underneath it all, he's a sweetie."

"Is that what you want?"

Cathy opened her mouth, then closed it. "I don't understand the question."

"Do you want to go back to work?"

She still wasn't sure what information he was after. Her heart sank. Maybe he was trying to tell her that it was time to move on. After all, she was fairly mobile, and the doctor had said she was cleared to drive.

Disappointment overwhelmed her. She wished they were back in the dark so she wouldn't have to guard her expression. Of course, she thought. He wanted her gone and his house to himself. She should have figured that out sooner.

"I do plan to take the extra couple of weeks," she admitted. The prospect of returning to her graveyard shift at the answering service was not appealing. "But I won't wait that long to get out of your way. You've been more than kind, and I don't want to take advantage of your hospitality. I probably should have left sooner. I apologize. It's just everything has been so lovely, I didn't really think about it." She shrugged lamely, then cleared her throat. Please God, let her not cry until she was alone.

"No!" Stone said forcefully. "I'm not hinting that I want you to leave. Quite the opposite. I want you to stay with me as long as you like. At minimum, until you're ready to go back to work. No arguments. I insist."

"I—" She didn't know what to say. The truth was she wanted to be with Stone for as long as possible. His dark gaze was so intense, she decided she could believe him. After all, he was a successful businessman. He wouldn't be where he was today if he had trouble telling people no.

One corner of his mouth twisted down. "Unless you'd rather leave. You're not a prisoner here."

"No," she said quickly. "I'd like to stay. Thank you for asking me. You're very kind."

"I'll make you a deal, kid. Stop telling me I'm kind, and you can move in permanently if you like."

He was teasing, but for a second she allowed herself to believe it was true. That the fantasies that filled her night were real and that Stone cared about her as more than a friend.

"You are kind," she said, "but I'll stop saying it."

"Then we have a deal?"

She nodded.

He finished his iced tea. "I have fourteen phone calls to return," he said, then rose to his feet. "Thanks for letting me join you."

He circled around the table and paused by her chair. Before she could figure out what he was going to do, he leaned down and pressed a kiss on the top of her head. Then he was gone.

Cathy watched him walk into the house. She knew that his mind was already a million miles away, or at least up in his office dealing with business. She knew that the gesture had been friendly and even absentminded. He probably didn't know what he'd done. But she could still feel the soft pressure of his lips on the top of her head and the way he'd briefly squeezed her shoulder in passing. She would remember and tonight, before she slept, she would play out her fantasy of the two of them. She would pretend that his touch had meant so much more.

"You've promised," Pepper said two weeks later as she folded up her table.

Cathy grinned. "I know and I mean it. I'm going to work out at least five times a week. Forty-five minutes of aerobics, and I'm going to keep up the weight training, too."

"Three times a week is best on that," Pepper reminded her. "I'll let you slide with twice a week, but only when things are really hectic. You've done great and you don't want to lose that, do you?''

Cathy shook her head. She followed her physical therapist to her van and helped her stow the equipment. Pepper turned toward her and gave her a hug. ''You've worked really hard and it shows. Be proud of yourself, okay?''

''I will.''

Cathy stood in the driveway and waved as the other woman drove down to the street. When Pepper was no longer in sight, Cathy bounded up the steps to the big house, then let herself in the front door.

She paused in the foyer. She wasn't really sure what to do next. The truth was she had to make some decisions with her life. She'd been at Stone's house for nearly six weeks, and she couldn't hide out here forever.

''Time to act like a grown-up,'' she told herself as she settled on the bottom step and drew her knees up to her chest.

As much as she would like to stay here and enjoy the life of the rich and reclusive, that wasn't an option. She had her job back at the answering service waiting for her.

Cathy wrinkled her nose. She *really* didn't want to go back to her old, boring life. She'd come so far in the past six weeks. She was eating right and exercising. She felt positive about herself; she was sleeping great. Just to make life even better, she'd lost fifteen pounds and nearly two sizes. Just five more pounds to go.

So her world had taken a turn for the better. The fire and her injuries could have been a horrible situation. Instead, she'd come through even better than before. She didn't want to lose the momentum. She didn't want to go back to what she'd been before. None of which answered the question, now what?

College was a possibility. Maybe a few classes while she

was working. If she kept her night shift, she could take morning classes, then come home and sleep until she had to leave for work. She would have plenty of time to study at night. After midnight, the answering service really slowed down and Eddie had never cared if she read. Studying would be a more productive use of her time.

She didn't have a clue as to what she wanted to study, but right now that wasn't important. She could take a few general-education courses and get her bearings. It had been a long time since high school, and she was sure it was going to take some effort to get her brain used to studying again.

"That's decided, then," she said aloud, and rose to her feet. But instead of climbing the stairs, she sighed. She didn't want to go. Not because the house was beautiful, or that there was someone to cook and clean, but because she didn't want to leave Stone. She liked him. She certainly had a crush on him. She was probably a little in love with him. He would go on and forget all about her, but she would always remember him. He was the highlight of her life.

Still, she'd stayed as long as she dared. She was ready to go back to work and couldn't think of a single excuse not to go.

"Like I said," she reminded herself. "Time to be a grown-up. Better to go on my own than be asked to leave."

She started up the stairs. On the second floor, she turned right and headed down to his office. The door was ajar. She knocked as she pushed it open and stepped inside.

Stone looked up from his computer and smiled. "This is a nice surprise. Are you finished with Pepper?"

"Yes, it was our last session. She left me with firm instructions about continuing on with an exercise program, and I'm determined to do it."

"Good for you." He motioned to the chair in front of his desk.

As she took the seat, she studied him. The contrast of thick scars and perfect male beauty never ceased to move her. He was the most amazing man. Truly kind, although she wasn't allowed to say that anymore.

"Are you just visiting?" he asked.

She shook her head. "I have an announcement. I've imposed on your life enough. You have been more than generous with your home and your time, but I need to get back to where I belong. I start back to work on Monday."

Stone stared at her so intently she wanted to check her cheek for a smudge. "Is something wrong?" she asked.

The corners of his mouth turned up, but it was a pale imitation of a smile. "I don't want you to go," he said simply.

Cathy blinked. Had she heard that correctly? He didn't want her to go? "But I'm just in the way," she blurted out.

"Not at all. I enjoy your company." He picked up a pen and turned it over in his hands. "Sometimes this house gets a little too quiet. I don't get out as much as some think I should." He motioned to his face. "For obvious reasons."

"It doesn't have to be like that," she said quickly.

"That's not the subject under discussion," he reminded her. "We were talking about you leaving. Would you reconsider?"

"I—" Her heart pounded in her chest. What was he saying? Was he telling her that he was really going to miss her? Had she come to matter to him the same way he mattered to her? Were they more than friends?

She leaned forward in her seat and clasped her hands together. "Stone, I don't know what to say."

"Good, because I haven't made my offer yet. I know

you still have your job at the answering service. You're very good at it, but then, why wouldn't you be? You're personable and very bright. The truth is, Cathy, you're not challenged there. I realize I'm overstepping my bounds, but this is important. You could be so much more.''

He continued talking, but she couldn't hear him. He thought she was bright and efficient. Great. Lovely. A combination of a good computer and favorite dog. Next he would go on about how tidy she was.

Cathy tried to keep her emotions from showing on her face. Why had she let herself hope? It was silly. She knew better. Stone was not like her. They had very little in common. He didn't see her as a woman, at least not as one he would be interested in.

''I'm offering you a job,'' she heard him say.

That got her attention. ''I'm sorry, what was that?''

''I said I'm offering you a job. As my personal assistant. I've needed one for a long time. I want someone to act as a liaison for me with certain people at my office. There will be meetings, some occasional travel. At first you're probably going to feel that you're way out of your league, but I think you can do it. Actually I think you'll be terrific.''

''A job?''

He frowned. ''I would really like you to consider this, Cathy, but only if you feel the opportunity is right for you. I'm not trying to insult you or tell you what to do.''

''I understand that,'' she said. Her head was spinning. A job? Working with him? ''You'd want me to go talk with people at your company?''

''Yes. Currently we have meetings with me attending via speakerphone. That would still happen, but I would want you there as my personal representative.''

''I don't have a college degree, let alone any experience in business.''

"I'm aware of that. You'll have to work hard to get up to speed. It's a daunting task, but if you're up to it, I'd like to give it a try. We could agree to a six-month trial, after which time we both get to evaluate the situation."

She pressed her lips together just to make sure her mouth wasn't hanging open. Okay, this wasn't the declaration of love that she'd imagined, but it was a great second prize. Working with Stone? It would be exciting and different. She would learn a lot. She didn't fool herself about the hard work. She knew the hours he kept. Just because Stone used his house as his main office didn't mean he wasn't driven.

Now that they were discussing business, everything about him had changed. His posture was stiffer, his gaze more direct. Even his word choices had taken on a business flavor and a hard edge. Could she survive that?

Cathy wasn't sure, but she also knew she would never forgive herself if she walked away from this once-in-a-lifetime chance.

"I think the idea has possibilities," she said, trying on business-speak for the first time.

Stone grinned. "I'm glad. Before you decide, there are some logistics. I would prefer you to live in the house. You would be more accessible to me. I'm sure it wouldn't be difficult for you to rent out your house. However, if you hate the idea of staying here, I would appreciate it if you would live someplace closer than your home in North Hollywood."

He wanted her to stay in his house? "Um, staying here wouldn't be a problem."

"Good. The company has an excellent benefit package. You can make an appointment with the director of human resources to discuss that with her directly. Which leaves the issue of salary.'' He named a figure that made her head spin.

She opened her mouth to tell him that it was too much, then swallowed the words. What did she know about the starting salary of the personal assistant to the president of a very successful company? Maybe Stone was padding it a little because he knew she didn't have much, but she doubted it. This was business, and for him that was very separate from his personal life. So what if she was about to earn over three times what she'd been making at the answering service? She thought she just might be able to suffer through that.

"I accept," she said.

"Was that a yes?"

She grinned. "Absolutely. You're right—I'm sure I am going to be in over my head, but I want to learn. I'm not afraid of hard work. I'm honest and dependable and I'll give a hundred percent every day.'' Now she sounded like a loyal dog, but she no longer cared. Not only did she get to stay with Stone, but she also was going to be working for him.

A flash of self-doubt filled her, but she pushed it away. She *would* make this happen, she promised herself. She would earn his respect.

"I'll notify human resources,'' he said, and rose to his feet.

He came around his desk toward her. Cathy stood up. When he held out his hand to shake on the deal, she reacted impulsively. She reached out to hug him.

Even as she moved forward, she told herself to stop. But it was too late, and the momentum carried her into him. She tried to pull back, to save the potentially awkward situation. Then large, strong hands settled on her back.

"Your way is much better," Stone murmured, and bent his head to hers.

The hug had been an unplanned act. She'd meant it as a friendly gesture. She had no idea what *he* meant by the kiss, but as his mouth gently touched hers, she found she didn't care.

He was warm and firm, and she felt as if she'd come home. Cathy didn't have enough experience to compare his kiss to others, but it was plenty wonderful on its own. He didn't move much, or try to deepen the kiss. He stayed still. She didn't know if he was savoring the experience or giving her a chance to get used to their closeness, and soon she found she didn't care. It was enough to be in his arms, his mouth against hers.

She moved her hands to his shoulders and squeezed the hard muscles. In response, he tilted his head slightly and pressed a little closer. She inhaled the scent of his body— the scent of him. Clean and masculine, and maybe a little dangerous.

They weren't touching in many places, and she longed to lean against him. That's what she always read about. Couples pressing together, breasts straining. She had never understood how breasts could possible strain, but now she did. Hers ached. She would have sworn they were swollen, too, longing to be flattened against his broad chest. Shivers rippled through her, starting at her toes and working their way up to her scalp. Her fingers tingled; so did that secret place between her thighs. She thought—

His mouth parted, and he touched the tip of his tongue to her lower lip. Instantly her mind shut down, as did her ability to breathe. None of that mattered. She focused all her energy, all her senses, on that single damp spot.

He touched her there again, this time pressing a little more as if urging her to comply with his wishes. Before she could figure out what to do, her mouth parted, almost without her realizing it, and his tongue slipped inside.

He was warm and sweet and tasted better than any chocolate she'd ever had. He didn't attack or act as if he was there to map out the points of interest in her mouth. Instead, he moved slowly, almost reverently, first exploring the tender skin on the inside of her lip before gently stroking her tongue.

She supposed the fire was inevitable. Between the shivers and the sparks and goodness knows what other sensations, she already felt as if she were in danger of going up in flames. So when the heat licked against her skin, she simply surrendered to the hot need. She leaned against him, at last giving her breasts what they'd been screaming for. The relief was instant, and over just as quickly. For as her breasts nestled against the hard planes of his chest and the aching eased, her hard, sensitized nipples began to tighten even more. She'd never felt anything like this in her life. She wasn't sure what was happening or what it meant. She only knew she didn't want Stone to ever stop kissing her.

As if he read her mind, his arms tightened around her. She had leaned into him, but he pulled her even closer. Their bodies pressed together, just like she'd read about. He *was* hard to her soft, just like those authors had promised. It was so incredibly perfect. Especially the hardness she felt pressing into the spot between her stomach and her left hipbone. He was aroused and ready. Kissing her had done that to him!

She must have made a sound of pleasure and gratification, or somehow indicated something had changed, because Stone pulled back. He broke the kiss gently, cupping her face as their lips parted. Still, she was loath to let him go.

"Wow!" she said without thinking.

Fortunately he grinned. "Yeah. Wow." Then the smile faded. "I'm sorry," he said. "I don't usually welcome employees to the company like that."

His words had the effect of an ice bath. She forced her smile to remain in place even as she took a step back. "I guess a lot of the guys would really object, huh?" She waved as if it had meant nothing to her, either. "Don't worry about it, Stone. We're friends, right? It was a very nice kiss."

"I agree. And I promise it won't happen again."

Great. He was probably the kind of man who gave blenders and vacuum cleaners for birthday presents, too. She sighed. Well, it had been a wonderful experience. She would have a lot to think about when she was alone in her room that night. In the meantime, she must never let him know that her knees were still weak and her breasts would probably be aching for days.

So this was desire, she thought. At least she knew what it felt like. For a while, she'd thought she might go her whole life and never experience it.

"Thank you for understanding," he said.

"Sure. No problem."

She left his office with a promise to see him at dinner. Once out in the hall, her good humor faded and confusion took its place. What exactly had happened back there? If he didn't mean it, why had he kissed her like that?

"So much for being a grown-up," she whispered as she started shaking. She felt strange inside. Tense, but not tense.

Now she was supposed to work for the man. Fine. She would figure out a way to put this behind her and she would work for him. She wanted the chance. She would be a fool to mess that up by getting too caught up in what had obviously meant different things to her than to him.

He'd thanked her for understanding. Great. The problem was she didn't understand. Not even for a minute.

Chapter Nine

Stone walked the few steps to his chair, then collapsed. Every cell in his body ached with a need he couldn't control. He'd wanted before—he'd even wanted Cathy. But he didn't remember ever feeling this overwhelming desire. He was having trouble focusing on anything but how she'd felt in his arms and the way his world had exploded into passion when he'd kissed her.

Talk about stupid, he told himself. First he asked the woman to work for him. A smart move. After all, she was bright, energetic and willing to get the job done. The way she'd tackled her recovery and physical therapy had shown him that. Better yet, he sensed he could trust her. There weren't many people he could say that about. But then he had to go and blow it by kissing her.

It had been the hug. He knew that, but told himself it was a pretty poor excuse. Women had hugged him before. Admittedly none had since the accident. Not that there had been any opportunity. So maybe that was the reason he'd overreacted. He'd been caught off guard. The unexpected contact with an enticing female had left him vulnerable to his physical needs. Apparently that part of him wasn't as dead as he'd imagined.

That's all it was then—animal lust. Nothing more. A physical sensation, be it desire or pain, could be controlled. He'd done it all his life.

Stone sucked in a breath and exhaled it slowly. To be completely honest, he had a lot of experience controlling pain and virtually none controlling desire. Wanting had never been an issue in his life. In college he'd had a string of steady girlfriends more than willing to be intimate with him. He'd experienced desire, but nothing like this soul-wrenching wanting. Marriage to Evelyn had been difficult because he hadn't felt any sexual connection with her. So this experience with Cathy was new territory. Still, he *would* conquer it.

He pressed one foot against the floor and pushed until he'd turned his chair around and he could stare out the window. So far the lecture on managing the need wasn't helping. Every inch of him was still on fire. His groin throbbed to the point of pain. Part of the problem was his body sensed the possibilities. Cathy had responded to the kiss as if she, too, had felt the same passion flaring between them. Without closing his eyes, he could put himself back there—holding her, kissing her, bodies pressing, tongues stroking.

He groaned low in his throat. His hardness swelled to the point of explosion.

He could never do it again. Cathy had to be completely off-limits to him except as an employee and a friend. She was too softhearted. She only saw the scars on the outside, and they would never bother her. Even though he'd tried to warn her off, she thought he was a normal, decent guy. She didn't have the life experience to know that inside he was little more than a monster. An empty shell of a man who had lied to and betrayed the best person in his world.

If she knew the truth— He shook his head. He was a coward, as well, he realized. He didn't want her to know the truth about him. She would think less of him, and he knew he couldn't bear that. She was important to him and if she were gone, he would have nothing of value left. Work had long since ceased to be much of a challenge.

So he wouldn't tell her how he'd married Evelyn for all the wrong reasons. How he hadn't had the common decency to love or even desire his wife. How in the end, he'd allowed her to catch him in an act of betrayal and that she had died because of it.

Instead, he would remind himself of his plan and continue to act on it. Cathy was physically better. Now he'd offered her a job. He was well on his way to fixing her and her life. Soon she wouldn't need him anymore, and he could set her free.

But the idea of Cathy being gone was even more painful than the wanting, so he pushed that thought away. He was doing the right thing for the right reason. The desire had no place in this.

He shifted until he was facing his desk again, punched a button on his computer keyboard and went back to work. But it was nearly an hour until the throbbing subsided to a manageable level, and that night, despite a healthy dose of Scotch, he was restless. When he slept, he dreamed of making love with Cathy, waking to a sweat-slicked body and a hardness aching for release.

Cathy pulled back the drapes and stared out at the morning. As usual the sky was clear and the ocean a deep shade of blue. "I don't have to leave," she said softly to herself, and grinned. It was all too wonderful to believe.

As she showered and dressed, she made a mental list of everything she had to do. She agreed with Stone that she should rent out her house in North Hollywood. Today she would find a broker who handled that sort of thing and sign the necessary papers. She also wanted to pack up her personal belongings and store them in the little room off the garage. She should probably get a post-office box somewhere close, too, so she could have her mail forwarded. So many things, she thought, happy to be busy at last.

She returned to the bathroom to apply her makeup. It was Saturday. She would start working for Stone on Monday morning. A flutter of excitement rippled through her. The thought of the new job was a little scary, but she was determined to work as hard as she could to be successful. This was a terrific opportunity, and she wasn't going to blow it.

She reached for her compact of blusher, then stared at herself and laughed. She didn't need the color in her cheeks; she was already glowing. Cathy chuckled. Her happiness wasn't all about her new job, either. Some of it was about the kiss.

She sighed softly and closed her eyes. Instantly she was transported back to those few moments in Stone's arms. Her body began to tingle as she remembered being so close to him. She could recall the scent of him, his heat, the way his hands had felt against her back and waist. His had been the most amazing kiss of her life.

Cathy opened her eyes. "Not that I have a whole lot to compare it to," she reminded herself.

There had been a couple of kisses in high school at different parties when kissing games had been played. But she'd never had a boyfriend. She'd been shy and standoffish, mostly because of her mother. It had been too dangerous to let anyone get close. She couldn't have risked someone wanting to come home with her ever. So she'd refused the few tentative offers she'd had.

Her only other kissing experience had come at an acquaintance's summer party a couple of years after high school. Cathy didn't remember very much about the night, except it had been very hot and the college boys had spiked the drinks. She did recall one young man cornering her by the billiard table. He'd pushed her into the shadows, murmured something about her being quiet but sexy. Then he'd stuck his tongue in her mouth and his hand down her shorts. She'd been too stunned to react. He'd taken her silence as agreement and had started pushing her toward one of the bedrooms. Cathy had escaped by asking him to get her a drink, then ducking out a side door and walking home. At the time, she'd decided that the kissing they talked about in books was highly overrated and she wasn't ever going to worry if she didn't do it again.

But now everything had changed. Stone's kiss hadn't been anything like the ones she'd experienced before. She'd liked it and she wanted him to do it again. Not that he would, she thought as she put her makeup away and headed toward the door. She was going to be working for him, and that meant they would have a professional relationship. She just wished there was a way she could have it all.

Ula was in the kitchen when Cathy arrived. She quashed a flash of disappointment that Stone wasn't there. He rarely joined them in the morning, but sometimes he did and after what had happened yesterday, she'd been hoping this would be one of those special days.

"Good morning," the housekeeper said as she put a plate of cut-up fruit in front of Cathy. "How did you sleep?"

"Great. And you?"

"Well as always."

Cathy speared a strawberry. "Did Stone tell you?"

Ula poured them each a cup of coffee, then took her usual seat on the opposite side of the small table. The kitchen itself was large, with restaurant-sized appliances. The floors and countertops gleamed in the bright morning sun. The windows faced east and caught all the early light. Fresh herbs grew in a built-in planter, while several vibrant, healthy plants hung from hooks in the ceiling.

Ula's dark eyes brightened with curiosity. "Mr. Ward hasn't told me anything."

Cathy leaned forward. "I'm not leaving. Stone has offered me a job as his assistant. I start Monday. He said it would be better for him if I continued to live in the house." Some of her good humor faded. "I hope you don't mind the extra work."

"Child, you worry too much." Ula gave her a smile, then touched the back of her hand. "I'm delighted for you. I could never understand why someone as bright as yourself had gotten locked away in that boring job. Mr. Ward is a demanding boss, but he's fair. Besides, I suspect you've already seen much of his temper is more bark than bite."

Cathy relaxed into her chair. She hadn't realized how concerned she'd been about the other woman's opinion until she'd told her about the job offer. Ula wasn't an open person and she didn't let on either her feelings or what she was thinking. But over the past several weeks, Cathy had noticed a softening by the housekeeper. She was glad to know she had the other woman's approval.

"I have a lot to do today," Cathy said. She explained about renting out her house and getting a post-office box.

Ula nodded. "You might want to think about picking up a few things to wear, too. Everything you own is loose.

Besides, I suspect Mr. Ward will want you to go into the office for him, from time to time. It's some grand building on the west side. One of those high-rise places. They all dress nice over there.''

Cathy hadn't thought that far ahead. ''You're right. I still have a few pounds to lose, but I could get a couple of things now and fill in as I go. There's a nice mall at the intersection of the 101 and 405 freeways. I'll stop there on my way back.'' She smiled. ''Thanks for the suggestion.''

''You're a sweet girl. You'll do well for Mr. Ward. See that you do well for yourself, too.''

''I plan to learn everything I can.'' Cathy knew her happiness showed on her face. She couldn't help beaming. For the first time in her life, everything was going right.

''I've read the prospectus,'' Stone said into the phone. When Ula tapped on the door, he motioned for her to enter and put his breakfast tray on his desk. ''Yes, I understand what everyone is saying about the IPO. I don't agree. I think they're going out too high with their initial public offering of stock and I'm not going to buy. The company has merit and they're going to be successful, but wait a month. I'm betting that by then the initial price is cut nearly in half. Then we'll buy.'' He listened for a couple of minutes. ''Fine. If Johnson disagrees, he can risk his own money, but not my clients' funds. No, I don't want to talk to him about it. Uh-huh.'' There were a few more protests, then Stone realized Ula was still in the room. She obviously had something on her mind, which was unusual. She rarely interrupted his business day. ''I'll get back to you later,'' he said, and hung up the phone.

He turned his attention to his housekeeper. ''Have a seat, Ula. Tell me what's on your mind.''

Ula sank into the chair opposite his. Despite her petite

stature, she was a formidable presence. As always, her gray dress was perfectly pressed. Every dark hair was in place and her gaze was steady. Ula seemed unflappable. She would have been a great spy.

''You're not going to like this,'' she announced, and then waited, as if he would order her from the room.

''Unless you're telling me that you're quitting, I think I'm up for just about anything.''

She pressed her lips together. ''I'm not quitting. I like my job. It's about Cathy.''

For some reason, her words didn't surprise him. He knew Ula had been an interested bystander in the odd relationship he'd developed with his houseguest. Cathy was neither close friend nor family member, yet Stone had welcomed her into his home. He hadn't been willing to explain about their special relationship, nurtured by years of chatting on the phone. Nor did he want to discuss the psychology of his motives for helping her.

''What about Cathy?'' he asked, playing for time.

''You've offered her a job.'' She spoke as if that simple sentence explained it all.

''I know. As my assistant. I need someone and she's perfect. She's bright, trustworthy and looking to make a change. This is a better opportunity for her than that dead-end job she had at the answering service.''

''I don't dispute that this is a step up for her. What I question are your motives.''

''I'm trying to do the right thing.''

Her eyes darkened with disapproval. ''You're trying to make up for the past. This isn't right, Mr. Ward. Cathy isn't Evelyn, and all the fixing in the world isn't going to bring your wife back from the dead.''

Ula had always been one for plain speaking and this time was no exception. Stone had to swallow hard to keep from showing surprise or lashing out in a defensive move. Instead, he forced himself to relax back into his chair and appear calm.

"You're perceptive as always," he conceded. "I'll admit there are some similarities between Cathy's situation and Evelyn's life. But I know they are two different women. Nothing will bring Evelyn back." Or atone for what he'd done, but he was still working on the latter. "Cathy only needs a boost up in life. I can offer her that."

Ula leaned forward. "Mr. Ward, you have to think about what you're doing. Cathy is a very nice young woman. She is everything you've said. Bright, hardworking and someone you can trust. She'll be very loyal. But she's young and inexperienced. To her, you are a romantically tragic man. She will fall in love with you. Perhaps she already has. She will allow herself to dream, not knowing that you are incapable of loving her back. You will break her heart and then she'll be forced to leave. It would be kinder to let her go now."

Ula's words stunned him. He didn't want to think about Cathy loving him, or anyone caring about him again. He didn't want love. He didn't want to care about anyone. Being alone was so much safer.

"You're exaggerating. We're friends, nothing more." Memories of the kiss intruded, but he pushed those away. It had been a one-time occurrence, never to be repeated.

"Just because you won't acknowledge the truth doesn't mean it's going away," Ula told him. "I'm not saying it's wrong for her to love you. In many ways, you're a good man. But the scars go deeper than your cheek. We both know that. You'll never be able to give her what she deserves."

The truth was as ugly as his face. How long had Ula been able to see through him?

"Cathy isn't a toy," Ula continued. "You can't play with her until you're tired of her, then toss her aside. I don't think you'd do that on purpose, but it is a potential problem. You've seen Evelyn in her and you want to find a way to make up for what happened before."

"I'm giving Cathy an opportunity. Without this, she goes back to her go-nowhere job at the answering service. Is that what you want?"

"And when she falls in love with you?"

"She won't." She couldn't. He wasn't worth loving, and Lord help him, he couldn't risk caring back. He'd loved Evelyn and in the end, he'd been the cause of her death.

Ula clasped her hands tightly together. "You can't keep her safe like a princess in a fairy tale. She's not under a spell, and this isn't an enchanted castle. She needs to know the truth. She deserves that much. At least let the girl make a choice."

"She made a choice. She wants the job."

Ula stared at him for a long time. He forced himself to stay still, when in fact he felt like pacing the room. His housekeeper's words were hitting too close to home by far. Dammit all to hell, when had he become so transparent?

"Does she know the truth about Evelyn?"

"She knows about the accident, if that's what you're asking."

"It's not. Does she know you blame yourself for the accident?"

He thought about their conversations. "In a manner of speaking."

"I see. Does she know how you felt about your late wife?"

"She knows that we were very close. The best of friends."

Ula's dark eyes saw far too much. Her expression tightened. "So you're not going to tell her."

"Tell her what? You're making too much of this."

"Am I?" Ula rose to her feet. "What will you do when she falls in love with you? You talk of wanting to make it better for her, but I don't think she's going to thank you for breaking her heart. Because that *is* what is going to happen. We both know that. Even if you wanted to, you're not capable of loving her back."

With that, she turned on her heel and left.

Stone stared after her, then focused his attention on the view behind him. But for once the expanse of sky and ocean held little comfort. Ula had been wrong about many things, he told himself. He knew this wasn't a fairy story. There was no castle, although there was a beast in residence. Cathy was free to come and go as she liked. She'd made an informed choice about taking a job with him. He'd offered her the opportunity of a lifetime. Without him, she would have gone back to the answering service and her small, tedious life. He offered her the world.

As for her falling in love with him...it wasn't possible. He wasn't the kind of man to inspire strong feeling. He was too withdrawn, too physically unappealing.

What about the kiss?

The voice whispered from inside his head. He pushed it away, reminding himself that it had been a reaction of gratitude combined with the reality of two adults thrown together in close quarters. Nothing more.

That had to be true because Ula had been right about one important point. He would never risk loving anyone again. So he would never be able to return Cathy's affections.

Not that it was going to be an issue. They would work

together, they would stay friends. His housekeeper would see that she'd been wrong.

He turned back to his computer and began to work, all the while ignoring the burning in his gut that felt amazingly like guilt.

Chapter Ten

Cathy paused outside the door to Stone's office. Despite all the time they'd spent together, she was nervous. Probably because today was different. She was no longer just a friend, or someone he was helping out while she recovered from the accident. Today she was his employee.

"I can do this," she whispered. She'd repeated the phrase at least a hundred times over the past couple of days. So far she wasn't convinced, but she figured it had to sink in sometime and start working. She *would* be successful because the alternative was unthinkable. This mattered too much—she wasn't going to let herself fail.

She smoothed down the front of her tailored slacks. She'd bought a couple of pairs, along with some simple blouses and a pair of nice leather flats. The clothes were a far cry from her usual oversize jeans and T-shirts. The combination of low-fat food and Pepper's exercise program showed on her slimmer figure. Between that and her new haircut, she felt almost pretty. Perhaps for the first time in her life.

"Good thing," she said softly. "Today I'm going to need all the confidence I can get!"

With that she knocked firmly on Stone's office door and stepped inside.

He was already working. He glanced up and smiled. Cathy's stomach reacted with a predictable leap up against her ribs. She sighed. So much for getting used to being around him, she thought. Every time she thought she had the situation under control, something happened to change it. This time her nerves were a combination of first-day tension and lingering memories of the kiss they'd shared.

"Good morning," he said, and glanced at his watch. "It's barely eight, Cathy. I didn't expect you this early."

She shrugged and stepped into his office. "I wasn't sure what time you wanted me to start and I knew you would be here first thing." According to Ula, the man barely slept. He didn't drink, didn't eat much. Work was his life. Cathy had begun to wonder if the reason for that was work was all Stone could trust.

"Why don't we compromise on eight-thirty as a regular starting time," he said as he rose to his feet. "I would rather you stayed late than came in early. I have people on the East Coast to take care of the market opening, but not enough staff to cover the international comings and goings in the Far East. This way."

He led her to a side door. She followed him into another room. "You'll work here," he said.

Cathy glanced around in amazement. She hadn't really thought about what it would be like working for Stone. She'd known she would be busy, but she hadn't dwelled on the question of if she would have a desk or not. She certainly hadn't expected a whole office just for her.

The space was smaller than his, but there were large windows and the view was amazing. An L-shaped desk dominated the room. The short leg contained a computer complete with a printer. Against the far wall were several filing cabinets, along with copy and fax machines. Opposite the door to his office was another door.

"That leads to the conference room," he said. "Should you need to hold a meeting here, it's very convenient. Try to give Ula a day's notice if you want a meal served, although she's great about throwing something together at the last minute."

Cathy was stunned. Her head felt as if it were spinning, and she was having trouble concentrating on what he was saying. If *she* wanted to hold a meeting? Oh, sure, she did it all the time. Tons of meetings, just her and her laptop back at the answering service.

Doubts flooded her. What on earth had she been thinking? She didn't know anything about the world of investments or finance. She couldn't fake her way through this. Stone was crazy if he thought she wasn't going to completely mess up everything. She had to come clean and let him know that he'd made a mistake.

But she didn't want to. Maybe it was wrong, but she really needed this chance. What if she *could* do it? What if she was smarter than she thought, or the work wasn't that hard or any variations on that theme? What if this was exactly what it felt like—the opportunity of a lifetime? She didn't dare walk away. She might never get another chance.

"We're going to start you out slow," Stone told her as he walked to the computer and patted the top of the monitor. "I thought this morning you could answer some correspondence for me. I write my own memos and E-mail." He grinned. "This is the nineties, after all. But these are official letters, so I prefer to have them done. I've left you notes and some samples so you can see the format.''

He leaned forward and shuffled through the papers. Cathy watched him. The light-colored shirt he wore emphasized his dark good looks. She'd been around him so much, she barely noticed the scars on this face. As always he took her breath away.

Suddenly he straightened and stared at her. ''I never thought to ask. Are you familiar with computers?''

She sent up a prayer of thanks for her lone indulgent purchase a little over a year ago. ''Yes, I had a laptop. It was damaged in the fire. Eddie's getting it repaired for me.'' She moved to the desk and sat down. After feeling around on the front of the machine, she found the On switch and pressed it. The machine hummed to life.

''Good,'' Stone said. ''After you finish the letters, I'd like you to organize some information for me.'' He pointed to a stack of folders on the floor next to her desk and grimaced. ''I know, it's a mess. I've been meaning to get to them for the past couple of months and I haven't found the time. I'd like you to design a spreadsheet. One file for each client. I don't have any idea on the best way to sort the information, so I'll leave that up to you.''

He looked around. ''I guess that's everything. Oh, there's a small service room across the hall. Ula keeps the refrigerator stocked with snacks and soda. There's coffee and mugs. Let her know if you want anything else.''

''Thanks, I will.''

He gave her another smile. ''Then I'll leave you to it.'' With that, he was gone.

Cathy stared after him until he'd closed the door between their two offices, then she leaned back in her chair and covered her face with her hands. Now what? She didn't have the first idea about where to start. The letters would be easy. When she'd first bought her laptop, the computer store had offered a couple of hours of free instruction so she could learn how to use different software programs. But a spreadsheet? She remembered a little about what the instructor had showed her on those, but not enough to be proficient.

"Start with what you know," she told herself. "Try or leave. There's no middle ground."

She straightened in her chair. "Right," she said. "I'll do my best. No one can ask for more."

She moved the mouse until the arrow pointed toward "Programs," then she clicked. She read the display and was pleased when she realized the word-processing program was the one she was familiar with.

It took her an hour to write the letters and print them out. Fifteen minutes of searching yielded manuals for the various programs along with the physical equipment. She read the section on printing out envelopes, then took care of that. After a quick break for coffee, during which she found that Ula had left her fresh fruit and nonfat yogurt, she returned to her office and tackled the pile of folders on the floor.

The task was less daunting than she'd first thought. After sorting them by type of client—individuals versus corporate—and reading through Stone's notes, she designed a simple spreadsheet to track the requested information. She was hard at work on entering data on the third account when their common door opened and he walked into her office.

"You look busy," he said.

"I'm trying." She pointed to the neat pile of letters on the corner of her desk. "I didn't know if you wanted me to bring those in to you or wait for you to ask for them. I didn't want to interrupt."

"Good idea." The praise was absentminded as he leafed through the letters. "Nice work. Very clean style."

His praise made her glow.

He walked around the desk and peered over her shoulder. "What did you decide about these accounts? Hmm." He moved the mouse and clicked to expose more of the spreadsheet.

Cathy waited, her throat tight, her stomach doing its usual line dance under her ribs. This wasn't all about Stone's close proximity, although she could feel the warmth of his body as his shoulder pressed against her arm. It was also because she wanted him to be pleased with her work.

"I wouldn't have thought of sorting them this way," he said as he straightened. "I like your way better. It's simple and to the point. I'll have everything I need without flipping through pages. Well done."

She couldn't help smiling. "Thanks." She fingered the pile of folders left. "I should have these finished by the end of the day."

He waved aside her comment. "You can get to them in the morning. This afternoon you have a couple of notebooks to work through. Human resources insists that all new employees complete an orientation. There might even be a video. To be honest, I can't remember. Then there's the piles of paperwork for the government and our records, not to mention picking the health-insurance package you want."

"Just like a real job," she teased.

"Exactly." He moved around to the single chair opposite hers and sat. "Speaking of real jobs, how did your former employer take the news of your resignation?"

"Eddie wasn't happy, but he understood. He said if I ever changed my mind to let him know."

"I hope you're not considering going back."

"Not really," she said. Not in a million years, she told herself. Her morning's work had shown her she was capable, at least with the easy stuff. She would grow into the rest of it.

Ula knocked on the adjoining doors. "I've brought lunch. Do you want to eat in the conference room?"

Cathy glanced down at her watch and gasped. She would have sworn she'd been working for two hours at most, but it was already nearly one o'clock. The time had flown. At the answering service, every hour had been an eternity, except for the time she'd spent talking to Stone.

"You don't mind keeping me company, do you?" Stone asked as he ushered her into the conference room.

"Not at all," Cathy said. Being with Stone was hardly a hardship. She barely had a moment to take in the gorgeous view and rich wood tables and chairs before Ula was serving her a delicious salad. She caught the other woman's gaze. Ula gave her a quick wink as if to tell her that everything was fine, then left.

Stone poured them each a glass of iced tea from the pitcher Ula had brought. "I know this is none of my business, but I'm going to ask anyway."

Cathy took one of the rolls, but ignored the dish of butter. "What?"

"You're obviously bright and articulate. Why didn't you go to college? Was it because of your mother?"

She nodded. "By the time I graduated from high school, she was very ill. I had to take care of her. She lingered for nearly two years. By then I was physically and emotionally exhausted, and there were medical bills to pay. I couldn't imagine starting back to school, so I went to work instead. I used to dream about what I would do one day."

She thought about the past. She'd been so alone and so very lonely. Her life had felt like a trap, and she couldn't find a way out. "One day the dreams became more and more difficult to imagine. I finally just gave up, I guess."

Stone leaned forward and covered her hand with his. "We have an employee-assistance program," he said. "For employees who want to go to college while working. When you are more comfortable with your job and your responsibilities, I think you should look into that. You have a lot to offer, and it would be a shame to see it go to waste."

His dark gaze was steady. Cathy didn't know what she'd done to deserve his generosity, but she was grateful. Still, her throat was tight, and all she could manage was a strangled "Thank you."

Apparently it was enough. Stone gave her hand a quick squeeze, then he released her. He proceeded to bring her up-to-date on the workings of the stock market that morning. Cathy nodded and pretended she even had a clue as to what he was talking about.

Cathy knocked once, then paused.

"Come in," Stone called.

She stepped into his office with an armful of folders. He glanced at the clock and saw it was 3:10 in the afternoon. They generally had their catch-up meeting between three and three-thirty.

"You've been busy," he said as she set the pile on the corner of his desk.

"I know." She flashed him a cocky smile. "Here are the minutes from the meeting, as per your request." She handed over the first folder. "Mary faxed them this morning. The fax is pretty readable, although the machine is making this really weird noise. I called for service. The guy will be here around four. Second, two personnel problems, both executives, so now they're your problem."

Two more folders moved from her pile to his. He leaned

back in his chair and laced his fingers behind his head. "Go on."

"Oh, I plan to. I'm leaving all of this with you." She picked up the next folder. "Research I did on the Internet about that company you're thinking of buying." She hesitated. "Their website is very slick, but I don't know if that means anything. And here's the analysts' report on the IPO." The last folder moved from her pile to his.

He laughed. "Confess, Cathy. When you started a month ago, you didn't know an IPO from a type of washing machine."

She sank into the chair opposite his and grinned. "You're right. I still remember that first lunch we shared. You went on and on about the stock market and for all I knew, you were actually speaking a foreign language. But I've been studying and reading. An IPO is an Initial Public Offering. It's when a private company goes public for the first time and their stock appears on one of the stock exchanges."

"Very good."

Her increased knowledge wasn't the only change, he thought, studying her. She wore a sleeveless cream-colored dress that barely came to her knees. The tailored garment skimmed over slender curves, hinting at a fullness below that often left him in a very uncomfortable state.

She started work promptly at eight-thirty in the morning, but she was up long before that. He often saw her leaving the house around six-thirty to go jogging on the grounds. Between her flattering hairstyle, her new shape and the way she used makeup to emphasize her best features, she'd come a long way in three and a half months. There weren't any traces left of the unhappy, plump young woman who had lied to him over the phone.

She tilted her head. "You're staring at me. Do I have something in my teeth?"

"Not at all. I was just admiring the changes. You're jogging nearly every day, aren't you?"

She nodded as a faint blush stained her cheeks. "I promised Pepper, the physical therapist, that I wouldn't give up exercise. I've lost twenty-three pounds and I'm the size I've always dreamed of being." She paused, then leaned forward as if to confide in him. "I've been thinking of joining a gym. There are a couple around here, and I want to start lifting weights. Nothing heavy." She wrinkled her nose. "I want to tone up a little. Maybe get some definition in my arms."

She was classy and confident, but still as funny and bright as ever. He was pleased to have been a small part of the changes she'd made. Her world had opened up. That's what he'd wanted. To heal her. To make it right.

"You're welcome to use my weight room," he said. "The machines are fairly simple, and I would be happy to give you a demonstration if you have any questions."

A light flared to life in her eyes. Stone didn't know what it meant, and he wasn't prepared to ask. Affection, maybe? He would like Cathy to care about him a little. After all, he cared about her. They worked well together. They were friends. Ula had been wrong in her claims that Cathy would fall for him. There was no evidence that had happened at all.

"Thanks," Cathy said. "I'd love to work out in your gym. If it's close, I won't be able to come up with as many excuses to avoid the process. I'm still lazy at heart."

"We all are. How about today before dinner. Say at six?"

"Wonderful." Cathy rose to her feet and walked toward her office. "I'll see you there."

She closed the door behind her. Stone found himself unable to return his attention to work. Not only had Cathy started dressing differently, but also she now wore perfume. The soft, feminine fragrance lingered in the room and taunted him.

Just being close to her, even in a working situation such as this, left him hard with wanting. No, Cathy hadn't fallen for him, but he was having a difficult time controlling his unexpected needs. Sometimes he wished things were different, that *he* was different so he could approach her. But he couldn't. For one thing, it would be dangerous to her. For another, he had a goal and that didn't include a passionate affair with his new assistant. Besides, Cathy would never want him that way. She saw him as a combination of older brother and benefactor.

He pushed away the desire flaring inside of him and ignored the hardness throbbing between his legs. Just as he ignored the real reason he couldn't get involved with Cathy. That hadn't changed. He couldn't because of Evelyn.

"Well, it seemed like a good idea at the time," Cathy muttered as she climbed the stairs to the third-floor exercise room. It was at the east part of the house, over the garage. She'd had to go into the kitchen and ask Ula where it was. The housekeeper's expression had remained impassive as always when Cathy had told her what she wanted.

So here she was, climbing yet another flight of stairs on her way to work out with Stone. The bad news was she knew the pounding of her heart came solely from nerves. She'd been working out so much that a couple of flights of stairs didn't affect her at all. Which was *both* good and bad news. After all this time, she hated that Stone still got to her.

Or maybe it was just to be expected, she thought. They

spent part of each day together. They were co-workers, they shared lunch and usually dinner. They discussed world affairs, read the same books, occasionally watched television or a movie together.

''Just like being married without all the hassle,'' she told herself cheerfully. They were also missing all the good points, too, she thought. No loving, or lovemaking. No commitment.

She'd reached a point of confidence where she felt that Stone liked her. They were friends. He thought she was smart. But she wanted more than that. She wanted to matter to him. Because he mattered to her. He had for a long time, and working together had only increased her feelings. But she was determined that he would never figure that out. It would all be too humiliating. What if he felt sorry for her? She shuddered. Better to keep things the way they were.

So she would never tell him that her feelings had changed. That she thought about him all the time and wished they could be more than friends. She never told him about her daydreams for their future or how the fantasies sustained her through long nights when she couldn't sleep. She never mentioned how often she thought about that kiss they'd shared.

As she reached the third-floor landing, she heard rock music coming from down the hall. She followed the sound and ended up in a large mirrored room. Several pieces of weight-lifting equipment sat on the hardwood floor. There was a treadmill and stair climber. In the corner was a cross-country-ski machine. No wonder Stone was in such great shape.

He was already in the room, crouched down in front of a stereo system. He'd exchanged slacks and a shirt for shorts and a cropped T-shirt that exposed his flat, muscled belly. Cathy tugged on the hem of her T-shirt. It was oversize and fell nearly to the hem of her bicycle shorts. Over the past month, she'd been swimming on the weekends, so her legs were faintly tanned. She was the size she wanted to be, and with all the aerobics, she was in decent shape physically. But this was Stone, and she knew no matter what the circumstances, or how she was dressed, he had the power to leave her feeling breathless and inadequate.

He glanced up, caught her reflection in the mirror and grinned. "You made it."

She laughed. "This room is so far away, it's practically another country. I had to leave breadcrumbs to make sure I made it back."

"I can show you the way," he promised.

"Hah. Like I'd trust that." Her voice was teasing.

He rose to his feet and crossed to her. "Come on, kid. Let me show you how the big boys work out."

She glanced at all the gleaming equipment. "Don't hurt me or let me hurt myself."

"Never."

Oddly enough, she trusted him. At least in that.

"We'll start with light weights," he said, approaching a machine that looked like a medieval torture device. "The trick is to work big muscles first, then smaller ones. Here's what you want to do on this machine," he said, and described the mechanism.

She slipped into the seat and took the position he told her. "I think the trick is not to get maimed."

But it wasn't as hard as it looked. They took turns, with him going first, showing her what the exercise looked like. Then he would adjust the weight and the seat for her. They worked slowly. Cathy felt her muscles awakening, then protesting the unfamiliar activity. Stone was a patient teacher, guiding her slowly. She knew she should be grateful...and she was...if only the man would stop touching her.

A hand to her arm, fingers on her knee, a pat to her shoulder. He was driving her crazy. How was she supposed to concentrate on what they were doing? And he was so darn close to naked! Again and again she caught herself staring at his long legs or his firm belly. More than once she admired him as he bent over. The man had the best butt she'd ever seen. It just wasn't fair.

They took a break after about thirty minutes. Stone crossed to a small refrigerator in the corner of the room and pulled out two bottles of water. Cathy took one and gulped down half of it. Then she walked to the windows and stared out at the grounds.

She'd never seen the view from this side of the house. The ocean was behind them, but she could see trees and well-manicured grounds. In the distance was another large property.

He came up behind her and placed a hand on her shoulder. She didn't know whether to groan or swoon.

"How are you holding up?" he asked.

"Fine. I'm going to be sore tomorrow, though."

"Try a hot bath tonight. It works wonders."

Great. Now she could add thinking about him in a tub to her list of fantasies. If only she were his type, she might have a chance. But she wasn't. Stone was the kind of man who would date women who—

She frowned. She had been in his house nearly four months, and to the best of her knowledge he didn't go out with anyone. Evelyn had died over three years before. Was he still recovering? He must really have been in love with her.

"Did you live here with your late wife?" she asked.

Stone took a drink of water and nodded. "Evelyn is the

one who found this house. She adored it. When we moved in, she did a lot of the decorating herself. She'd grown up pretty poor. They lived in a trailer park, but she spent a lot of time at my place. She said that gave her ideas and she'd been dreaming about the perfect house for years. So when we bought this one, she already had most of the rooms planned out.''

Cathy was surprised she wasn't jealous of his relationship with Evelyn. She supposed it was because to her the woman wasn't real. They'd never met and there was no trace of her in the house. No pictures, no mementos that she knew about.

''Where did you meet?'' she asked.

Stone settled on a workout bench and rested his elbows on his knees. The water bottle hung loosely from his hands. ''Through some redistricting, the kids from the trailer park came to our elementary school. Talk about mixing the haves and have-nots. Evelyn sat next to me in class, and I was instantly smitten. We ate lunch together, and by the end of the first day of third grade we were fast friends.'' His gaze drifted from her to a past she couldn't see. ''Nothing ever changed that.''

''I'm surprised your parents approved of your relationship.''

He shrugged. ''Me, too. But as long as I did the appropriate 'heir' things, they left me alone. Benign neglect and all that. Evelyn was my real family. After high school, we went to the same college. She was on scholarship. She was amazing. So damn bright. She never let me get away with anything.''

Cathy leaned against the wall. She could hear the love in Stone's voice. That hurt a little. No one had ever loved her that much. Not even her parents.

''You miss her,'' she said.

"Yeah. It's better now, but I do miss her. She was my best friend and we'd been together so long, I didn't know what the world would be like without her." He straightened. "I'll never be able to replace her. Not that I'd try. She was unique."

Cathy nodded. Theirs would have been a special marriage, she thought. The years of friendship would have added a dimension to their love. No doubt the transition from friends to romantic partners had been exactly right.

She finished her bottle of water and placed it in the trash. She was a fool. All his kind acts, all her daydreams, even her change in circumstances couldn't shake the truth. She was living in a dreamworld.

It was a very nice dream, she reminded herself, and for now it was enough. She was here to do a good job and learn as much as she could. She wanted to grow as a person. But everything came with a price. For her, that price was falling for her boss. A man who was still in love with a woman who had been gone for three long years.

Chapter Eleven

Cathy paused at the bottom of the stairs. As usual her heart was pounding. She was getting used to the sensation. She worked with Stone every day and managed to act and even feel completely normal. But as soon as something happened to upset their routine, or they moved out of the comfortable employer/employee relationship—like tonight—she was a walking, breathing set of vibrating nerves.

"You'll be fine," she told herself as she smoothed her hair back from her face. She'd had it trimmed recently and she loved the way the soft, highlighted waves fell around her face. After her cut, she'd paid for a second makeup lesson and even bought a few products. Daily practice had made her confident about her abilities to duplicate what the makeup artist had done. Her dress was new, one of several things she'd purchased to flatter her trimmer figure. She still jogged regularly, and a few weeks of weight lifting had done their bit to tone her body. If she held her arm just right, she could even see a little muscle definition.

All in all, this was the best her life had ever been. If she could just get over what seemed to be a permanent set of nerves, everything would be fine.

She heard footsteps in the foyer. Ula walked slowly toward her holding something long and dark in her arms. The housekeeper stopped in front of her.

"You look very beautiful," she said as she smiled at Cathy.

"You're too kind." Cathy felt herself blushing. *Beautiful* was definitely an exaggeration. She looked pretty good. Although compared with her old frumpy, chubby self, the transformation could realistically be called amazing.

"The dress is lovely."

Cathy glanced down at the rust-colored knit dress she wore. It had long sleeves and was fitted through her waist and hips. Then the fabric flared out a little before softly falling around her calves. There was a low scoop neck in front and an even lower scoop in the back. The color brought out the red highlights in her hair and made her eyes as green as a cat's. The style flattered her figure and made her grateful for all the miles she'd logged.

"Thanks," she said. "I fell in love with it at the store. I've never really owned pretty things and I couldn't resist."

"Mr. Ward will be most impressed. To that end, I have a contribution to make. It's a little chilly tonight, and I thought you might like to borrow this."

Ula held out a stunning hunter green velvet cape. The lining was silk, and a darker green. Cathy stared in disbelief. "Ula, it's wonderful. But you can't mean to lend it to me. It's too fabulous."

The older woman shrugged. "I never wear it. Besides,

it's your twenty-ninth birthday, and you deserve something special.''

Cathy thought about protesting. After all, Ula had already baked her a special ''low-cal'' birthday cake that they'd shared at lunch that day. The housekeeper had also given her a hardcover book she'd wanted. But she couldn't speak just now. Not because she didn't know what to say but because her throat was tight with unshed tears.

''You have been so kind to me,'' she managed to say at last.

Ula tsked. ''There will be none of that,'' she said. ''No crying. You'll ruin your makeup. Then you'll get me going, and I hate to show emotion. So take it. On me, the cape drags to the floor, but I suspect it will hang just past your dress on you, so it will be perfect.''

Cathy took the offered heavy garment and swirled it over her shoulders. The silk lining was heavenly soft and cool against her neck and shoulders.

''I feel like a princess,'' she said, and bent down to hug the smaller woman. Hard to believe that when she'd first arrived, she had thought of Ula as cold and stern. Now she knew a warm heart beat behind the stoic facade.

Ula hugged her back. ''Have a good time, Cathy. Enjoy your birthday.''

''Thank you.'' She straightened her shoulders and walked toward the front door. The beautiful cape gave her that added bit of confidence she needed to actually step outside. With a little luck, Stone would never know she was nervous.

She walked out into the night. It was just after nine. When Stone had invited her out to dinner to celebrate her birthday, his only two requests were that he choose the restaurant and that it be later in the evening. She understood that he was nervous about being seen. Given his reluctance, she had been even more touched by his invitation. She wished there was a way to convince him how very little his scars meant to her. Perhaps if she—

She stared at the vehicle waiting in the circular driveway and felt her mouth part. She'd expected to see the BMW with Stone behind the wheel. Instead, a dark limousine waited at the foot of the stairs. Stone lounged next to it. She caught the flash of white as he smiled.

"You look surprised," he said.

"I am. I've never been in a limo before."

He opened the door and gestured for her to enter. "Then come have a look. They're fun."

As she walked down the stairs, she reminded herself this wasn't a date. It was dinner out with her boss. Nothing more. But as she approached and saw he was dressed in a perfectly fitted suit and tie, then bent to step into the limo and saw the champagne on ice waiting, she couldn't stop a flicker of anticipation from moving through her. It was her birthday, after all. And she knew exactly what she was going to wish for when she blew out her candles.

Stone settled next to Cathy in the back of the limo, then reached for the champagne. Perhaps it was overdoing things a little, but he hadn't been able to resist. He'd suspected that her previous life hadn't had much in the way of special surprises, and she deserved this and more.

He filled the two flutes, then handed her one. "Happy birthday," he said.

She smiled. "Thank you, Stone. You've made this evening very special."

"It hasn't even started yet."

"It's already wonderful."

In the dim light of the rear seating area, her eyes looked black. Shadows flirted with the lines of her pretty face, emphasizing her high cheekbones and full mouth. The long cape surrounded her, concealing her shape from him, but he knew what she looked like. He'd seen her in workout clothes and tailored dresses enough to know that her commitment to fitness had paid off. He'd always liked her and enjoyed her company. He'd found her physically appealing even before she'd started her quest for personal improvement. But now there was an extra spark. He'd admired her because he'd known who she was on the inside. Now any man would want her, simply based on her appearance.

Stone felt a hint of something primal stir, and it took him a moment to figure out it was the beginnings of jealousy. Ridiculous, he told himself. There was no one to be jealous of. Besides, he wasn't interested in Cathy that way.

But the lie was getting harder and harder to believe. Just being next to her was enough to turn him on. It had been that way for weeks. Still, he never hinted. She must never know. It was wrong of him to want her. First because of Evelyn, and second because of Cathy.

To the former, he owed a debt he could never repay. To the latter, he owed respect. While he didn't agree with Ula's assessment that Cathy could fall in love with him, he knew she was innocent enough that a physical relationship would give her the wrong impression of his feelings. She would want and expect more from him than he was capable of giving. He didn't want to set her up. So instead, he suffered, needing her in ways he'd never needed a woman before.

Cathy leaned back in the seat and sipped her drink. "It's a perfect night," she said. "When I was getting dressed, I noticed I could see stars from my bedroom window."

That was the difference between them, he thought. She would look at the night and see stars, while he was only interested in the safety and cover provided by the darkness.

"We'll have to admire them when we get to the restaurant," he said.

She looked at him. "You don't go out much, do you? I don't think you've left the house since I moved in."

"That's true." He'd been out to see her in the hospital, but not since.

She placed her hand on top of his. "You didn't have to do this for me."

Her touch was trusting, as was her expression. If she knew what the cool pressure of her fingers was doing to him, she would be afraid. In the past month or so, the wanting had become unbearable. He needed her all the time. Just being in the same room with her was enough to make him hard. He didn't know what had changed in his life and he knew he didn't like it. He wanted to go back to the way things were. He wanted to be dead again. Feeling nothing was better than constant agony.

But there was no way to turn back time. Eventually he would figure out how to deal with his wayward body. Eventually he would shut down again. He always had in the past. He didn't have a choice—he wasn't allowed to have more.

"I wanted to make the evening special," he told her. "Birthdays come around so seldom."

"Barely once a year," she said teasingly.

"I've noticed that. I spoke with Ula about what I wanted to do, and she made the arrangements. We'll be fine."

Her fingers squeezed his. "I'm not worried, Stone. I think the scars bother you more than they bother anyone else."

"Perhaps," was all he said, thinking she had never experienced the gasps or stares, the artless comments of children who didn't know better than to speak what they were thinking.

The limo drove north into Hermosa Beach. Stone recognized the area and knew they were close to the restaurant. As instructed, the driver pulled around back. After parking in the alley, he left the vehicle.

"He'll just be a moment," Stone said.

Sure enough, the man returned shortly. He opened the rear door. "Everything is arranged, Mr. Ward. If you'll follow me, please."

They were met inside by a young man named Art who showed them to a back room. As they entered, Stone saw it was big enough to hold a group of sixty or so. No doubt the restaurant used it for large parties. A small section had been partitioned off, and a table had been set for two.

Flowers, several potted trees and lengths of fabric draped over the screens gave the space an air of intimacy. Slow, romantic music played softly in the background.

Art moved to take Cathy's cape from her. Stone felt his gut tighten as he caught his first glimpse of her dress. The simple style belied the power of the outfit. A low round neck hinted at the curves of her breasts, while the clinging fabric outlined the perfect shape of her body. Art stared appreciatively, and Stone thought about bashing in his unscarred, handsome young face.

When he reached for Cathy's chair, Stone beat him to it. "I'll take care of this," he said coolly, and seated her.

Art took the hint, backing up to give them room. So far he'd only glanced at Stone's face. Ula must have warned him about the scars. While Stone appreciated her thoughtfulness, for a moment he wished it weren't necessary. Then he pushed the thought away. Not tonight, he told himself. Tonight was just about Cathy.

"The chef has prepared a special menu, as per your request," Art said. "The champagne is chilling. Would you like it now?"

"Please," Stone said, and took his seat opposite hers. They were across from each other, but the table was small enough for them to maintain intimacy. They were also alone and had no fear of being overheard by curious patrons.

When Art nodded and left, Stone turned to her. "So what do you think?"

She laughed. "I keep remembering a line from a movie I saw years ago. 'It's good to be the king.'"

"I'm hardly a king."

"You do all right." Her smile faded. "Seriously, Stone, I really appreciate this. You've made my time with you so incredible. I can't believe what's happened to me in the past few months." She faltered and some of her confidence faded. He thought she might be blushing, but it was hard to tell in the dim light.

"I'm glad I could help," he said as quiet pride swelled up inside of him. This is what he'd wanted—to make a difference in her life. He'd given her more than she'd had before. He hesitated to use the word *fix* but that's what he really meant. He'd wanted to fix her and he had. She was better off now for having known him. He was pleased, even though in time he was going to have to set her free to continue on without him. They had no future together.

The plan was sensible; at least he'd always thought so in the past. But now, in the dimly lit restaurant, with Cathy looking so lovely and the music in the background, he wasn't so sure. While he knew she still had to go, he also knew he was going to miss her. More than he'd planned. More than he wanted to. Even though it wasn't supposed to happen, even though it wasn't allowed, he'd come to care for her.

Still, when the time came, he would let her go and eventually he would forget about her. Because she was just a means to an end. A way to make up for the past.

But they had tonight, and the time that would follow. He would make the most of that.

Art returned with their champagne and poured. He asked when Stone wanted him to start serving dinner and was told to give them about twenty minutes.

Cathy stared at the intimate setting. ''I still can't believe how you pulled this off.''

''Ula did the work,'' he said.

Cathy laughed. ''She's an amazing woman. I'm surprised you haven't lured her into the business.''

''I've thought about it, but I think I want her more at home. She keeps everything running smoothly. With as much time as I spend there, I need that.''

Cathy leaned forward. ''It's none of my business and you're probably going to get angry...'' Her voice trailed off.

''But you're going to say it anyway,'' he told her.

She nodded. ''It's not that bad. I won't pretend people wouldn't notice, but you're seeing yourself in a far more harsh light than the rest of the world.''

They were talking about his scars. Stone resisted the urge to reach up and touch them. Tonight he didn't want to remember that he was physically a beast. He wanted to be a regular man out with an attractive woman.

''You don't know what it's like,'' he said at last when it became obvious she was waiting for him to respond.

''I can imagine.'' Her soft hair swung against her face as she tilted her head. ''I spent much of my life hiding away because I was afraid of what other people would think. At first I was worried because of my mother, but later it was just about me. Look at our relationship—how we met. Six months ago, it would never have occurred to me that you would be interested in me as a person just as I was. I felt the need to create a whole false world so that you would think I was interesting and had value. I'm not saying I'm completely over those fears, but I've come a long way.''

She had. Eventually she would no longer need him, he thought sadly. Then she would leave. Better for both of them. Even if he wanted to make it more, he could never give her what she needed. He didn't know how. In time she would see that. She would find someone who could give back as much as she gave, someone who would welcome and admire her generous spirit.

''Let it go, Cathy. You can't change me.''

She nodded. ''I'll do as you ask because it's my birthday and we're celebrating. But don't think I'm going to forget and not mention it again.'' She smiled. ''Your luck just isn't that good.''

''Oh, I think it's pretty great. After all, you're the one going to that meeting tomorrow instead of me.''

She groaned. ''Don't remind me. I've been trying not to think about it all week. I can't believe I let you talk me into that.''

''I didn't talk you into it. Attending meetings on my behalf falls under the category of your job description.''

She grimaced. ''You'll be sorry.''

''No, you'll be brilliant.''

She raised her glass. ''To brilliance. Or at least not putting my foot in my mouth.''

He touched his glass to hers and took a sip. Tomorrow there was a quarterly review at his office. In addition to his attending via speakerphone, Stone wanted Cathy physically at the meeting. She'd never been to his offices, and it was time she established her presence there. She'd come up with several good ideas of her own, and he wanted her to present them. His team needed a little shaking up, and she was just the woman to do it.

The song ended and another one began. A slow instrumental that made him long to hold her. Before he realized what he was doing, he was half on his feet, and asking, "May I have this dance?"

Cathy was too stunned to verbally accept. Instead, she let Stone pull her to her feet. Her body trembled as he took her into his arms. She told herself not to get too carried away by the moment, but it was far too late for those kinds of warnings. If she hadn't already fallen in love with Stone, tonight had sealed her fate.

Star-crossed lovers, she thought dreamily as he pulled her close. She closed her eyes and rested her cheek against his shoulder. He was warm, his body hard against her curves. They felt right this way, although she doubted that he would ever see it. He confused her. Sometimes she thought the distance between them was because of how he saw her and their relationship. Sometimes, though, she wondered if it was about the scars.

She supposed there was no way to ever find out. In the meantime, she would enjoy the good times as they occurred and try not to think about the future.

They circled the room, moving in time with the music. Stone didn't say anything; he just held her tenderly. If only it could be like this forever. Just them, the night and the song.

Loving him had been inevitable, she thought. First, on the phone they'd had a fantasy relationship. She wouldn't have thought anything could be better than that. But she'd been wrong. Life with him was even better. He was a wounded warrior, a man who thought of himself as a beast, and she was his only link to the world. How was she supposed to resist that?

She raised her arms and wrapped them around his neck.
He placed his around her waist. They pressed tightly
against each other. She could feel the beating of his heart,
and against her belly, the hard proof that he wanted her.

Fierce gladness filled her. She needed to know that. It
was just physical; it didn't necessarily *mean* anything more
than a natural reaction to their close proximity, but it was
more than she'd ever had before.

Slowly, carefully, knowing he might pull back and destroy her with a few words, she pressed her lips to the side
of his neck.

His breath caught in an audible gasp. Every part of him
stiffened, including the hard ridge of his desire. His arousal
flexed against her. Stone swore under his breath. He turned
his head toward her, but before they could kiss, Art appeared with their salads.

Reluctantly they drew apart and returned to the table.
Over the mundane issues of what dressing and did they
want ground pepper, the mood shifted from passionate to
friendly. When their server left, they talked about work and
the books they were reading.

Cathy finally understood what was going on. In that moment when she'd felt his reaction to her light kiss, everything had become clear. Stone was first and foremost a
man. He might think he was a monster and might still be
in mourning for his late wife, but he had physical needs.
For reasons Cathy didn't understand but that made her very
happy, he wanted her in his bed.

She also knew he would never make a move toward her.
Not only was she living in his home, but she also worked
for him. He would never allow himself to take advantage
of the situation. He wouldn't come to her, but she could
go to him…if she was willing to put it all on the line.

She broke a roll in half and took a bite. That was really

what it came down to, wasn't it? Was she willing to take the chance? Would she walk into the situation with her eyes open, fully realizing he was only interested in a temporary affair. It would never be more, no matter how long it lasted. In the end, she would lose him.

There was no point in asking the questions. Of course it was worth it. She was tired of not knowing, of hiding from life. She wanted more. She wanted to live. She wanted Stone to be her first time.

She gazed at him. Not tonight, she thought. She needed to think some things through, to be prepared. But soon.

"I know what you're thinking," he said.

She laughed. "I doubt that."

"You're wondering if you get a present from me."

"Not at all." She waved at the restaurant. "This is my present and it's wonderful."

"That's not all." He reached into his jacket pocket and pulled out a small box.

Cathy stared at it. The trembling started again because she knew it was going to be amazing. "Thank you," she whispered, and had to fight back tears.

"You haven't opened it yet."

"Oh, you're right." She fumbled with the small box, then finally pulled up the lid. Nestled on a bed of white velvet was a pair of square-cut emerald earrings surrounded by diamonds. They glittered in the candlelight.

Her breath caught in her throat, and she could barely speak. "They're stunning."

"Don't you dare say they're too much or some of that other nonsense women insist on mouthing at times like this. I wanted to get you something nice, so I did."

The gruffness in his voice gave him away, she thought as she reached out and touched his hand. "Then I won't say any of that. They're the most perfect present anyone has ever given me. Thank you, Stone. I'll treasure them always.''

''That's better,'' he grumbled.

She pulled out her simple gold hoops and exchanged them for the emeralds. Then she tucked her hair behind her ears and turned her head back and forth for his inspection. ''What do you think?''

''They're very nice.'' He frowned.

''What is it?''

''I was just thinking, you need somewhere special to wear them.''

''This is special.''

''That's not what I mean.'' His frown deepened.

''Stone?''

''It's nothing. Just that this is the first time I've been out to dinner since—'' He shrugged. ''In a long time.''

Since Evelyn had died, she filled in silently. ''You should get out more. I've been telling you that for months.''

''I know. I'm not comfortable with that, but I do have social obligations I've been ignoring. Perhaps there's a way to take care of that.''

''I'm intrigued. What did you have in mind?''

The frown faded and he smiled. ''A masked party. I'll be the phantom of the opera.''

They both started to laugh. They were still laughing when Art returned to take away their plates. He stared at them strangely, but they both ignored him.

''I can't do this,'' Cathy whispered into the cellular phone, even though she was alone in the car and there was no one to hear her.

''Then why did you agree to go?'' Stone asked.

She exhaled sharply and glanced around at the parking

lot. "If you're going to be logical, I absolutely refuse to have this conversation with you."

"Cathy, you'll be fine. They're expecting you, they know you're brilliant and they'll go out of their way to make you feel comfortable."

She closed her eyes and rubbed the bridge of her nose. "Like I believe that."

"You're going to be reporting back to the boss, whom most of them have never met. Are you kidding? They'll want you to say wonderful things about them to me."

She brightened at the thought. "Oh, I really like that."

"I thought you might."

She glanced around the plush interior of his BMW. "Thanks for letting me borrow your car."

"I thought driving it would terrify you enough that you wouldn't have to time to worry about the meeting."

She laughed. "It worked...right up until you told me your logic."

"Take deep breaths. You look great, you know your subject and if any of them bug you, you have the power to get them fired."

"Really?"

"Sure."

"I'd never do that."

"I know, but remember you are in command. Anyone gets out of line, zap 'em with a ray gun. Or tell me about it, which is probably better."

"I would guess. What with ray-gun technology not being perfected yet."

"That's what you think. You should see some of the high-tech firms we own stock in. They have some amazing developments in the works."

Cathy laughed. "I don't have time to debate futuristic

weapons with you, Mr. Ward. I have a business meeting to attend. Thanks for the moral support.''

''Call me as soon as you get back to the car. I want to know everything.''

''Promise. Bye.'' She hung up the phone and smiled. She'd known Stone was going to make her feel better. That's why she'd called. Well, that and to hear his voice. She wished he were with her. This meeting would be a lot easier if they were in it together. But Stone Ward of Ward International did not attend meetings. At least not anymore.

She picked up her briefcase, a surprise that had been waiting on her desk that morning, and her slim handbag. After locking the car and setting the alarm, she made her way to the elevator that carried her to the twenty-fifth floor and the reception area for Stone's firm.

As the small car moved vertical, she checked her suit. It was a linen blend that looked expensive but didn't wrinkle. Her silk blouse was the same color, as were her shoes. She'd been poring over fashion magazines for the past month and had been shopping several times. A monochromatic look gave her authority, she had decided. Anything else tended to look too, well, sexy.

Cathy smiled. Who would have thought that would ever be a problem? But it was. With her newly toned body, she actually attracted attention on occasion. She didn't want that for the meeting. She wanted to look as if she'd been in business for years.

The doors slid open, and she stepped out into a large, elegantly decorated reception area. She hadn't realized Stone's firm took up the whole floor. Her stomach headed for her toes. Even so, she raised her chin slightly and ordered her lips into a faint but confident smile.

Before she could approach the waiting receptionist, two men in their thirties stopped her. ''Ms. Eldridge?'' the taller of the two asked. They were both well-dressed and blond with blue eyes.

"Yes?"

"I'm Eric McMahn. This is Bill Ernest. We'll be running the quarterly review this time. Nice to meet you."

As they shook hands, Cathy realized she was never going to be able to keep names straight. With luck there wouldn't be a quiz later.

"You found the building all right?" Bill asked.

"It wasn't that difficult, what with the street address being on the front in big letters."

She meant the comment as a slight joke to ease the tension coiling inside of her. But instead of smiling, Bill looked vaguely panicked. "Of course. I didn't mean to imply you wouldn't be able to find it."

"I know. I was teasing."

"Oh. Of course."

Cathy drew in a deep breath and relaxed. They were as nervous as she was, although for different reasons. For her, she was terrified of making a big mistake that would not only reflect badly on Stone, but that would point out that she had never been to college or worked in business before. However, for them, she was a frightening unknown—an emissary sent by the big boss. Someone who had his ear and could say anything she wanted about them.

Power, she thought ruefully. Who would have guessed she would ever have power?

The heady feeling lasted right up until she walked into the meeting room. The table was huge, and nearly every seat was filled. Everyone turned toward her and stared.

Cathy worked hard to keep her expression pleasant. "Good morning," she managed to say, and was pleased when her voice didn't shake.

Murmured greetings came in response. Eric, or maybe

Bill—she'd already forgotten which was which—introduced everyone. Cathy nodded and didn't even try to remember names. That would be her goal for next time. This morning it was enough to get through the next few hours.

The conference table was extrawide, which put two people sitting side by side at the head and the foot. Cathy found herself next to Eric. She knew it was him because each of them had a three-ring binder in front of them and the names were printed at the top of the binder.

"We'll be going in order," Eric said, pointing to the book. "I'll be able to answer any questions or clarify anything. Mr. Ward has his own copy of the report. It was delivered to him this morning."

"Good."

"Hi, Cathy."

The familiar voice made her smile. She glanced up and saw that someone had put a speaker in the center of the table.

"Morning, Stone." She spoke without thinking and saw several people exchange startled glances at her use of their boss's first name.

"Are they treating you right?" he asked.

"Of course."

"Are you ready?"

"Yes." She drew in a breath for courage. "Let's begin."

Cathy washed her hands, then dried them on the small plush towel provided. Apparently both sexes had executive washrooms, and she'd been shown to the ladies' version of that time-honored perk. She gazed around at the light-colored fixtures, the tray of toiletries and grinned. She'd come a long way from the woman who had worked the graveyard at the answering service, she thought.

They'd taken a fifteen-minute break from the meeting.

Everything was going well, and her butterflies had finally gone to sleep. She was able to follow most of what people were saying and she made notes about what confused her. Stone had promised they could discuss everything when she got home.

She headed for the door. She passed through a small sitting area on her way out, then remembered she'd left her purse on the shelf by the sink. She spun back to retrieve it and saw someone else had entered the room.

She paused, waiting for the other woman to say something. Then her mouth fell open as she realized there wasn't anyone in the rest room but herself. She was staring at her own reflection in a full-length mirror.

While she'd known she'd lost a lot of weight and that her hairstyle had improved her appearance, the changes had happened gradually. She'd never really taken a look at herself in comparison to what she'd been before. Her reflection showed a tall, slender woman in a fashionable suit, elegant shoes, with a great hairstyle and perfect makeup. Had Cathy met herself a year ago, she would have been intimidated and assumed the worst.

Fierce gladness filled her, and she sent up a quick prayer of thanks. For Stone for giving her the chance to change, and for the fact that she'd had the courage and conviction to make the most of the opportunity.

Chapter Twelve

Cathy ran up the stairs to the second floor, then hurried to Stone's office. He stepped into the hall and grinned at her.

"You were great!"

"Thanks." She followed him inside and laughed. "I was so terrified that they would think I was an impostor or stupid or something, but it didn't happen like that."

"Of course not. You're intelligent, articulate, knowledgeable."

She tossed her purse and briefcase on the chair in front of his desk, then allowed him to lead her to the sofa against the far wall. She sank down onto the smooth leather and sighed. "You flatter me, but I like it. Don't stop." She smiled again. She'd been smiling on the whole drive home. Everything had gone perfectly.

"So what did you think?" Stone asked as he settled next to her.

"You've got a good team. They work hard for you. They're also terrified of you, but then you probably like that."

"You're right."

They giggled together like schoolchildren. While Cathy had greatly enjoyed the opportunity and it had been fun getting out to face down her fears, she was pleased to be back where she belonged. Here, in Stone's presence, her world was right.

He asked about different people. She answered as best she could, trying to put faces to names. As they spoke, she studied him, the way he moved his hands when he talked, the slight tilt of his head as he unconsciously kept his scarred side turned away from her.

She *had* grown to love him. She'd figured that out last night at her birthday dinner, and today only confirmed that information. She wanted to do him proud. Not just because she worked for him or cared about him, but because he was the most important part of her life. She didn't want to think about a world without him, even though that was inevitable.

He leaned forward and gave her a quick hug. "You did great, and I'm very proud of you."

He started to release her almost as quickly as he'd reached for her. As if he'd just realized what he was doing. Cathy had a split second in which to make a decision. She knew it would never be more than physical—at least not for Stone. It would never be emotionally meaningful or anything permanent. Stone would offer her an affair, and if she could live with that, if she could make it enough, then this was her moment.

In an act she knew would count as one of her bravest, she let him release her, but kept her hands on his shoulders. His expression shuttered. Her heartbeat increased and the butterflies returned, bringing all their friends and relatives to the party. She told herself that she would survive the rejection, that emotional pain was rarely fatal and that for once in her life she would be regretting action instead of passive acceptance. Then she pressed her mouth to his.

She waited for the heat and tingling that had engulfed her the last time they'd kissed, but there was only a painful pause during which she wondered if he would respond or push her away. She realized then that the sparks between them had required both their participation. Her heart thundered twice more before she figured out he wasn't going to kiss her back. Instantly humiliation flooded her. She'd been wrong last night. He wasn't interested in her in that way. How could she have made such a mistake?

She pulled back. Hot color flooded her cheeks. "I'm sorry," she managed to say. "You must think me..." Her voice trailed off. She didn't know what he was thinking and she didn't want to know. She'd been a fool. She wanted to die. She wanted to run away and never see him again. Most of all, she wanted to turn back time a little more than five minutes and have this to do over again.

She tried to stand, but her legs were trembling. She pushed off the sofa again, this time using her hands for extra leverage. Suddenly Stone grabbed her upper arm. His firm grip held her in place.

"Why did you do that?" he asked. His voice was low and harsh. Obviously the moment had been so repugnant, he could barely speak.

"I'm sorry," she whispered again.

He shook her. "Why?"

Compelled by reasons she couldn't explain, she looked at him. Something dark and dangerous lurked in his blue-gray eyes. His mouth was stern, and a muscle clenched in his cheek.

"I thought you were interested in me. Not romantically,'' she added hastily, not wanting to increase her humiliation more than necessary. She swallowed and averted her gaze. "I thought, last night, when we danced…'' She shrugged.

"I was aroused,'' he said flatly.

She nodded. "I thought that meant you wanted me.'' The last two words were barely audible. An hour ago, she'd been on top of the world, confident of her looks and her capabilities. Now all she wanted was to crawl away and hide under a rock like a slug or a roach.

"I can't—'' He hesitated. "My past,'' he began. "There are things that I can't explain.''

"I know. I wasn't expecting anything more, Stone. I thought it would be nice.''

For the first time since she'd kissed him, his expression softened. "If it was just 'nice,' we would be doing something wrong.''

She didn't respond. After all, she had no frame of reference. "I'll understand if you don't want me to work for you anymore. I'd rather not quit, but I will if you'd prefer. However, if you're willing to give me another chance, I promise I won't ever say or do anything like this again. I'm so very sorry.''

He released her arm and raised his hand so that he could cup her cheek. "Cathy, I wonder if you even know what you're saying. You act as if I'm angry or insulted.''

"Aren't you?''

"No. I'm flattered. I can't promise you very much, but I do want you. Make no mistake about that. My concerns are all for you. That this isn't what you really want.''

Some of the humiliation faded. "I kissed *you*. How could I not want this?''

He gazed at her for a while. "We are talking about becoming lovers.''

Thank goodness she was already blushing so he wouldn't notice the fresh wave of color that swept over her face. That word. No man had ever said it to her before.

Lovers.

"Yes," she murmured.

He rose to his feet without saying anything. When she spoke his name, he pressed his fingertips to her mouth, then took her hand. They left the office and walked down the hallway, turning left at the end and stopping in front of a closed door.

There he stopped and faced her. "Are you sure?" he asked. "Because once you come inside and I begin to touch you, I won't be able to stop."

Cathy looked from him to the door. So this was his bedroom. She'd known it was at this end of the house, but she'd never explored much. She hadn't wanted to pry.

There were a thousand ways she could have answered. She could have explained that she wanted him to be the one to teach her the secrets between a man and a woman. She could have tried to tell him that she loved him and that being intimate with him was as close as she could come to perfection. She could have gone on about how many nights she'd lain awake in her bed reliving their kiss and wanting to repeat it.

But the words got tangled in her mind. She didn't know where to start or how much he would want to hear. So she simply put her hand on the doorknob and turned it. The door swung open, and she stepped inside.

She had a brief impression of a large bed, a wide window with a perfect ocean view and sunlight spilling onto thick carpeting. Then Stone took her into his arms and drew her close. When his hands held her against him, thoughts of the room faded. When he kissed her, she couldn't think at all.

As soon as his mouth moved on hers, the tingling began as her whole body focused on the feel of his lips pressing, caressing, moving on hers. He was all damp heat and passion, drawing her closer still, as if he couldn't possibly get enough of her. This is what she wanted, she realized. Not just the lesson, not just the intimacy, but the wanting. She craved his desire for her. No man had ever felt those needs, not for her, and as she shifted against him and felt the instant hardness that surged against her belly, her trembling turned into shivers.

He touched the tip of his tongue to her bottom lip. Instantly she parted for him. He slipped inside, rediscovering her. Her hands fluttered helplessly as she tried to figure out where to touch him first. His arms? His shoulders? Then she wrapped one arm around him and settled her free hand on the back of his head.

His hair was silky and cool, a marked contrast to his heated body. She felt her breasts flatten against his broad chest. When he stroked her back then moved lower and cupped her rear, she gasped faintly against his kiss. Involuntarily her hips arched forward, bringing her belly more firmly in contact with his arousal.

There was too much to think about, she realized with mild panic. She couldn't keep track of what was happening. There was the kiss, and the sensations brought about by the kiss. The feel of their tongues stroking and circling, the sweet taste of him, the way he growled low in his throat and she both felt and heard the sound. There were the signals from her body—places he was touching, the way his fingers felt, the pressure and sureness of his hands. Her breasts were achy, her nipples hard. Her thighs felt hot, and she could feel dampness forming in her most secret place.

To complicate matters, her brain was getting fuzzy. She didn't want to think anymore. She just wanted to feel. She wanted to do all the things she'd read about. She wanted to feel his body on top of hers, wanted him to touch her breasts, perhaps even to kiss them. She wanted him to touch her down there.

That last thought made her blush return. Stone didn't seem to notice. He cupped her face in his hands and pulled back enough to trail kisses across her forehead, then her cheeks.

"I want you," he breathed in her ear. The warm air made her shiver. He followed the breath with a soft kiss that made her want to melt right there. "I want you," he repeated. "Naked, in my bed. I want to be inside of you. I want to fill you up and pleasure you until you can't think about anything but how we are together."

His words created an erotic image that both aroused and terrified her. He was a strong man, extremely focused on whatever he set his mind to do. She hadn't realized that when they made love, all that attention would be centered on her. She wasn't sure she was up to it. But she was willing to find out.

"Cathy," he murmured, and kissed her mouth. "Sweet Cathy."

His hands dropped to her shoulders, and he eased her suit jacket from them, then tossed it over the back of a chair. As his mouth teased hers, his fingers reached for the first button on her blouse. She felt her breathing increase, although not all of her reaction was from passion. He was going to touch her breasts. She just knew it. She was desperate for that. Maybe he could ease the aching there. But she was also terrified. What if he hated them? What if it hurt? What on earth had she been thinking? This was all a hideous mistake and she was going to tell him, too. Just as soon as they stopped kissing.

Because while the rest of it was frightening and something she was beginning to think she could do without, the kissing was still very nice. So she concentrated on that. She closed her eyes and lost herself in the kiss and almost managed to not notice when he finished unbuttoning her blouse and pulled it free of her skirt. She was so successful that she actually jumped when warm male hands settled on her bare rib cage.

He broke the kiss and moved down to her throat. Cathy wanted to protest, then he licked the sensitive skin under her left ear and she found that was nearly as nice as kissing. She would insist he stop doing that in just a second or so.

His mouth moved lower, down her neck to her shoulder. He nibbled along her collarbone. She was vaguely aware of her arms falling to her sides and her blouse sliding down before drifting to the floor. It seemed so unimportant.

He kissed down her chest until he reached the swell of her left breast. Her breathing quickened, but there wasn't any fear now. Just the wild hope that he could soothe the ache, that he could somehow give her what she'd just realized she needed.

He licked the valley between her breasts. She shuddered and whispered his name. But then he was gone. She opened her eyes. He walked to the window and drew the drapes partially closed. There was still plenty of light, but it wasn't so bright. Cathy wasn't sure if Stone was doing that for him or for her and she found she didn't much care.

While his back was to her, she slipped out of her pumps and her panty hose. In all her romantic imaginings, she'd never once figured out an erotic way to remove panty hose. But she left on her skirt.

As he returned to her side, he pulled his shirt free of his jeans, then sat on the edge of the bed and removed his shoes and socks. When he held out his hand to her, she took it and joined him on the bed.

He ran his fingers through her hair. "How scared are you?" he asked.

"Somewhere between very and petrified."

A smile tugged at his lips. "That's honest." He pressed a kiss to the tip of her nose. "For what it's worth, I haven't made love in a very long time. There's every chance that I've forgotten how."

"Don't even expect me to believe that," she told him, but his confession made her feel a little better. Maybe he wouldn't notice how awkward she was.

He chuckled and pressed his mouth to hers. Even as she parted to admit him, she felt his fingers against her bra hooks in back. She fought against the need to fold her arms against her chest to keep the undergarment in place. This didn't seem the time or place for modesty, she thought. After all, she'd been the one to initiate their lovemaking. So when he slipped a finger under the shoulder strap of her bra, she relaxed and let him pull it down and toss the undergarment aside.

The air felt cool on her breasts. At least her eyes were closed, and they were kissing. She couldn't see what he was doing, and he probably couldn't stare at her *and* kiss her at the same time.

He eased his hands behind her and urged her to stretch out on the bed. Unfortunately that meant they had to stop kissing, but she tried not to think about that. Before she could well and truly panic, he placed a hand flat on her rib cage.

Here it comes, she thought, hoping she didn't do anything stupid and that it wasn't horrible and—

His hand slid up to her right breast. She braced herself, not sure what to expect. Then he touched her. A gentle, sure caress. A warm palm cradled the fullness of her curves while thumb and forefinger teased her tight nipple.

The pleasure was as intense as it was unexpected. She'd thought it might be nice—at least alone in her bed when she'd imagined it, she'd thought it would be very pleasant. In the past couple of minutes, she'd assumed the worst. But now that he was touching her, she didn't know what to think. And then it didn't matter and she didn't want to think. She only wanted to feel how wonderful it all was with him stroking her like that.

He dropped his hand, and his mouth touched her other breast. Hot breath warned her of what was to come, but even so she gasped with the wonder of it. Lips closed over her nipple while his tongue brushed against the very tip. Unable to control herself, she grasped his head as if to hold him in place. It was too perfect, she thought.

"Please," she whispered urgently, not sure what she was asking for. But Stone seemed to know. He chuckled low in his throat.

"I knew it would be like this with you," he said, raising his head enough so that he could look into her eyes. "I knew we would be good together."

Are we? she wanted to ask, but didn't. If he said it, she would believe it.

All will had drained away and she didn't bother to protest when he stripped off her skirt and panties. Her skin was hot, and everywhere he touched, she felt fire. Her body trembled as he stroked her thighs, across her belly, then over her breasts. She grew wanton and drew him up for a kiss. They arched toward each other, and as he gripped her hair to hold her still, she felt the pressure of his arousal against her hip and was filled with a sense of feminine power. She had done this to him. He wanted her. Nothing had ever been so right.

Still his hands moved over her. At last one of them slid between her thighs. She was too weak to stop him. She wanted it all and she wanted it with Stone. Her legs fell open.

He stroked the insides of her thighs, moving higher and higher with each caress. At last his fingers sought out her most feminine place.

"You're so ready," he said as he lowered his head to her breast and suckled her. His tone was reverent, his body taut. She assumed this was a good thing.

He moved slowly, discovering her, allowing her to discover what he was doing. He slipped one finger deep inside of her, and she caught her breath as she imagined his hardness filling her. Then he withdrew and began circling around, searching. She wanted to help but she didn't know what he was looking for. Right up until he found it.

It was as if someone had connected her to a source of pure pleasure. His fingers produced magic sensations, feelings, heat and desire that she hadn't known she was capable of. Every cell in her body focused intently on that single point. She half rose into a sitting position.

"Don't stop," she gasped as she clutched his arm.

His smile was slow and satisfied. "I won't. I promise."

She sank back onto the bed. The world was spinning. She wanted to reach, but she didn't know for what. The tension was unbearable…and she never wanted it to stop.

He touched her and spoke to her and urged her on. She followed his voice, trusting him to know where they were going.

"Give in to it," he whispered. "Now."

She didn't know how to give him what he obviously wanted. "I don't know—"

And then she did know. Her body tensed as she felt herself pushed up higher and higher until there was nowhere to go but through the clouds. She felt herself flung into nothingness. Into the most exquisite pleasure and peace she'd ever experienced in her life.

She knew she spoke. She heard sounds, but she couldn't have said what they were. She thought she might have cried out Stone's name. She clutched at him and gave in to it all, as he'd requested. Then, when her body relaxed and the last of the aftershocks had faded, she pressed her head against his chest and asked him to hold her for a little while.

Stone wrapped his arms around her and hugged her close. She was still trembling. "I really want to take credit for what just happened," he said, "but you are obviously a very responsive woman."

She didn't answer. He supposed it wasn't the kind of thing a woman wanted to talk about the first time she made love with a man. To be honest, he didn't want to hear about lovers from her past. He just wanted to be joined with her.

He sat up and pulled off his shirt, then slipped out of his trousers and briefs. Before lying down beside her again, he took a moment to study her beautiful body.

"You're lovely," he said as he touched her full breasts, then stroked her flat tummy.

She laughed. "I've worked hard for this."

"It shows." He frowned. "I do like how you are now, but I wanted you before," he said.

She shook her head. "Not possible."

"I felt the attraction back in the hospital." He shrugged. "I wanted you to know it was more than just how you looked."

She smiled. "I know. We were friends for nearly two years before we met. It was definitely my sparkling personality."

"Brat. I'm trying to be a nice guy here, and you're making it difficult."

"Oh, sorry. I didn't recognize the action for what it was."

Her teasing made him smile. "You'll pay for that." He lunged at her and pulled her close. He'd thought to start tickling her, but then his hand closed over her breast and passion took the place of playfulness. His erection flexed painfully.

"I want you," he said before claiming her mouth.

He knew she was ready. What they'd done before had prepared her for him. So as he deepened the kiss, he slipped between her thighs and pressed the tip of his maleness against her waiting warmth.

"This isn't going to take very long," he said ruefully. "I promise a better performance next time."

She wrapped her arms around him. "I don't care how long it takes. I just want to make love."

He was too much of a man to resist an invitation like that. He pushed his way inside, then gasped and muttered, "You're so tight. I'm going to lose it right here."

He withdrew to plunge in deeper. His hips thrust him forward so quickly, he barely felt the barrier as it gave way. But he felt Cathy flinch.

Reality crashed in around him. Reality and truth. She'd been a virgin. Even as the questions formed and he told himself to stop, he couldn't. He was too far gone. Half a dozen more thrusts, and he shuddered in release, emptying himself into her.

Sanity returned slowly. He stayed where he was, inside of her, on top of her, savoring the intimacy even as he fought the panic.

"Why didn't you tell me?" he asked, careful to keep his voice gentle.

"It didn't matter," she said. Her eyes were wide, and

her mouth trembled slightly. But she didn't seem upset. Or was that wishful thinking on his part?

At least she wasn't trying to pretend she didn't know what he was talking about.

"It matters to me," he said. "I would have done things a little differently."

"Like what?"

He thought for a second. "That's not important. The point is, I would have liked to have known."

She bit her lower lip. "So you could have stopped."

It wasn't a question. "No. I wouldn't have stopped." Unfortunately he wasn't that noble.

He withdrew and stretched out next to her. "I'm sorry, Cathy. Your first time shouldn't have been like this."

She turned toward him. "Yes, it should have," she said fiercely. "This is exactly what I wanted. Don't forget who started this."

He wrapped his arms around her and pressed a kiss to her mouth. He wasn't likely to forget anything about this afternoon. Her virginity was a surprise to him, although knowing what he did about her past, maybe it shouldn't be.

"Don't be angry," she whispered. "I couldn't bear that."

"I'm not angry. Never that. I'm honored. Truly."

Her gaze was trusting as she looked at him. He gave her a quick smile, then urged her to rest her head on his shoulder. She snuggled close.

"Thank you," she murmured. "Thank you for making my first time so lovely."

He tightened his arms around her in reply, but he couldn't speak. What was there to say? He couldn't undo what had just happened, and except for the fact that she'd been a virgin, he didn't want to.

But that was a huge fact to overlook, he thought grimly

Once again he'd been a woman's first. He knew there were men who never experienced that, and he'd done it twice. Cathy, and before her, Evelyn.

He didn't want to think about his late wife. Not now, not with Cathy so soft and wonderful in his arms. But the lines were starting to blur. It wasn't that he couldn't tell the two women apart—it was that he was finding it difficult to remember the ground rules. He wasn't supposed to be enjoying himself. He was supposed to be making up for the past, not repeating it. What happened now? What did she expect from him?

Cathy exhaled slowly. "I swear I'm suddenly so sleepy. But it's the middle of the day."

"It's all right," he said. "I'll be right here, holding you."

"That's all I've ever wanted," she murmured. She snuggled a little closer. There were a few moments of silence, then she whispered, "I love you, Stone."

He forced himself not to react physically. Cathy sounded as if she was already fading fast, and he doubted she realized she'd said the words aloud.

He believed them, though. Ula had been right. He'd tried to convince himself otherwise, but his housekeeper had seen the obvious. Cathy had fallen in love with him. She'd given her heart to a scarred, broken man who had sworn never to love anyone again.

Now what? he wondered. Did he let her go or keep her close? He didn't have the answer. He would miss her dreadfully if she was gone. He didn't know which act would be kinder for her. Loving her back wasn't an option. It wasn't allowed and even if that issue was resolved, he wasn't capable anymore.

Not knowing what else to do, he pulled her close and silently promised he would never hurt her the way he'd hurt Evelyn.

Chapter Thirteen

"You know, when he first mentioned this, I thought he was kidding," Cathy confessed.

Ula glanced up from the list she was reviewing. "When Mr. Ward first spoke about the party to me, I wanted to ask if he was feeling all right."

The two women smiled conspiratorially.

"It's too late for him to change his mind," Cathy said, pointing to the list of acceptances that had quickly followed the mailing of the invitations.

"No one has seen him in years. They're all curious." Ula raised her eyebrows. "Then there's the issue of his new assistant. Word has spread since your meeting at the office two weeks ago. I can't tell you how many people have asked about you when they called to accept."

Cathy ducked her head, partially in pleasure, partly from nerves. She was glad the meeting had gone well and that she hadn't embarrassed herself or Stone. While she wouldn't mind meeting those people again, she was sure she wouldn't remember any of their names, and how on earth was she supposed to fill an evening with small talk? Except for Stone, she wasn't going to know anyone.

You can do this, she told herself. That was her new trick. When something new threatened to overwhelm her, she reminded herself of how far she'd come. In the past five months, her entire life had turned around. There was very little she couldn't accomplish. And she was not about to come undone over a simple party.

Her gaze fell on the guest list, and she sighed. "Here I am giving myself a pep talk when the reality is there are going to be nearly two hundred people coming here. Where on earth will we put them?"

Ula waved her hand. "I've done this dozens of times. There are going to be tents set up on the grounds. The weather is perfect—warm in the day, but cooling slightly at night. A valet service takes care of the cars. I've hired the caterer. Best of all, you have your dress."

Cathy smiled. The cream-and-gold off-the-shoulder gown had been in the window of the first store she'd gone to. She'd tried it on and known instantly that it was right. As if proving it had been made just for her, it hadn't required a single alteration.

"Did you get your mask?" Ula asked.

Cathy nodded. "I picked it up yesterday, along with Stone's." While his was a large affair, designed to cover half his face, hers was a small wisp of silk and sequins and barely covered her eyes.

She laughed with delight. "I can't believe I'm actually going to attend a masked ball."

"Imagine how I feel," Ula told her. The housekeeper rose and collected the coffeepot, then refilled each of their cups. "For three years, this house has been shut up as tight as a coffin. All of a sudden, Mr. Ward wants to throw a party.'' Her expression softened. "Just like it used to be.''

"Did he and Evelyn entertain much?'' Cathy asked.

"Some. Their wedding reception was held at the country club, but as soon as they moved here, they had a big open house. There were the usual Christmas parties and barbecues in the summer. Evelyn wasn't one for entertaining, but she did it to please Mr. Ward. That woman would have done anything for him.''

"She loved him very much, didn't she?''

Ula glanced at her, then returned the pot to the stand and took her seat. The slight pause told Cathy that the housekeeper was weighing her words carefully.

Cathy understood her reluctance. Not only did Ula not want to betray a confidence, but she was also caught in the middle of a new situation.

For the past two weeks, Cathy and Stone had been lovers. After that first afternoon, he'd asked her to move into his bedroom. She'd accepted gladly. While she understood the limitations of their relationship, she greedily wanted as much as she could get for as long as possible. He might not love her, but she cared about him deeply and she wanted to be with him.

So every evening, she retired to his bed. He pulled her close and they made love. Every night they slept cuddled together, bodies satisfied and entwined.

While Ula didn't know the details, she was aware of the change in circumstances. She hadn't commented, although she'd put Cathy's clean laundry into the drawers of Stone's dresser without being prompted.

"It's all right,'' Cathy told the other woman. "I didn't mean to make things awkward for you. This is confusing for all of us.''

Ula nodded. "I know you have questions. Some I'm

comfortable answering, but others, well, you're going to have to talk to Mr. Ward. As for Evelyn, she did love him. Had since they were children. He was all she'd ever wanted.''

Cathy found herself regretting the question. The information wasn't a surprise, but still it felt strange to hear it. Probably because she didn't know how to compete with Stone's past. Telling herself it wasn't a contest didn't help at all. Because it was, and Evelyn had already won.

She held in a sigh. Night after night, Stone pulled her close and made love with her. Night after night, he touched her body, he kissed her, he taught her pleasures she hadn't known existed. Night after night, they drifted to sleep without saying anything of importance. He never said he cared for her. Just that he wanted her. They were physically as close as two people could be, yet emotionally she felt as distant from him as ever. Her feelings hadn't changed. If anything, they'd grown stronger and more secure. But his? She'd never known what he thought and now she was terrified to find out the truth.

Because he still loved Evelyn?

''Things would have been different if they'd had children, I think,'' Ula was saying. ''I know they both wanted little ones, but they weren't in any rush. Then she was gone.'' The phone rang. Ula shook her head. ''Another acceptance. There are always those who call at the last minute.''

She rose to get the call. Cathy stared after her. Her mind had started racing as her blood drained from her head. For a second, she thought she was going to pass out.

Little ones, Ula had said. As in babies. As in she and Stone hadn't once discussed the issue of birth control.

She sucked in a breath. It just hadn't crossed her mind, she admitted. She'd been a virgin and had no experience in the matter. Stone had been celibate for years. Disease-wise they were fine, but what about being responsible adults and thinking ahead?

"The average teenager knows better than to do this," she muttered under her breath as she stood up and gave Ula a quick wave.

Okay, so she couldn't undo the past, but she could improve the future. She would go directly to her office and make an appointment with her gynecologist. She would go on the Pill and solve the problem. Thank the Lord no damage had been done.

Stone adjusted his mask and tried to tell himself he was having a good time. Nothing helped. The truth was he'd given the party for Cathy—in an effort to give her something fun to look forward to. He'd done it to show her he wasn't completely cut off from the world, and maybe a little to show off. No expense had been spared.

None of the reasons were especially impressive, and he wasn't proud of any of them. As the noise level increased and the crush of people grew, he was sorry he'd ever suggested the idea. He didn't want these people in his home and on his grounds. He didn't want the stares, the questions he wasn't supposed to hear. There was curiosity, but that was manageable. More difficult were the looks and kind words from people he'd actually cared about. The ones who had tried to stay in touch with him after the accident. The ones he'd shut out by refusing their phone calls and not acknowledging their notes.

"Stone?"

He turned and saw Meryl Windsor walking toward him. Despite the mask and the full skirt of her costume, he recognized her.

"Hello, Meryl," he said, and accepted the hand she held out.

She leaned forward and kissed his cheek. "How on earth did you recognize me?" she asked. "It's been years, and I was sure this was a perfect costume. At least as a disguise."

"I remember what your voice sounds like."

She pursed her lips together. "Done in by too many years at an English boarding school. I will forever be paying for that, in one way or another," She sighed dramatically, then laughed. "My very proper English instructors never did approve of my humor."

"I've missed it," he said in an attempt to be polite, then he realized he was telling the truth.

She was a tall, stunning redhead who had been happily married for years. Her husband had once been a close friend. "How is Ben?" he asked.

"Fine. He sends his regrets. Business takes him to Paris."

"Why aren't you with him?" Meryl had always traveled with her husband.

"I wanted to go but the children have just started a new term and I hated to miss that. I simply had to take photos on the first day of school." Her smile was impish. "Fortunately for you, my handbag was too small for me to slip them inside. Otherwise, I would torture you with them unmercifully. I'm quite the doting mother."

"I remember that," he said.

Meryl stepped close and linked her arm with his. "Oh, Stone. We've missed you. And I haven't given up. I'm still regularly sending cards at the holidays, and I do call to check on you."

"So Ula tells me."

The tent was large, with a small combo at one end by the wooden dance floor. Round tables and crowds of people filled in the remaining space. She slowly led him to the edge of the tent.

"Stone, why do you insist on playing the martyr? No one blames you for what happened. I'm sure Evelyn doesn't."

He could always count on Meryl to be direct. But she didn't know all the facts. He wished it could be different. He wished he could believe her.

"Are you still involved with your charity work?" he asked.

"That wasn't even a subtle change in subject," she chided, then obligingly talked about her efforts to raise money for the local children's hospital.

At first he listened to her words, then a flash of light caught his attention. He looked toward the entrance and saw that Cathy had walked into the tent. She was surrounded by a group of young male admirers. She was incredibly beautiful, and as he watched her he found it hard to believe that she was a part of his life.

The overhead light caught the red highlights in her hair and made her skin glow. The off-the-shoulder gown she wore made her creamy skin look like satin. The shape of the small mask hid only her large eyes. She was a vision. That's what he'd thought when he'd first seen her in the dress. So much so that desire had overwhelmed him.

He'd come up behind her, intent only on kissing her bare shoulder. But when he'd touched her, he was instantly aroused. She'd turned to face him and had seen the passion in his eyes. As always, she denied him nothing. Instead, she'd carefully pulled up the skirt of the gown to reveal stockings, a garter belt and a tiny scrap of silk pretending to be panties. The latter had been quickly pulled off. In seconds, he'd buried himself inside of her. He'd moved his hand between them, rubbing her sweet spot until she convulsed against him, the contractions of her release sucking him dry.

The memory was enough to make him want her again. It was always like this with her. He couldn't get enough of her. Even knowing that she was in love with him couldn't keep him away. And it should have. After all, he could never give her what she wanted...what she deserved.

"You're not even pretending to listen," Meryl said, and sighed. "At least Ben pretends."

"I'm sorry," he said. "I was—"

"I know exactly what you were doing." Meryl nodded toward Cathy. "Who is she, Stone? Are you letting go of the past at last?"

"She—" He paused, not sure how to explain Cathy. She was a friend. Someone who worked for him. She was also a project, his way to atone for what had happened before. She was to make up for Evelyn.

"She's my assistant," he said at last.

"Ah, so she's the mystery woman. I've heard about her." She patted his arm again. "I demand an introduction, and as soon as Ben returns from Paris, the two of you are to dine with us."

He murmured something unintelligible. Meryl accepted it as assent, even though that wasn't what he meant. He wouldn't be going anywhere with Cathy. The party was special. The mask he wore offered him protection. But Meryl's house would be different. Bright lights, unfamiliar surroundings, children to stare and be frightened. No, he wasn't going to be visiting with them any time soon. But he wouldn't spoil her evening by saying that. He would explain it all at another time.

When a handsome young man dressed like a matador claimed Meryl for a dance, Stone retreated to the far side of the room to watch the party. Cathy kept glancing at him, but he motioned for her to continue circulating and to enjoy herself. This party was for her, and he wanted her to have a good time.

He found pleasure in just watching her. He liked watching the young men flirt with her because he knew she wasn't interested. Unfair and ignoble of him. After all, he wasn't planning on claiming her emotionally or permanently. But for tonight he was pleased that while these other physically perfect specimens tried to capture her interest, her body was still wet from their lovemaking. He knew that as she walked she could feel the slight ache left over from the heated rush they'd shared only a few hours before.

He was playing a dangerous game. He knew that. He was having trouble keeping his distance. In time that was going to have to change. He would have to learn how to pull back again. For now he'd lost perspective. This was supposed to be about his late wife. He knew that. Yet somehow it had also become about him, and what he wanted, as well.

Cathy moved through the party with an ease she didn't feel. Every time she tried to get close to Stone, he shooed her away to experience all the excitement on her own. As if being with him would get in the way of her fun. She frowned slightly. Didn't the man realize that being with him was all she wanted? Obviously not, she thought, wondering why someone who could be so bright about business could also be so silly about women.

She put down the glass of sparkling water she'd been sipping and made her way to the exit. Across the lit path were double glass doors and the entrance to the ladies' rest room. She had to admit this was the only private residence she'd ever been in with such a huge powder room. There was a sitting area, and two private stalls. She supposed the space had been designed for entertaining.

She stepped inside and checked her makeup. The lighting was soft and flattering. She touched her hair and fished in her small handbag to get her lipstick. The door opened and two women entered. Their costumes were elaborate, obviously rented from an exclusive store. They were tall, slender and very beautiful. Six months ago, Cathy would have found herself shrinking out of the way. But now she met their gazes in the mirror and smiled.

"Is there a line?" the brunette asked.

"No. I'm just hogging the mirror. The stalls are empty." Cathy motioned in that direction and turned her attention back to the lipstick. The color was a brownish coral. At first she'd passed it over, thinking it was too muddy. But the women at the cosmetic counter had insisted she try it. Cathy was pleased. The lipstick had—

"He's as handsome as ever," one of the women said, her voice slightly muffled by the distance and the closed door. "In that mask and cape, he looked just like a Broadway star in *Phantom of the Opera.*"

Cathy looked over her shoulder. Both women were using the rest room. Apparently they'd forgotten they weren't alone, or they didn't care. Either way, as they were talking about Stone, she felt free to eavesdrop.

"A tragic figure," the other one said. "It's a pity he withdrew so completely after his wife died."

"What was she like?"

"Not what you'd expect. Not our type at all."

"Really?"

"Yes," the first woman continued. "Very plain. Apparently they'd been friends for years. Then one day he up and married her."

"Sounds romantic."

"Oh, it wasn't. His parents were insisting he marry someone appropriate, and apparently he wouldn't have any part of that. He said he would pick his own bride, then he married Evelyn."

"That's right. Evelyn. I couldn't remember her name. I met her a few times. She seemed very sweet, but not attractive at all. Still I never had much to do with her. I hadn't known she wasn't from a good family."

"That's not the worst of it. She adored him. You could read it on her face. While he—"

The sound of running water drowned out the woman's words. Cathy nearly screamed in frustration. All she'd wanted was to listen. Was that too much to ask? But the sound of the water reminded her that she wouldn't be alone much longer. She quickly pulled a couple of pins from her upswept hair and concentrated on the mirror as if her minor style disaster was all that was on her mind.

The women walked out together. They hesitated when they saw her. She moved to the right to give them more room, then offered an absentminded smile.

The blonde began to wash her hands. "He never loved her at all," she said, her voice low. "She was nothing but a friend. He took her on as a project—you know, as a way to help her better herself. Of course, he knew she loved him, but that only made him pity her."

Cathy nearly stabbed herself with the hairpin. She didn't know what to think. The woman couldn't be telling the truth. Of course Stone loved Evelyn. He'd been in mourning for her for years.

The brunette voiced her opinion. "Then why has he withdrawn from everyone? This is the first party he's held in years. And no one has seen him anywhere since the accident."

"That's not about her. It's about the scars. Remember,

he was hurt in the accident. How like a man to hide away, when women find that sort of thing very sexy. Of course, if a woman has so much as a pimple on her face, men go screaming in the other direction.''

The two women laughed and left the rest room. Cathy stared after them, not sure what she was supposed to think. They couldn't be talking about Stone, but of course they had been. Yet everything had been wrong. He loved Evelyn. She'd been his whole world. He'd as much as told her that himself. It had to be true. The alternative was too unthinkable.

She finished fixing her hair, then sank into the upholstered chair in front of the mirror. Her head was spinning. Was any of it true? Could it be? Had he really not loved Evelyn?

A project, the blonde had said. Someone he could feel sorry for. Someone he could fix.

Her blood ran cold. She told herself that none of it was true, that even if it was, she wasn't Evelyn. But the parallels were too clear, she thought unhappily. She, too, had been plain. She was poor and alone in the world except for him and what he offered her. Worse, she'd fallen in love with him.

''Please God, it can't be like that,'' she whispered.

A group of women entered the rest room. They looked at her oddly. She rose to her feet and took a deep breath. She had to get out of here. Maybe she could make her escape and walk around the grounds until her head cleared and she could think again. She felt as if her whole world had suddenly shifted and she didn't know how to keep her balance. Anything but pity, she thought fiercely. She could stand anything but that.

She stepped out into the foyer, then walked toward the doors. Strains of music drifted out from the tent. She was about to duck around it when she heard someone call her name.

The man approaching her didn't make her heart beat faster. All that happened was that she felt even more frantic about being on her own. Unfortunately Eric, one of the men from Stone's office, couldn't read her mind. He stopped in front of her and smiled. "They're playing a waltz, Cathy. May I have this dance?"

Before she could think of a polite way to refuse, she sensed more than heard Stone approach. He took her hand in his. "I'm afraid the lady has already promised this dance to me," he said, and led her off.

Cathy gave Eric an apologetic smile.

"I've been watching for you," Stone said as they entered the tent. "I was afraid you weren't feeling well."

"I'm fine. I had a bit of trouble with my hair."

"It and you look very beautiful tonight," he murmured as he took her in his arms.

The music was lovely, a steady three-three beat that allowed her to follow him around the tent. There were more dancers now. Cathy stared at the costumes, tried to absorb the spectacular scene, anything to avoid thinking about what she'd just learned. There was no point in trying to talk to Stone now. Later, when they were alone, she would seek the truth.

But even the pleasure of being in his arms wasn't enough to keep her mind from racing. She didn't know what to think. How much of it was true? What if it was all true? Then she was just another project to him. She wasn't anyone special at all. She'd never thought he would love her but she had hoped that he would care...at least a little.

She reminded herself that they were lovers. He wanted her in his bed, if nowhere else in his life. He couldn't fake that kind of passion. Was it enough? She didn't have an answer, but as her body grew cold, despite his closeness and heat, she had a bad feeling that it was going to have to be. Just like for Evelyn, her story wasn't going to have a happy ending, either.

Chapter Fourteen

Stone watched Cathy remove the pins from her hair. She'd already hung up her dress and taken off her makeup. She wore a short peach-colored robe with a matching nightie underneath.

He stretched out under the sheets and waited for her impatiently. While he enjoyed her bedtime rituals, tonight he was already aroused and ready for her. He wanted her in his bed, his arms around her, her body pressing against his. He wanted to kiss her and taste her. He wanted to reach between her thighs and find her already wet for him. Then he wanted to plunge inside of her and take them both to fantastic release.

"Thinking about it doesn't make the wait any easier," he mumbled to himself.

Cathy glanced up and looked at him. "What was that, Stone?" she asked. She finished pulling out the pins, then reached for her brush.

"Nothing. I was talking to myself."

"Oh."

She returned her attention to the mirror. He frowned. There was something different about her tonight. Instead of joking, she was quiet.

"Is something wrong?" he asked.

She put down her brush, turned out the lights on the vanity, then crossed to the large bed. But instead of joining him under the covers, she settled on top of the blanket and pulled her knees to her chest.

"I heard people talking at the party tonight," she said.

So that explained it. "I'm not surprised. A lot of them haven't seen me in years. A few probably thought I was dead."

That earned him a quick smile. "I'm confident they were pleased to see that you weren't."

"Don't be so sure about that. My competitors would like nothing more." He stuffed a second pillow behind his head. "Tell me what bothered you."

Cathy drew in a deep breath. "I wouldn't say bothered, exactly. It's just—" She shrugged. "I know it's none of my business."

"I don't have very many secrets."

"I heard two women talking about Evelyn," she said. "One of them knew her, and the other had only met her a couple of times. They said you weren't in mourning for her because you'd never loved her."

Now it was Stone's turn to hesitate. He shouldn't be surprised that people were talking. After all, he was prime fodder for the gossip mill. He had been for years. His time in solitude would have only made him more interesting…at least to some people.

In the back of his mind, he'd always known the truth was going to come out. It had to at some point. Cathy was too much a part of his world to be kept in the dark, he decided. As long as he didn't tell her everything.

"I guess it's time to come clean," he said lightly. "It's a long story, so you might want to get comfortable."

He patted the pillow next to him, but she shook her head. "I'm fine here."

She was sitting on the bed, but he felt as if she were a million miles away. He realized he would have been more comfortable telling her this while she was in his arms. At least then he wouldn't have to depend just on facial expressions. He could read her thoughts in the tension in her body and the way she pulled back or hugged him close. This way she could keep her thoughts to herself. Which was probably what she wanted. Well, there was nothing he could do about it.

"You know that Evelyn and I were friends," he began. "After college I went to work in the family business. Evelyn was staying in school to get her MBA. My parents realized they had a son in his midtwenties and they decided it was time for me to get married. They threw a series of parties and invited all the young women they considered eligible. I knew that I was expected to choose one of them."

He thought back to those days. It had been summer, he recalled. Because Evelyn had been around a lot. His parents hadn't wanted to include her but they knew better than to exclude his best friend.

"I didn't think it would be that big a deal," he admitted. "I had never been in love, but I'd always had plenty of girlfriends. I thought this would be more of the same. But marriage is a serious business. Somewhere along the way I decided they weren't going to make me choose someone just because of who her parents were and how much money she would bring to our family. Tensions got very high between myself and my parents.''

He remembered the fights. His mother's pleas, his father's cold anger. The older man had taken him aside and informed him that every Ward for generations had been marrying for the good of the family. It was the first time he'd realized that his parents hadn't been a love match.

''I wanted more,'' he said simply. ''At least that's how it started out. Then I got stubborn and decided that I wasn't going to pick someone they approved of. One afternoon I was complaining to Evelyn about the situation. I told her all the qualities I wanted in a wife. Someone bright, easy to talk to, with a great sense of humor. I remember we were sitting on the beach. I'd escaped for the afternoon. She looked up, smiled and said, 'Someone like me.' I knew then she was right.''

''So you proposed,'' Cathy said.

''Yes. And she accepted.'' He rubbed his eyes. ''I don't know what I was thinking. In a way I thought we were just joking. But when she started talking, I realized she was serious and she thought I was, as well.''

The past returned, as it had many times before. ''She said we would be good together, and I knew she was right. We'd always gotten along well. We liked the same things, had the same dreams. So I decided to go along with it, at least for a while. My parents were furious. They reacted in the worst way possible—they forbade me to marry her.''

Cathy nodded. ''That just made you more determined, right?''

''I was twenty-six years old. Of course I dug my heels in.'' The story was harder to tell than he'd realized. He knew he was to blame for what had happened between them back then. There had been so many signs.

''We had a long engagement,'' he said. ''Over a year.

I'm the one who pushed for that. I guess there was a part of me that knew what we were doing was wrong, but I didn't know how to stop it or make it right.'' He cleared his throat. ''A couple of months into our engagement, I realized that Evelyn was in love with me. She had been for years. Marrying me was all she'd ever wanted.''

''And you didn't want to hurt her,'' Cathy said softly.

He nodded. ''She was so incredibly important to me. I thought I could make it work. I loved her, but as a friend. At the time, I didn't think there was a big difference. I was wrong.''

There were many things he wouldn't tell Cathy. Personal things that he and Evelyn had shared. He still remembered the first time they'd made love, but not the way most men remembered that event. Evelyn had been so eager. He'd known she was a virgin and he'd put it off as long as he could.

Because he'd cared for her and they'd always had fun together, he hadn't had any trouble getting hard. But there wasn't any passion or fire between them. After a few times together, he found himself avoiding her physically. She'd been inexperienced enough that she hadn't realized how little they were intimate compared with most other married couples. In the end, he hadn't even been able to fake it.

''The marriage was a disaster,'' he said. ''She couldn't figure out what was wrong, and I felt guilty all the time. I tried to make it up to her but I didn't know how. All I could think of was that I was the only man she'd ever been with and I never really wanted her that way.''

Cathy hugged her knees closer to her chest and reminded herself that she'd been the one to initiate this conversation. For reasons she couldn't remember anymore, she'd *wanted* to know this information. Now she was sorry. The more he told her, the more real Evelyn became to her. Worse, the more similarities she saw in their situations.

She loved Stone and she knew he didn't love her back. She was from a different world; she'd been a virgin. The only differences she could see were that she and Stone weren't married and that he wanted her in his bed…at least for now.

Her body ached. It was as if every bone had been clubbed. It hurt to breathe, and her eyes felt gritty. His words cut her like daggers. She half expected to feel warm blood oozing down her arms and legs. It didn't matter that she wasn't really Evelyn. They were too similar by far.

Unrequited love is one of the oldest stories around, she thought to herself. Lord, but she hated to be a cliché. Unfortunately she hadn't had a choice in the matter. She couldn't help loving Stone any more than she could help breathing. It was as involuntary.

"Are you all right?" he asked. "You've gone pale."

He must never know, she told herself as she gave him a smile. "I was just thinking about what you said. I'm sorry things didn't work out with you and Evelyn. She sounds like she was very nice."

"You would have liked her."

Cathy doubted that, despite the fact that the two women had something in common. And she didn't think Evelyn would have liked her. They would have known each other to be the competition in a game they were both destined to lose.

He pulled back the covers and patted the sheet. "Come to bed," he said.

She nodded, then stood up and slipped off her robe. Wearing only a short nightgown and panties, she joined him on the wide mattress. There was more to the story, she thought. But she wasn't going to push to learn it all now.

His arms closed around her and pulled her close. "Are you sorry I told you about Evelyn?" he asked.

"Not at all." Better to know, she thought.

He brushed her bangs off her forehead, bent his head and kissed her. "I want you," he murmured against her mouth.

He did. She could feel his hardness pressing against her hip.

Cathy kissed him back and willed herself to respond. But for the first time since they'd become lovers, she wasn't instantly ready for him. When he reached between her legs, he gave a start of surprise. She could feel that she wasn't ready yet. To divert any questions, she plunged her tongue into his mouth. He stroked her breasts, and in a few minutes she felt herself preparing for him.

Later, when they'd both been lost in passion and had found their way back, she lay on her back in the dark. Stone slept next to her. Their hands were still entwined.

She told herself that it didn't matter. She wasn't Evelyn, and this was a very different relationship. But the words offered no comfort. Mostly because they weren't true. It *did* matter. There was no way for her to ignore the past, or the truth inherent in his story about his late wife. He hadn't loved Evelyn, just as he didn't love Cathy. Yet both women had loved him. In the end, that fact had destroyed Evelyn. What was it going to do to her?

Stone closed the file. "That's enough for now." He glanced at the clock on the wall. "Ula will be bringing lunch soon. She told me she'd made that mango-chicken salad you like so much."

Cathy gave him a quick smile that didn't quite reach her eyes. "She's very sweet, but I'm not hungry. Could you ask her to save it for me?"

He frowned. "You aren't eating lunch?"

"Maybe later. I want to go for a run." With that, she rose to her feet.

The early-September day was warm, but there was a pleasant breeze blowing off the ocean. Cathy wore a short skirt and sleeveless blouse. Both showed off her figure to perfection, and he found himself wanting her. No matter how many times they made love, he was still hungry for her. But she walked into her office without turning back, and suddenly he wasn't sure what she would say if he asked her to join him for a quick lunchtime tryst.

Something had changed between them. He'd noticed it a couple of days after the party. He kept telling himself it was hormones or work pressures, but he didn't believe that anymore. Was it because of what he'd told her about Evelyn? He didn't want to connect the two but couldn't figure out what else it could be.

Was she jealous? He shook his head. She couldn't be. He'd explained about his first marriage. Cathy knew that he hadn't loved Evelyn, at least not that way. He'd certainly never wanted her the way he wanted Cathy. She had to know that. Barely a night went by that he didn't reach for her. Their lovemaking was wonderful for them both, and she was always ready for him when he touched her. They were perfect together. So what was the problem?

Maybe she was feeling as confused as he was, he thought. He enjoyed having her in his life. They got along together. Despite his attempts to avoid it, he'd come to care about her. He wasn't worried about loving her—he would never love anyone ever again—but he didn't want to lose her. He wasn't sure where that left him.

There was a tap on the door. For a second, he thought Cathy was coming back. He looked up eagerly. Then he realized the noise had come from the door leading to the hallway, not to her office just to the right of his.

"Come in," he called.

Ula entered. As always she was perfectly tidy in a plain gray dress. Her dark gaze was unwavering. "I've set up lunch."

"Thank you. Cathy is going out for a run, so she'll be eating later."

Ula nodded. "I passed her in the hall. She mentioned that." She paused, and he knew she had more to say.

"What is it?" he asked, knowing it was pointless to avoid the inevitable.

She took a step into the room. Despite her height—or lack of—she was imposing as she stared at him. "You can't keep doing this much longer."

He wasn't sure what the *this* was, but he had a feeling she was going to fill in the details. He leaned back in his chair and kept quiet.

"She isn't a plaything," Ula told him.

The *she* being Cathy, of course. "I know that. I respect her. She works for me and does a great job." He knew this wasn't about work, but it was the only card he had.

"The girl is in love with you. You're treating her as if you have strong feelings for her. In the end, she's going to face heartache at your hand. You must let her go."

"It's not like that," he said lamely, trying not to remember the first time they'd made love. As Cathy had fallen asleep, she'd whispered that she loved him. Since then she hadn't repeated the words. He'd almost been able to make himself believe she hadn't really said them...or if she had, that she hadn't really meant them.

Unfortunately even he couldn't make that one fly. She cared deeply about him. He wasn't sure if it was love, but it was strong enough that she could be hurt. He didn't want her to love him—he wasn't worthy. And he knew better than to love someone else.

"I never told her it could be more," he said by way of defense, as much to Ula as to himself. It was true, he thought. He'd made it clear that he wasn't interested in any kind of a relationship. He ignored the voice in his head that asked what they had now, if not a relationship.

Ula shook her head. "She deserves better than this. She's been wonderful to you, and this is how you're repaying her. Stringing her along as if she's not a real person, worthy of consideration."

He hated her assessment even as he thought she might be right. "It's not like that."

"It's exactly like that. I don't know which would be worse. That you're lying to yourself about the truth of it, or that you're so blind and caught up with yourself and your own problems you can't see what's really going on."

Cathy stared at the small, wide-mouth plastic cup. "Do I have to?"

The curly-haired nurse grinned. "'Fraid so."

Cathy groaned. "But I just went before I left the house. I don't think I have it in me. And I mean that literally."

"There's a water cooler at the end of the hall," the nurse said helpfully. "You could try downing a couple of glasses."

Cathy shook her head. "Let's see what I can do on my own first."

When she was done, the nurse led her to an examining room and handed her a paper robe.

"I'm sure you know the drill," the young woman said. "We keep the air-conditioning cranked up, so feel free to leave on your socks."

"Oh, yeah, that's really going to help."

Cathy stepped behind the curtained dressing area. While she hated going to the doctor, she knew it was important to get her annual checkup. And she wanted to get a prescription for birth-control pills.

She folded her clothes, then slipped on the robe. As usual she felt exposed and foolish as she perched on the edge of the examining table. To distract herself, she thought of Stone. As her good mood faded, she realized that had been a mistake.

How much longer until Stone noticed something was wrong? She suspected he already knew but he was giving her time to work it out on her own. She was having trouble pinning down the exact problem herself. Some of it was that she was afraid she was little more than a good deed for Stone. A good deed he enjoyed sleeping with.

On the other hand, she reminded herself that she'd known going in that he would never fall in love with her. She'd decided that knowing what it would be like with him, then losing him, would be better than always wondering. She couldn't forget that. She'd promised herself no regrets.

"An easy promise when I didn't know how much it was going to hurt," she admitted.

Sometimes the pain was so sharp, she could barely breathe. She thought she'd known what she was doing when she'd started their affair, but now she wasn't so sure. She still loved him. If anything, her feelings had grown stronger. She believed that it was just a matter of time until he tired of her. Then where would she be? Where would she go? Could she still work for him? Would he even want her to?

Those questions were too dangerous, she thought, and shied away from them. She loved her work and would hate to think he'd created the job out of pity. If nothing else, she wanted him to respect her abilities. Maybe she could—

The examining-room door opened and the doctor stepped

in. The gray-haired woman smiled at her. "Cathy? I'm Dr. Chastin, but please call me Maddy. How are you feeling?"

"Good. A little nervous. I don't think anyone *likes* their yearly exam, but I know it's important. Oh, I told the nurse that I would like a prescription for birth-control pills."

"Yes, she mentioned it." The doctor settled on the stool next to the table. "You're in a relationship?"

"Yes. I'm monogamous, if that's what you're getting at."

"I am, but not for reasons you're thinking." The doctor had a kindly expression. The lines around her eyes and mouth hinted at a happy nature. She made Cathy feel very comfortable.

She took Cathy's hand in hers. "You're a little late for the birth-control pills. We check all our patients' urine samples, and yours came up positive. You're pregnant."

Chapter Fifteen

Cathy didn't remember much about the rest of her appointment. When she was next aware of herself, she was sitting in her car staring at a handful of brochures and pamphlets on prenatal care. She also had another appointment for a check-up. She would have to come in more regularly now that she was going to have a baby.

A baby! Dear God, she was pregnant.

She pressed her left hand against her still flat stomach. There was life growing inside of her, and she hadn't even known. She vaguely recalled the doctor calculating her due date based on her last period.

"I'm so late," she told herself as she stared out the windshield and tried to make sense of it all. "Why didn't I notice?"

Maybe she hadn't wanted to, she thought honestly. She and Stone had been pretty hit-and-miss with the birth control, and she had to take responsibility for that. She had been a virgin, but that was no excuse for being irresponsible. Now there were serious consequences for their actions. She was going to have to make some difficult decisions.

Cathy set the brochures on the seat next to her and fastened her seat belt. Then she started the car. She supposed she should go home and discuss this with Stone. But the truth was she wasn't ready to talk to him yet. Her head was spinning. She needed some time to come to terms with what was happening.

She left the parking lot without a particular destination in mind. Ten minutes later, she saw a large bookstore up ahead on the right and quickly changed lanes. Cathy parked and walked inside. After a couple of minutes of searching, she found the child-care section. She collected several books on pregnancy, took them over to a chair in the corner and sat down.

Not knowing what to expect, Cathy flipped through the books. Several had pictures of ultrasounds, line drawings and computer images of the different stages of development. She stared at them, but didn't feel any connection. The doctor's statement that she was pregnant made about as much sense as saying she was going to be abducted by aliens.

Cathy looked through the rest of the books, then picked two that seemed to have comprehensive information. Whether she wanted to believe it or not, she was about to be responsible for another person. She was going to have to learn what to do to stay healthy for both herself and the new life growing inside of her.

She thought about the past few weeks. Oddly enough, she hadn't had anything to drink. Not even at the masked ball. She'd been so nervous that she'd been afraid alcohol would upset her stomach. That was something. She figured she could talk to Ula about a healthy diet, although she was already consuming plenty of fruits, vegetables and lean protein. She was going to have to increase her calcium, the doctor had said.

Cathy paid for the books and returned to her car. She had to go home. She had to talk to Stone.

What was she going to say to him? What was he going to say in return? She shivered and realized it came from fear. She was terrified.

She knew that he wanted to be with her. She knew that they had passion, but what else? Anything? In her heart she was afraid that if she pressed him for more, he would simply turn away from her. He'd never once indicated that he was interested in them being more than friends.

She bit down hard on her lower lip and fought back tears. It was all going to fall apart. She could feel it in her gut. He hadn't loved Evelyn, even though she'd loved him desperately and had even been his wife. They'd grown up together. She'd known him for years. If Evelyn hadn't been able to make him fall in love with her, what hope did she, Cathy, have?

History was repeating itself, she thought sadly. He would let her go without a second thought.

As she pulled into the driveway and parked her car, she tried to tell herself she was jumping to conclusions. After all, Stone might surprise her.

''How?'' she asked aloud. ''Will he suddenly realize he can't live without me?''

Not likely, she thought. Not likely at all.

It didn't matter, she told herself. Either way she had to find out the truth. She owed them both that…make that she owed the three of them that.

She stuffed the brochures into the bag with the books and made her way inside. The foyer was still overly large and very impressive. The curved staircase led up to the second and third floors. There were too many rooms. She'd never counted or visited them all, but she knew that to be true. Stone lived in a different world from her. He was wealthy and he'd been wealthy all his life. She was a nobody he'd practically taken off the streets. What on earth had she been thinking?

She climbed to the second floor and walked down the hall to her office. Maybe if she worked for a while she could clear her head enough to make sense of it all. She walked into her office and stared at the familiar furniture.

More games of pretense, she thought as the rest of the truth sank in. She hadn't fooled anyone but herself. She wasn't a businesswoman. She was a rich man's mistress playing at having a "real" job to justify her presence in his life. Now she was a pregnant mistress. Nothing about her story was unique…including the fact that Stone was going to want to get rid of her as quickly as possible.

The pain was so sharp she couldn't catch her breath. It was all going to end, she thought. And there was nothing she could do to stop that from happening.

For a second, a voice in her head said that she could keep the pregnancy from him, at least for a little while. Maybe…

She pushed the voice away. No. She wouldn't play that game. If nothing else, she wanted to be honest. Their relationship had begun in lies, but it would end with the truth. She had survived without Stone for most of her life. She could do it again. As for the baby, they would be fine together, she and her unborn child. She would make sure they were fine. She wasn't the same meek, insignificant person she'd been six months ago. She'd grown and changed. She was strong. She would do well to remember that.

She drew in a deep breath for courage, then walked to the door separating her office from Stone's. She knocked once, then let herself in.

He was on his computer. When he saw her, he looked up and smiled. The sunlight reflected on his dark hair. The unmarked side of his face was toward her, and as always, his pure male beauty took her breath away.

"How was the doctor's appointment? I hope he didn't make any advances."

She sank into the chair opposite his desk and tried to smile. She wasn't sure if she succeeded or not. "No advances. For one thing, most doctors are professional. For another, 'he' is a she."

"Ah, a woman doctor. I'm glad. Seriously, that probably made the exam easier for you. So everything is all right?"

She knew how he meant the question so that was how she answered it. "I'm perfectly healthy."

She stared down at her hands. Usually she wore a dress or skirt and blouse when she worked. Today, because of the doctor's appointment, she'd dressed in tailored pants and a blouse. She fingered the linen blend. With Stone's generous salary, she'd been able to afford pretty clothes. She'd paid off all her bills and the house, put some money away and had bought a new car. Currently the car payment along with utilities on the house in North Hollywood were her only steady bills. She wasn't going to need much, which was good. She didn't think she was going to have much.

"Cathy, what's wrong?"

How well he could read her, she thought sadly, knowing that was just one thing she would miss about him. He'd always been able to sense what she was thinking. Of course, that wasn't the only thing. There was the laughter, their intense discussions about business, the passion, the holding, the fact that someone somewhere knew where she was during the day and would miss her if she was late.

''I've been thinking about us,'' she said at last. ''About our future. Where exactly do you see this relationship going? The personal one, I mean. Not the professional.''

He hit the save key on his computer, then turned his chair and faced her. Not for the first time she wished *she* had the ability to read *his* mind. His expression didn't give anything away. It remained pleasantly neutral.

''You're seeking my thoughts on whether or not I see this as continuing indefinitely?'' he asked.

His voice was low, almost formal. As if he were addressing a group, or giving a presentation.

She nodded. ''Yes, that's it.''

''I see.'' He folded his hands together on top of the desk. ''I care about you, Cathy. I think you know that. We're good friends. We work well together and we live well together. I think that's important.''

Her body felt as if it were being pierced by thousands of tiny arrows. In a way, there was no point in continuing the conversation. She already knew how it was going to end. But there was a part of her that needed to hear the words. If he spoke them, she would be able to remember them. She would be able to let go of her hope. But first she had to hear them, despite what that would do to her.

''You don't love me,'' she said.

''No.''

Something inside of her twisted up and died. Coldness swept through her. The room spun once, then stilled. She couldn't breathe, but that seemed unimportant when compared with what he'd just told her.

''It's not you,'' he added. ''Please, don't take it personally. I couldn't love anyone. I want things to be different.

If I was able to change, I know it would be with you. I'm sorry."

Yeah, her, too, she thought. So the fact that it wasn't personal was supposed to make her feel better? "It feels very personal to me," she managed to say, and was pleased when her voice didn't shake.

"Cathy, no. Don't take it that way. I…" His voice trailed off. "It's because of Evelyn."

That didn't make sense. "You never loved her. I know you're not in mourning for her. You told me that yourself."

"I know and that's true. The point is I should have. I owed her that." He grimaced. "She was jealous. When I stopped—" He cleared his throat. "The physical side of our marriage deteriorated rapidly. After a while, she became convinced there was someone else. There wasn't, but I couldn't get her to believe me."

His dark eyes focused on a past she couldn't see. "I tried to make myself fall in love with her. I thought if I could just do that, everything would be fine. I learned that I couldn't force it or bargain it into happening. I respected my wife, I enjoyed being with her, I loved her as deeply as I've ever loved anyone, but as a friend. Nothing more. Then we went to that damn party."

He shook his head. "I wish I could tell you I was so drunk I didn't know that woman was coming on to me, but I did know. I had no intention of following through when she kissed me. But I let her do it. I let myself be cornered by another woman and I let her kiss me. Then I kissed her back." He rubbed his eyes. "The hell of it was, I got turned on."

He dropped his hand and stared at her. "That's what Evelyn saw. She saw me kissing another woman and when I pulled away, she saw that I was aroused. The last time we'd tried to make love, I couldn't, but there I was, hot and ready for someone else.''

Cathy didn't want to hear any more. She knew how the story ended, and she was reasonably sure she knew what it had to do with her. Stone was right. In a twisted way, this wasn't personal. But for her the bottom line was that as much as she loved him and wanted him, he didn't return her feelings.

"Needless to say, we left right away," he said. "I was too drunk to drive, so Evelyn took the wheel. We started fighting as soon as we got to the freeway. She finally had the proof she'd been looking for. Her fears about my supposed infidelities had been confirmed. I tried to explain, but she wouldn't listen. All she knew was that she couldn't turn me on anymore but this other woman could. I'd devastated her. I'd always loved her and cared about her and in the end I'd hurt her more than anyone ever had before.''

He was silent for a long time. Cathy picked up the story. "That was the night of the accident." It wasn't a question.

He nodded. "She was killed instantly, but I survived. Evelyn died thinking that I'd betrayed her. All she'd ever wanted was for us to love each other. It was the only thing I couldn't give her. I'll never be able to make up for that. I can never heal her or fix her, and that makes me crazy.''

The pieces of the puzzle fell neatly into place. Cathy had thought she understood the ending of the story, but she'd been very wrong. The point wasn't that Stone wouldn't love her because he hadn't loved Evelyn. No, that would be too simple. It was worse.

He wanted to make up for what had happened between him and his late wife. He wanted to fix Evelyn. But she was gone. So he'd found someone else to fix. In some twisted way, she'd taken Evelyn's place in his life. Maybe he thought if he did enough good deeds, he could atone for the past.

"You think I'm Evelyn," she breathed.

He stiffened. "Of course not. You two have nothing in common."

She rose to her feet because the need to move was overwhelming. After folding her arms protectively across her chest, she paced to the window. "I don't know why I didn't see it before," she said, more to herself than to him. "There were so many similarities."

"You're nothing alike."

She glared at him. "Then tell me how we're so different."

"I want you," he said simply. As if the passion were enough. As if the fact that he wanted her in his bed would make up for him not loving her.

She shook her head. "That's not good enough. You've used me as a means to an end. I'm just a project to you. Not even a real person."

She thought about the unborn child she carried. If she wasn't real, what would he think of the baby? She shuddered at the thought.

"Cathy, you don't understand."

She spun toward him. "I understand perfectly. You've been playing with my life. You can't do that, Stone. You can't pluck people out of their worlds, change their circumstances and not accept responsibility for what you've done. What did you think? That I would accept all of this, then one day politely leave and never give you another thought?"

"No. Of course not. I didn't set out to do anything like that. I care about you. I thought we were friends. I just wanted to help."

"In the meantime, you might also ease a little of your guilt about Evelyn."

His expression hardened. "Nothing will ever change what happened there."

She stared at him. "You're right," she said. "Why didn't I see that before? Nothing will ever change how you feel about the past. I guess we were both acting without thinking."

He spoke, but she didn't hear him. The need to escape was overwhelming. She left his office and hurried into hers. Once there, she grabbed her purse and left. She didn't know where she was going; she only knew it had to be away from here.

He sat alone in the dark. He didn't want to see the room they'd shared together. In shadows he could pretend he was somewhere other than the bedroom where they'd spent so many happy hours together. Unfortunately the darkness couldn't hide the scent of her body or her perfume. The sweet smell lingered in the air. The darkness also couldn't erase his memories of what they'd said to each other earlier that day.

He knew he'd hurt her. Inadvertently he'd done the one thing he'd tried to avoid doing. He'd thought they could just be friends. But Cathy had been right about everything. He *had* interfered with her life without considering the consequences.

She'd seen right through him. She'd seen that he'd thought of her as little more than a project. A way to, if not make up for the past, then at least to make sense of it. It had taken a while for him to come to realize she was a person in her own right. By then it had been too late. They'd been involved.

He'd acted selfishly and thoughtlessly. Ula had tried to

warn him, but he hadn't listened. He'd done all the wrong things for all the right reasons, and now Cathy was paying the price.

He'd only wanted to help, he thought. Why had everything gone so wrong? Why hadn't he seen what he was doing?

He sat in silence for a while, waiting for the answer. At last it came to him. In a moment of self-revelation followed by self-loathing, he realized he was a selfish bastard who assumed he was smarter than everyone else. He'd assumed he knew and worked for the greater good when in fact everything he'd done had been for his own self-interest. No one else's.

There was an old saying that the truth hurts. He knew that to be true. Unfortunately his pain and truth had come too late to help Cathy. He didn't even know where she was.

He glanced at the clock. It was nearly midnight. She'd been gone for hours. What if she didn't come back? What if she did? What was there to say to her? He could apologize, but that was such a feeble effort after all he'd done.

As if his thoughts had conjured her, he heard her footsteps in the hallway. He reached for the light by the chair just as she walked into the room.

Her hair was tousled, and there were shadows under her eyes. Despite the bit of makeup still clinging to her cheeks, she looked pale and drawn.

"Are you all right?" he asked, half rising from his seat. She waved him back in place.

She remained by the door as she spoke. "I don't know what your plans are as far as work is concerned," she began. "But they don't matter to me."

He had thought she might not want to be his lover anymore, but he'd never considered that she would be quitting too. "I thought you liked your job," he said. "I would like you to stay on. You're excellent in that position."

"I'm also excellent on my back in your bed, but that doesn't mean I'm willing to keep doing it," she countered. Her eyes were dark green and they brightened with rage. "I will not be a man's mistress. Not even yours."

If she'd intended to cut him to the bone, she'd succeeded. "Please stay," he said before he could stop himself.

"No. I can't."

"You won't. There's a difference."

"Spare me the semantics, Stone. There was a time I would have accepted your offer. I would have stayed, even knowing there was no future here. But I've changed. I believe I'm worth more. You taught me that. I guess next time you should be more careful about who you're bringing in from the streets."

"Don't," he said. "It wasn't like that. You know it. Stop making yourself into an object. We were friends for two years before any of this started. I value that even if you don't."

"I'll agree that you were an important part of my life. Too important. That's what made it so easy for me to fall into your life here. But I need more now. I need to find my own way. I need to belong."

"You belong with me."

"As what? An employee? As the woman who services your physical needs? I won't be your whore."

That pushed him to his feet. He glared at her. "I've never treated you badly. You had my trust, my respect and my affection from the moment you arrived here. I wasn't the one to initiate our physical relationship. I would never have done that because I didn't want to put you into a difficult situation."

The fight crumpled right out of her. She sagged against

the door frame and closed her eyes. "You're right, of course. I know that. You were decent to me. But you also used me to make yourself feel better. I've been a project to ease your guilt."

He shouldn't be surprised that she put the pieces together, but he was still embarrassed that she knew.

"Cathy, I—"

She cut him off with a shake of her head. "You wanted to fix me and you did," she said as she looked at him. "Thank you for all your good intentions. Perhaps they should have been enough, but they weren't. You're trying to fix the past, but that isn't the problem, is it? The real issue is that you're terrified of loving anyone. You loved Evelyn and you believe that love destroyed her. So you promised to never let that happen again. Unfortunately, not loving again is a pretty lousy goal in life."

It was as if she could see to the scarred blackness that was his soul.

"You didn't destroy Evelyn," Cathy said. "I wish I could convince you of that, but I can't. You were wrong to marry her after you figured out you couldn't love her the way a man is supposed to love his wife. But she was wrong, too. She was wrong to keep you and try to make you feel guilty enough to love her. As you learned, you can't have romantic love on command."

She took a step toward him, then paused. "I know," she said softly, "because I've loved you for months and I've been hoping you would come to love me." She shrugged. "You haven't. There's nothing I can do about it now. It's not your fault or mine. It just happened. The thing is, loving you and knowing you'll never love me back makes it impossible for me to stay.

"I grew up taking care of my mother. I lost my hope and my dreams. Well, thanks to you, I finally have them back. I'm not willing to lose them again. So I have to go and make them happen. I'd thought we might do that together, but I can be just as successful on my own.''

She spoke so easily, he thought in disbelief. He could barely remain on his feet, but she looked fine. As if this was of no consequence to her.

She loved him. He supposed he'd known that for some time, even if he hadn't wanted to see it. She'd woven herself into his life and now she was leaving. How was he going to survive?

''Cathy, don't,'' he said. ''It doesn't have to be like this.''

''Yes, it does,'' she told him. ''You want to live with your pain and your scars. You're very comfortable here—hiding away like a wounded animal. I knew the risks I was taking when I fell in love with you. I knew there was a very good chance that you would never return my affection. But I did it anyway. I took the chance. It was probably the first brave act of my life and it felt good.''

She straightened. ''It hurts now. It hurts to breathe and talk and to be standing here in front of you acting as if I'm not bleeding to death on the inside. But I'm doing it. I'm risking it and I'm going to survive. I'm willing to take the chance and you're not.''

''I've taken chances,'' he said in a feeble effort to defend himself. Everything she said was the truth…about them both. She *was* brave, and he was simply a coward.

''I'm not talking about business,'' she told him. ''I'm talking about your personal life. You hide away and you refuse to take responsibility for your feelings or what you do to others. It's not just that you won't let yourself love anyone—it's that you won't let yourself love *yourself*.''

Her words made him flinch. ''I take responsibility for

what I did to you. I was wrong. I'm sorry. I never meant to hurt you.''

"Yeah, well, you did." She looked around the room. "I'll miss this place. It was a very nice fantasy." She turned her attention back to him. "I'll call Ula in the morning and have her pack up my things. I'll come back and get them later, if that's all right with you."

He took a step toward her. She couldn't be leaving. Not like this. Not without giving him another chance. "Don't go. We can still make this work."

"No, we can't. Besides, it would hurt too much to be with you every day and know that you didn't love me. I need a clean break."

"What will you do? Where will you go?"

Her gaze was level. "That's not your concern. You have done what you set out to do. You fixed my life. Congratulations."

He winced. "Cathy, don't leave like this. Let me at least write you a check. You'll need money to tide you over. Maybe you can start a business or something. I would be happy to finance anything you want."

Her gaze turned icy, and he saw something he'd never expected to see in her eyes. At that moment she hated him.

"If you think any of this is about money," she said curtly, "then you never knew me at all."

Chapter Sixteen

Cathy sat on the bed where she'd stayed the first few months she'd lived in Stone's house. She pulled her knees to her chest and hugged them tightly against her, but it wasn't enough to hold in the feeling that she was going to fly apart into a thousand pieces.

Every part of her hurt. Just the act of breathing was more pain than she'd ever experienced before in her life. She kept repeating that she'd known it was going to be like this, that she'd long suspected he didn't care about her— at least not the way she cared about him. But thinking it might be true and hearing it were two different things. She hadn't realized how true that was until she'd come face-to-face with her worst fear.

She shook her head back and forth in an effort to deny the truth. She wished she could cry. Maybe that would make her feel better. Maybe then she could heal. But for now there weren't any tears. There was only the ache inside of her and the sinking feeling that it was going to take more than one lifetime to get over loving Stone.

Even as she tried not to think about them, about all that he'd said to her, even as she tried not to place blame or think about what had gone wrong, she kept replaying his words in her mind.

She swallowed hard, but the bitter taste stayed in her mouth. He'd actually offered her money, as if she were some woman he'd bought and paid for. As if she really were just a whore. She supposed that's what hurt the most. She could understand someone not falling in love. It happened all the time. As Stone had learned with Evelyn, love couldn't be forced. But to have had him treat her like that. She shuddered. That made her less than a person to him, and it was more than she could bear.

She rolled onto her side and pulled her knees up tight again. A plan. She needed a plan. Think about what to do next, she told herself. That would help distract her.

First, she thought, she had to get out of here. In a few minutes, just as soon as she was able to actually draw in a breath, she was going to leave. It was after midnight, so she wouldn't bother taking much. Her purse, maybe a couple of things to wear. In the morning, she would call Ula. Cathy stiffened in anticipation of the humiliation, but oddly there wasn't any. She didn't know what the older woman would think about what had happened, but she knew in her heart that Ula would only be kind to her.

Okay, so a phone call to Ula to ask her to pack up her things. She would make arrangements to have them picked up by a delivery service or something.

Item two, she would make some decisions about her future. A job and maybe a couple of business classes at the local college. If nothing else, her time with Stone had taught her that she liked the world of business.

She would have to start saving because she was about a month and a half pregnant, and the baby was going to require—

The unexpected sob tore at the back of her throat. A baby. Dear God, she was going to have a baby. Tears trickled down her temple and dampened her hair. She pressed one hand to her mouth and the other to her belly where a tiny life grew.

She wasn't sure what the tears meant. While she hadn't planned on getting pregnant anytime soon, she'd always wanted a family. Ideally she would have preferred a husband at her side, but she'd recently learned that she was strong. She and her child would be fine on their own.

Cathy sniffed as the tide of tears slowed. Eventually she was going to have to tell Stone the truth. He deserved to know about the baby. It was the right thing to do, even if there wasn't any point. He hadn't been interested in her, so she doubted he would care about an infant, either. But she wouldn't make that decision for him. She would tell him. Just not tonight. She needed a few days to get strong.

She wasn't sure how long she lay there working on gathering her strength and her courage. Finally, when she'd run out of excuses, she sat up, then rose to her feet. She felt shaky and tired, which probably wasn't a surprise considering all that she'd been through in the past day.

She pulled an overnight suitcase out of her closet and quickly filled it with what she would need to see her through until she had the rest of her things. It didn't take long. Then she was out of excuses and it was time to leave.

She walked down the hall toward the stairs. On a whim, knowing it was a big mistake, she moved past the stairs to the opposite side of the house where a patch of light shone out of an open office door.

Stone was still up. The fact shouldn't surprise her. The

man hardly slept. She hesitated, knowing there was nothing for them to say, yet wanting to see him one last time.

She drew back her shoulders and walked into his office.

Stone sat behind his desk, staring into space. He obviously hadn't been to bed yet and from the look of him he wouldn't try to sleep that night. Stubble darkened his jaw. His mouth was weary, his scars especially pronounced.

He looked up as she entered. His gaze settled on her bag. "You're leaving."

It wasn't a question, but she answered it anyway. "Yes. I'll send for my things."

He looked at her face. She felt the attention as if it were a touch, as if his hand had brushed against her cheek.

"Don't go," he pleaded. "Don't leave me. It doesn't have to be like this, Cathy. What we have is very special, and I don't want to lose that. I don't think you do, either."

She hadn't realized she'd hoped until her hopes crashed onto the floor and shattered into slivers. He'd asked her to stay because they had something special and he didn't want to lose her. It was something, she supposed. Not what she wanted, though. Not a relationship built on mutual respect or caring. Not love.

"I can't," she told him. "I want more than that. I've learned that I deserve more. I have to be more than your current fix-it project and a convenience."

He stiffened. "That's not fair. While I'll admit that the reasons I wanted to help you were complicated, you make it sound like you were a faceless person in all of this. That anyone would have done. That's not true. I do care about you."

"Like a friend."

"Yes."

"A friend you sleep with."

"We're lovers."

''But not in love.''

His gaze shifted. There wasn't any point, she reminded herself. She couldn't change his feelings.

''I wish you the best, Stone. I hope that you can get it together. I love you enough to want to see you happy, but that's not going to happen until you can let yourself love someone. And that will require you to let go of the past. I hope you can, but I doubt it. Self-pity has become too familiar a companion, and I think in your heart you're afraid to let it go. You live this half-life, hoping it will make up for what happened to Evelyn. The truth is the accident wasn't your fault. But if you see that, you have to be willing to forgive yourself and admit it was all right for you not to have loved her. For some reason, you've decided Evelyn was perfect—therefore you have to be the wrong one. I suspect you were equally at fault.''

She shrugged. ''But what do I know? Good luck, Stone. Try not to stay in your beautiful prison forever. There's a big world out there, and it still has a lot to offer you.''

''Will I see you again?''

She wanted to say no. It would be easier for her to just cut him out of her life. But it wasn't just her decision. In a few days, she was going to have to tell him about the baby.

''I suspect you will,'' she said at last, then turned and left.

Stone watched her go. When the front door closed, he slumped back in his chair and tried to tell himself that it was for the best. Cathy was getting too close to him. If the situation continued, she would only get hurt. Better for her to move on now, while she still could.

As for him, well, he would be fine, he told himself. He ignored the anguish inside, the gaping hole that used to be his heart.

But as the night wore on and the silence grew, he found it more and more difficult to dismiss the sensation of his lifeblood flowing away. He didn't want his life to return to the emptiness he'd known before Cathy. It was one thing to never see her again, but he'd also lost the right to be her friend. She had been his only link to the world. Now there was no one.

"Cathy," he said aloud, already missing her more than he'd thought possible. He'd wanted so much for her, and he'd never realized that part of that wanting was to never let her go.

What did that mean? He couldn't really care about her. This wasn't…love.

Love. He turned the word over in his mind. He didn't know what it meant to love a woman. Not romantically. He never had. Besides, it wasn't allowed. He wasn't entitled. Not after what he'd done.

It always came back to the past. To Evelyn. To the horror of that night.

"I'm sorry," he said into the darkness. "I should never have married you. I see that now. I should have told you the truth. It would have been kinder. Instead, I let you hope."

Cathy had said there had been nothing wrong with not loving Evelyn back. He wondered if that was true. Did it matter? In the end, he'd betrayed her.

The thoughts filled his mind. He went through the past again and again, trying to figure out all the places he'd failed and what he could have done differently. He thought about Cathy, about what they'd had together. About all she'd given him and how much she'd come to mean to him.

After a while, he realized the light wasn't just coming

from the lamp on his desk, but instead spilled in through the window. Morning. The first day without her.

Sometime later he heard footsteps. When Ula entered the room she walked right up to his desk and stared at him.

"She's gone?"

He nodded.

"I see." His normally unflappable housekeeper looked as if she was having trouble controlling her tears.

"I'm sorry," he said. "She wanted to leave, and I couldn't make her stay."

"Of course you could." Ula practically spit the words at him. "There's always a choice. But this was easier, wasn't it?"

He felt as if she'd slapped him. "Cathy deserves better than me," he said lamely.

Ula rolled her eyes. "We all know that, but for some reason, you're the one she wants. She loves you, Stone Ward. She is perfect for you, but you're too stubborn and too caught up in the past to see that."

He touched his face, his fingers sliding over the familiar pattern of scars. "I have nothing to offer her. She can't want me like this."

"Then change. Make it right. I loved Miss Evelyn as if she were my own daughter. I know the two of you had troubles. You were wrong in some of it, but so was she. Let it go. Let her go. Keep the good memories in your heart and release the rest. If you continue to live like this, then you might as well have died in that car accident." Her anger and frustration were tangible. She was shaking as she stood in front of him.

"Don't you dare abuse the gift of life you've been given," she ordered him. "Don't you dare. You've wasted too much time already. You'll never get those days back. You can be happy for the rest of the time you have, or you can die a miserable old man. For once in your life, don't be an ass.''

She spun on her heel and walked out.

Stone rose as if to follow her, then sank back into his chair. Was Ula right? Was Cathy right? Had he been a fool, a coward hiding behind guilt? Was he afraid of risking it all just because he was afraid? Was he willing to lose someone as wonderful as Cathy just because there was some risk involved?

Was he, as Ula had so eloquently told him, an ass?

Cathy pulled into the driveway of her house in North Hollywood. It had been two weeks, and this place still didn't feel like home. She wondered if it ever would.

She collected her groceries and went inside. When she'd first come back, she'd spent four days giving the house a thorough cleaning. She'd gone through much of what her mother had left behind, a task she'd been putting off for years. Then she'd sewn new curtains for the kitchen, bought an inexpensive comforter for her bed and a window box for the front window. She figured she and the baby would both like looking out onto fresh blooming flowers every day. Then she'd gone back to her old job.

Cathy walked into the kitchen and started putting away the groceries. Her body felt thick, as if she were moving through water. The world appeared to be in black and white now, instead of the color she was used to.

"Time," she reminded herself as she stored the half gallon of milk in the refrigerator. "It will take a little time. Then I'll get over Stone. Eventually I'll feel like my old self again." She thought for a second, then smiled. "Okay, not too much like my old self."

She didn't want to go back to that empty life she'd had before. It had been too horrible. She'd been given a second chance and she was going to take it. But sometimes it was so hard.

When she finished with the groceries, she sat at the small table and pulled out the college catalog. She was too late to enroll officially, but the college had a special program that allowed returning adults to go to the first day of class. If there was enough room for the professor to allow them into the class, then all they had to do was pay a fee and they were officially a returning student. Cathy had already picked out three classes she wanted to take. They started that afternoon.

She'd worked out a schedule. She had her old job at the answering service, working evenings, but she got off at midnight. She would be home and asleep by one in the morning, then get up at nine. If she got the classes she wanted, she would be in school three days a week, from noon to three, and that gave her just enough time to get to work by four. She would have her mornings and weekends to study. Unfortunately, because of the baby, she would have to skip next semester, but she would start back up in the fall.

In the meantime, she would get going on her degree. She had some savings, decent health insurance and the house was paid for. All in all, she was very fortunate.

She only had one thing left to do.

Cathy stared at the phone. She'd already put it off too long, she thought. And she didn't want to admit the reason, not even to herself. She hadn't called Stone to tell him about the baby because she'd been hoping he would contact her.

"Foolish dreams," she said sadly. But they'd been *her* dreams, and she'd clung to them like a drowning man cling-ing to a life preserver. Every night she'd come home hoping to find her answering-machine light blinking. She'd even thought he might call her at the answering service. But it had been fourteen days and Stone hadn't tried to contact her once.

He'd let her go so completely, she wondered if she'd ever mattered to him at all.

She drew in a deep breath. It was time to put the fantasy to rest. She had to put the past and her feelings behind her and get on with reality. She had to tell him the truth.

"No time like the present," she said as she glanced at the clock above the clean but ancient stove. It was barely ten in the morning. She could call Stone and still easily make it to her first class.

She punched in the number, trying to ignore the way her hands trembled and the knot of fear in her stomach. She had no idea what she was going to say to him. There was only so much chitchat she could hide behind before she got to the truth.

"Ward residence."

Despite her terror, she smiled. "Hi, Ula. It's Cathy."

"It's about time. You said you'd keep in touch, and I believed you. But have you called?"

"You could have called me," she countered.

"I know, but I didn't want to be a reminder if you were trying to put all this behind you."

Cathy knew the *this* was actually Stone. "I appreciate the concern."

"So how are you?"

"I'm doing well." Cathy brought her up-to-date, then said, "Thanks for having my things delivered. You didn't have to do that. I could have made arrangements."

"I wanted to help, and it was all I could think of to do."

They talked for a few more minutes, then Cathy gathered up her courage. "I need to speak to Stone, Ula. Could you get him for me?"

The housekeeper was silent for a long time. Cathy began to wonder if he'd given instructions that she wasn't to be put through.

"I can't do that," Ula said. "Mr. Ward isn't here."

Cathy stared at the receiver, as if she'd suddenly heard a foreign language. "What do you mean?"

"Mr. Ward is gone. Cathy, I'm sorry. I don't know what to tell you. Five days ago, he came downstairs with two suitcases. He said he was going away and that I was to look after the house until he returned. I thought—" Her voice shook. "I thought he'd decided to go to you."

Cathy didn't think she could take any more. Stone hadn't bothered to get in touch with her and now he was gone.

"You don't know where he is?" she asked futilely.

"No. I swear I would tell you if I had any idea. That man is a complete—" She paused and sighed. "That doesn't matter now. I wish there was something I could say. I know how you felt about him. You were wonderful to him and for him. If he'd let you, you could have helped him heal. He's going to regret losing you."

Cathy hoped the other woman was correct, but right now that was cold comfort. Tears spilled from her eyes. She hadn't told Stone about the baby and now he was gone.

"Can I help?" Ula asked.

Cathy shook her head, then realized the other woman couldn't see her. "No," she managed. "I just..." She swallowed and tried to hold back the tears. "I have something important to tell him. If you hear from him, could you please ask him to call me?"

"Of course. I'm so sorry, Cathy. I hope you'll stay in touch with me."

"I'll try." It was the most she could promise. Right now she didn't think she could ever talk to Ula or anyone else again. "I have to go," she said. "Take care of yourself." Then she hung up the phone.

She wasn't sure how long she sat there. Stone was gone. He wasn't going to come for her; he wasn't going to be calling. He'd disappeared from her life. She'd never mattered at all.

Finally she placed her arms on the table and lowered her head. She sobbed until there weren't any more tears.

When she finally straightened, she saw it was eleven-thirty. Time for her to leave for her class. She stood up and started to collect her catalog and purse, then stopped. What was the point? Who was she kidding? College? Her? She couldn't make it. She was too old. She had a baby on the way. It would take too long.

"Just forget it," she said aloud. "Go to work, come home, wait for the baby. That's enough. You don't really need to have a life. Look how long you survived without one before."

Without thinking, she crossed to the kitchen cupboard. She pulled it open, then wrinkled her nose. Whole-grain bread, low-fat crackers. Soup. Not a cookie or a candy bar in sight. She needed chocolate and she needed it right now.

Cathy grabbed her purse and headed for the front door. As she stepped out on the porch, she noticed the mail had been delivered. She took the stack and prepared to toss it on the tiny hall table behind her. Then familiar handwriting caught her eye. Stone's writing.

Her heart jerked hard in her chest. The envelope was thick and business sized. She tore it open, wondering what he'd sent her. A note? A ticket? An explanation?

Money. She stared at the stack of hundred-dollar bills, then counted. Five thousand dollars. There was a folded piece of paper with a single sentence: "You can expect this same amount every month."

The bastard hadn't even bothered to sign his name.

Cathy looked at the money. So that was all he thought of her. Fine. She would put the money away for the baby. Maybe start a college fund. All the investment people said it was never too early, right?

She glanced around as if she couldn't quite remember where she'd been going. Oh, to get chocolate. Cathy frowned. No, that wasn't what she wanted. She didn't want to eat; she wanted a life. And by God, she was going to have one.

She turned around and marched into the house. After picking up the catalog and her notebook, she hurried to her car. There was still time to make the first class. She would convince the instructor to add her to that class list and she would get the other two she wanted, as well. She would make a success of this. Just to make sure there was no mistake, she was going to take a seat in the front row!

Fourteen weeks later, Cathy pulled into her driveway, still grinning like a fool. She was tired, but happier than she'd been in months.

She done it. She'd just taken the last of her three finals. She'd completed her first semester of college.

"Are you proud of your mama?" she asked as she placed her hand on her swelling belly. She was five months along, and the pregnancy was no longer easy to conceal. Cathy had found that hadn't mattered. The students in her classes hadn't judged her because she was pregnant and unmarried. If anything, they'd been kind to her.

She thought back over the past few months. College had been hard. She'd loved finance, had tolerated economics but who in the world would ever want to be an accountant? She shuddered at the thought of more balance sheets in her future. She'd only made a B in that class, but she was confident that her other two grades were As.

She was exhausted. All that studying, the tests, forcing herself to work hard even when she was tired and her body kept betraying her by getting bigger and bigger.

"It was worth it," she told her stomach, talking to her child as she often did. "You'll be worth it, too."

She turned off the engine and stepped out of the car. It was nearly nine in the evening. She'd joined a group of students for an after-finals dinner at the local Italian restaurant. She'd enjoyed the easy conversation and the laughter. There hadn't been enough of either in her life.

Eddie, her boss at the answering service, was so proud of her for finishing her first semester, that he'd given her the night off. She was grateful. All she wanted was to crawl into bed and sleep for twelve hours.

She walked up toward the house. A shadow moved. Cathy was too startled to be afraid. The shadow moved again, and became a man. Then she knew.

After all this time, Stone had come back. She didn't know what to think. What to say. He'd sent the money every month. Most of it she put away, though some she kept out to buy things for the baby. She'd talked to Ula a few times, but the housekeeper hadn't had any news.

She stood there on the path and tried to figure out what she felt. Not anger, even though she should be furious. Not even sadness, although there were tears on her cheeks. Despite everything, she'd never stopped loving him. The love moved through her, filling her with a warmth she hadn't felt in a long time. The same love she'd experienced before, with only one difference. The past four months had taught her how to be strong. She'd survived without him. She would continue to survive. She loved him and wanted him, but she didn't *need* him in order to feel that she had a life.

"Hello, Cathy."

He moved off the porch and approached her. The night was still with bright stars but no moon. She searched his face, but she couldn't see him clearly. It was just like when she'd first been at his house. Meetings in the dark.

"Stone. This is a surprise."

He stopped in front of her. "Are you angry?"

"I probably should be, but I'm not." She took a step toward the house. "Let's go inside and you can tell me why you're here."

"As calmly as that?"

She shrugged. "What did you expect? A scene?"

"No. I suppose you've forgotten all about me. I wouldn't blame you. I don't deserve more."

"You're right, you don't. Unfortunately I haven't forgotten. But at least I've learned to live without you." A cool breeze made her shiver. "Come on, it's cold. Let's go inside."

She led the way. Well, he was going to get quite a shock when she took her coat off. The thought was almost enough to make her smile. Whatever he had to say, she would handle it, just like she'd handled everything else recently. She'd learned that she was pretty tough.

She unlocked the door, then reached for the light switch. Stone placed his hand on top of hers. "Please don't. Not yet anyway."

"I've seen the scars."

"I know. Humor me."

He closed the door behind them, and they stood there in the dark.

"I'd ask you to sit down, but I'm afraid we'd both crash into something." She took a breath, prepared to add something witty yet biting. Something to show how well she'd done without him. But he touched her face. Strong, warm fingers stroked her cheek, and she melted.

"I've missed you," he said, his voice low and husky. "Every day, every hour. I was an incredible fool. You are an amazing woman. You're everything I've ever wanted, and I was so stupid. I lost you. I don't know if it was pride or anger at myself or guilt. It's taken a while, but I've learned to let go of the past, just like you told me."

She opened her mouth, but couldn't speak. Was Stone saying what she thought he was saying? She couldn't be sure.

"You were right," he continued. "About everything. Ula was right, too. She said I was an ass, and I was."

"Ula said that?"

"More than once."

She felt more than saw him move closer. He cupped her face. "I'll understand if you've moved on and left me behind. Or even if there's someone else. But if neither is true, would you please give me a chance? I love you, Cathy. I believe I always loved you, but I was afraid to admit it. That business about fixing your life was just an excuse to have you near me and not have to take responsibility for my feelings. I love you. Please come back home with me."

She couldn't believe. "Are you really here?" she asked. "Are you really saying these things to me?"

"Yes. All of them. I love you."

"Oh, Stone."

She threw herself at him and kissed him. Their bodies pressed together, and in the darkness they clung to each other.

"I love you, too," she said, pulling back enough to catch her breath. "There's no one else. How could there be? I gave you my heart and I don't have it back to give again." She laughed. "This is so amazing."

"So you'll come back?"

She hesitated, not sure what he was asking. "I love you and I want to be with you. But I can't be a rich man's mistress. I'll see you whenever you want, but I'm going to live here. I've also gone back to college. I refuse to give that up."

Stone chuckled. "So I really blew that one, huh? I wasn't asking you to move in, love, I was proposing. I want you to marry me."

"Oh." Marriage? To Stone? "Oh."

"Oh yes, or oh no?"

Tears flowed again, but this time they were from happiness. "Yes," she said, and kissed him over and over. "Yes, yes, yes."

"And if we're married, you will live in our house, right?"

"Of course."

"I think college is a great idea. You'll do well."

"I already have."

He laughed.

Cathy leaned against him. Her belly brushed his, and she caught her breath. "Stone, I have something to tell you."

"I have something to tell you, too."

"I'd like to go first," she said.

"Actually so would I." Before she could protest, he reached behind him and flicked on the light.

She blinked in the sudden brightness, then her gaze focused on his face. Her breath caught in her throat. On the left side of his face, thin pale lines took the place of the ridged scars.

He rubbed the lines self-consciously. "The doctor assures me they'll fade quickly. I'll always have a few marks, but nothing like what was there before." He shrugged. "I didn't want you to be married to half a man. I want to show you the world. At least what I remember of it. The rest I thought we'd discover together.''

"You're so beautiful," she murmured, in shock. "I can't believe how good-looking you are. Women will be all over you.''

"But I'm yours. For always.''

She touched his face. "I never cared about the scars.''

"I know. That's one of the reasons I was ready to get rid of them. The other…'' He shrugged.

She understood. They had been his strongest ties to the past and he'd let them go. It had been time.

She realized she had to expose her secret, as well. She took a couple of steps back. "I haven't been eating chocolate again. I know I didn't tell you when I first found out, and that was wrong. I should have. But it was the day I left and I just couldn't bear to talk about it. I tried calling a couple of weeks later, but you were gone. I hope you won't be angry. If you are, if it means you don't want to marry me, I'll understand.''

The last bit was a complete lie. She *wouldn't* understand at all, but she felt as if she had to give him an out.

She shrugged out of her coat and let it fall to the floor. Stone stared at her belly. "You're pregnant," he breathed.

"Five months.''

His expression softened. "A baby. You're having my baby. A new life and a new chance.'' He dropped to his knees and reverently pressed a kiss to her belly. "I've been incredibly stupid. Can you ever forgive me?''

"Yes.''

He hugged her tight. She stroked the top of his head. She knew there would be questions later. They weren't important now. It was enough that they were together.

He rose to his feet and took her hand, then led her to

the sofa. "I just want to hold you," he said. "I've been so empty without you."

She went with him, finding peace in his arms. He placed his hand against her tummy and grinned. "It's going to be a boy."

"Oh, please." She laughed. "That's just so typically male."

He hugged her close. "Promise me you'll never leave me again."

"I promise."

"And I promise you forever. I love you. You are the best part of me."

Cathy rested her head on his shoulder and listened to the steady beat of his heart. Together they'd healed each other and found their peace.

Forever, she thought happily. Now, there was a promise to hold on to.

* * * * *

Also, don't miss Susan Mallery's upcoming duo,

BRIDES OF BRADLEY HOUSE
in spring 1999
DREAM BRIDE—March 1999
DREAM GROOM—May 1999

Only from Silhouette Special Edition

FOLLOW THAT BABY...

the fabulous cross-line series featuring the infamously wealthy Wentworth family...continues with:

THE MERCENARY AND THE NEW MOM
by **Merline Lovelace**
(Intimate Moments, 2/99)

No sooner does Sabrina Jensen's water break than she's finally found by the presumed-dead father of her baby: Jack Wentworth. But their family reunion is put on hold when Jack's past catches up with them....

Available at your favorite retail outlet, only from

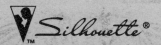

Bestselling author
LINDSAY McKENNA

continues the drama and adventure of her popular series with an all-new, longer-length single-title romance:

MORGAN'S MERCENARIES

HEART OF THE JAGUAR

Major Mike Houston and Dr. Ann Parsons were in the heat of the jungle, deep in enemy territory. She knew Mike's warrior blood kept him from the life—and the love—he silently craved. And now she had so much more at stake. For the beautiful doctor carried a child. His child…

Available in January 1999, at your favorite retail outlet!

Look for more **MORGAN'S MERCENARIES** in 1999, as the excitement continues in the Special Edition line!

Silhouette®

PSMORGMERC

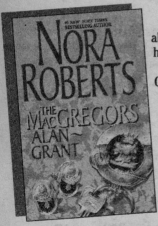
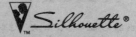

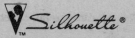

Silhouette®

SPECIAL EDITION™®

COMING NEXT MONTH

#1225 BABY, OUR BABY!—Patricia Thayer
That's My Baby!
When Jake Hawkins returned to town, he discovered that one
unforgettable night of passion with Ali Pierce had made him a daddy.
He'd never forgotten about shy, sweetly insecure Ali—or how she
touched his heart. Now that they shared a child, he vowed to be there
for his family—forever!

#1226 THE PRESIDENT'S DAUGHTER—Annette Broadrick
Formidable Special Agent Nick Logan was bound to protect the
president's daughter, but he was on the verge of losing his steely self-
control when Ashley Sullivan drove him to distraction with her feisty
spirit and beguiling innocence. Dare he risk getting close to the one
woman he couldn't have?

#1227 ANYTHING, ANY TIME, ANY PLACE—Lucy Gordon
Just as Kaye Devenham was about to wed another, Jack Masefield
whisked her off to marry him instead, insisting he had a prior claim
on her! A love-smitten Kaye dreamt that one day this mesmerizing
man would ask her to be more than his strictly *convenient* bride....

#1228 THE MAJOR AND THE LIBRARIAN—Nikki Benjamin
When dashing pilot Sam Griffin came face-to-face with Emma Dalton
again, he realized his aching, impossible desire for the lovely librarian
was more powerful than ever. He couldn't resist her before—and he
certainly couldn't deny her now. Were they destined to be together
after all this time?

#1229 HOMETOWN GIRL—Robin Lee Hatcher
Way back when, Monica Fletcher thought it was right to let her baby's
father go. But now she knew better. Her daughter deserved to know
her daddy—and Monica longed for a second chance with her true
love. Finally the time had come for this man, woman and child to
build a home together!

#1230 UNEXPECTED FAMILY—Laurie Campbell
Meg McConnell's world changed forever when her husband, Joe,
introduced her...to his nine-year-old son! Meg never imagined she'd
be asked to mother another woman's child. But she loved Joe, and his
little boy was slowly capturing her heart. Could this unexpected
family live happily ever after?